ALICE BLACK

J. SCHLENKER

Binka Publishing, LLC

To my husband, Chris

Contents

Alice

E veryone in the two-story brick house on 123 Tucker Street in Queens eventually vanished. It was as if the house spit them out one by one.

Every family has their own peculiarities, something distinctive. Alice's family excelled at the art of *disappearing*. Her father disappeared. Her brother disappeared. Then what remained of her mother, her bodily shell, disappeared, the part that hadn't already disappeared with her father and brother.

With her father and brother, the elimination was swift, leaving a trail of unanswered questions. With her mother, it was gradual—a lingering constipation offering no resolution. It had been a year since the undertaker took her mother's body away, and along with it, any answers she hoped to find.

Intellectually, Alice knew it wasn't the fault of the house, but it was easier to blame the house and all the secrets it possessed rather than entertain the assumption its entire occupants fell into the category of black sheep. It was hard to accept every single member of a family of four shared the dominant gene of dysfunction.

With a bottle of Merlot, Alice, on the verge of turning

twenty-five, sat on the porch steps of the house she had spent all but five years of her life in. Pondering the one time she managed to escape along with her new chance at freedom, she also lamented her failure at expunging the secrets that lingered within the now dingy eggshell walls and thin-planked oak floors and every threadbare piece of furniture that inhabited the house— secrets threatening to cause an implosion if the wrecking ball didn't shatter them first.

With each swallow of wine, she contemplated the house and its ghosts, the ones who infiltrated her psyche, while at the same time, celebrating the freedom she hoped to gain from their demise. Like a magician, she scrutinized her own vanishing act.

The one ally she should have had through all of this was her brother Jack Jr., but Alice and her brother hadn't been close. There wasn't much opportunity as Jack Jr. left when she was six. He would return later, so one might have to say Jack Jr. only partially disappeared, but during all those years he was absent, the only explanation Alice's mother gave was that he went to live with an aunt, one Alice had never met or even knew existed.

"What aunt? I have an aunt?" Alice asked.

"Alice, you ask too many questions."

Lack of explanations was also a peculiarity of the Black family.

Alice knew Jack Jr. had been a problem child. Those were her mother's exact words. Jack Jr. was the only thing she remembered her parents fighting about when her father was still there. It was as if a black cloud hung over their family, a commonality that Alice hoped might bring her and Jack Jr. together again. Instead, it drove them apart. Like the house, the black cloud's layers clung to Alice and repelled Jack. It was so strong it blotted out the main connection they shared—their nemesis, their mother.

As far as Alice knew, her mother went to her grave not

knowing Jack Jr. had returned. He begged Alice to keep his secret, and she did.

It was during Alice's senior year of high school while walking home that she spied a scraggly dark-haired guy standing outside the bay door of an auto repair shop. His uniform indicated he worked there. It was instinct that first caused her to look his way. The uncanny resemblance to their mother and the fact he looked to be the right age for her brother made her stop dead in her tracks. Seeing the blotched blue-ink design of a knife on his forearm sealed any doubt in her mind. It also triggered the memory of all the yelling when her mother had discovered the tattoo on his twelve-year-old body. He immediately looked her way when she yelled out, "Jack Jr!"

He wrinkled his forehead in puzzlement before responding. "Alice?"

On some days, she stopped to talk. She kept a respectable distance lest a spot of oil or the smell of the garage greases penetrate either her skin or clothing. Her mother would be sure to notice and ask questions. Normally, her mother was detached, severed from the world as if she had been transplanted on earth from a totally different planet. If she suspected something was going on behind her back though, she was like a bloodhound, the kind with red blood, not the icy blue she suspected her mother of having.

On other days if she saw Jack Jr. standing near the garage door, which is where she knew he took his smokes, she merely shouted his name when she passed, and they both waved. Seeing her brother again didn't evoke the warm fuzzy heavily embracing reunion she might have hoped for—him pulling out pictures of a wife and a niece or nephew he couldn't brag enough about and couldn't wait for her to meet, but the casual, aloof chit-chat they shared on some days was better than nothing. Alice provided the chit-chat; her brother contributed the aloofness.

Her mother would have been appalled if she knew Jack Jr. smoked. She always said smoking was a nasty habit. Why it would matter to her mother, Alice didn't know since she rarely ever mentioned Jack Jr., except maybe to say he was a drifter like his father or he had been such a problem child. Alice had to admit, she thought smoking *was* a nasty habit as well and cautioned Jack Jr. he should quit. His reply was to blow smoke in her face. She coughed and could see how her brother might have indeed been a problem child. On the days he blew smoke on her, she quickly ran into the house and up the stairs, yelling to her mom and Clara if she were there, she had to use the bathroom. She quickly changed her clothes and brushed her teeth lest her mother should think she was sneaking cigarettes behind her back.

As for drifting, Jack Jr. hadn't drifted too far since he worked less than a mile from their home. He bragged of his plans to travel. Maybe it was just talk. But one thing stood out about Jack Jr.—his restless nature.

When agitated, her mother sometimes compared Alice to Jack Jr. Alice's mother's nerves were complex. Her stability depended on prescription pills. Sometimes one got taken late or was even forgotten. At other times, the cause of her mother's distress was due to some disruption in what little television reception they had. How could her mother know what was happening on her soap operas? Alice, knowing one or the other was the cause of her mother's state of anxiety, reminded her mother to take her pills or she fiddled with the rabbit ears until a clearer picture came in. Then Alice retreated to her room. Like clockwork, an hour later when the soap opera concluded or when the effects of the pills set in, there would be a knock on Alice's door. Her mother would peek in, sometimes with a smile on her face.

"Alice, I know you are the responsible child. You will care for me in my old age." Her mother said it with a nod of her head as if it was a done deal. Alice thought the reason her mother repeated it so often was to convince them both.

Yes, people had a way of disappearing on her mother. But in another sense, they disappeared on Alice as well. Alice knew little about her father. All that remained of him were a few faded images in a picture album, three to be exact, the ones Alice surmised that cutting him out of would produce weird bodily mutilations and an oddly shaped picture, something resembling a jigsaw puzzle piece. In those that remained, his face was fuzzy. Alice wondered how many photos of her own infant and toddler years were missing due to her father's clear image being in the picture. She worried if she were ever to run into her father, she wouldn't recognize him.

Alice gave up asking about her father before she started high school. The mere mention of his existence brought on one of her mother's anxiety attacks, resulting in a flareup of shingles, for which Alice felt responsible.

There were times when Alice thought her mother might recover from her depression and be a normal mom, the kind she remembered so long ago, the one she had before her father disappeared. If Alice had been more mature at the time and had not had typical adolescent stuff invading her mind, she might have noticed it was never going to happen. Her mother was doomed to a downward spiral of despair and was trying to take Alice with her. Doug had offered her an escape hatch.

Alice returned home five years later. She tried to convince herself it was only for a visit before moving on to something new, but found both her mother and the house to be in a deplorable condition, more so than she remembered. She had not only returned to her mother's bouts of depression but to a physically altered woman.

Alice was a mid-life baby, so her mother was older than most. Priscilla Black had been forty-three when she gave birth to her. Guilt swept over Alice as she looked around, noting the many changes that had taken place. She gasped when she saw the prescription bottles she remembered being confined to a corner of the countertop now took up half of the kitchen table.

There was a pleading in her mother's faded blue eyes when she said, "Alice, you will stay this time, won't you? You'll take care of me?"

So much for the escape being permanent. Alice had spent what little money she had to return home. In fact, it was Doug who gave her the bus fare. She was twenty-three when she returned with no money, job, or plans.

Before Priscilla Black's mind completely failed, she'd had the foresight to leave the house and all of its bleak and worthless possessions to Alice. Blessing or curse? Alice would have to say *curse*.

MAC'S BURGERS, the diner where she took a job as waitress at a couple of days after her mother's funeral, even with all the overtime she could get, did not afford her a way out of her situation. It wasn't until a year after her mother's death that Alice labeled the inheritance of the crumbling house a blessing. For it was at that time, the also crumbling for sale sign that reminded her of the Leaning Tower of Pisa in the narrow yard of the house she still lived in disappeared. It wasn't because some nice couple wanted to live out of the city in an affordable first home. No couple or anyone but a demented scientist would want the house. As luck would have it, a real-estate developer wanted the whole row of houses for a strip mall.

The one holdout had been Clara Jenkins who lived two houses down. It was only after her son, almost by physical force, carted her off to an assisted-living home did the sale go through.

Clara was an odd bird—purportedly her mother's only friend, the only friend Alice knew of. Alice was maybe three when Clara moved to the neighborhood after her husband died. This was when her father was still there, when her mother was sane, when the smell of chocolate chip cookies wafted from the oven, and when the four of them did normal family things.

From the time Alice was six until she graduated from high school, Clara was a fixture at their house. She was always *just leaving* when Alice came home from school. Alice remembered all the times Clara rose from the kitchen table where she and her mother talked over coffee. Clara would grip her arm, saying with a look of pity, "You be good to your mother, you hear?"

Alice's only response was to say, "Yes, ma'am." Her mother told her to be polite to her elders. After Clara released her grip, Alice ran up the stairs to start her homework before dinner, counting down the number of math problems she could complete before the red marks from her arm faded. It took longer for the image of Clara's bony, veiny hand to fade from her mind. Clara was old, how old she didn't know, but much older than her mother. Even as a small child, Alice didn't like Clara nor did her opinion change as she grew older.

Alice was standing on the porch when Clara left with her son. She knew it was Clara's son. She'd seen his face on real-estate billboards but had never seen him visit.

Alice raised her hand in a half wave on the day Clara walked away holding onto the arm of her son. There was no gesture from Clara other than the normal pitying look. There was something strange about the relationship between Clara and her mother, more than strange—peculiar. Whatever it was, it was behind her now.

So here Alice sat, planning her encore disappearance from 123 Tucker Street with a bottle of twenty-dollar wine, the most expensive bottle the convenience store on the corner offered. She purchased it using her tips from MAC'S BURGERS. The pimply-faced kid at the register had looked at her like she was rich when she placed the bottle on the counter. Or maybe he had been salivating for a greasy burger, the kind that went well with a last course of CLEARASIL. She was still wearing her uniform which reeked of inferior ground beef, pickles, onions, mustard, and ketchup. Sadly, the smell didn't stop with her clothing; it spilled out of her pores.

Her mother didn't allow drink in the house. It wasn't in honor of her mother's memory or her rules that she drank the bottle outside on the porch. It was so the bouquet of the wine wouldn't be confused with the odor of the house. There was a certain odor dying things gave off. Her mother had it during her last days. And now, the house that knew its own days were numbered also had it.

She breathed in the smell of the old oak that hovered over the house, held up the bottle, and said, "Here's to you, old oak. I both climbed and swung from you in my youth. I apologize that you must go along with the house."

A bluebird had made its home in the birdhouse that hung from the tree almost every year. When the tree was young, the house seemed like a home. The tree reminded her of one of the earliest and few memories she had of her father: a smile, white teeth shining in the sunlight, smiling at a job well done as he hung the birdhouse. She tried to remember the rest of his face, his figure, but only a blurry image of his smile remained. Time after time, she concentrated hard, trying to remember her father, but nothing came. The memories that *did* surface came in fragments, spurred on by something ordinary, like a little girl riding her bicycle with training wheels down the sidewalk. At one time, she was that little girl being pushed along and encouraged by her father.

The shed her father did his woodworking projects in eventually fell down, and its remains were removed. Alice never knew what happened to her father's tools. Maybe he took them with him when he left or maybe her mother sold them.

What would the bluebirds do now with the tree gone? She drank the rest of the wine. As she grew lightheaded from the alcohol—drinking was a rarity for her—the memories of the house faded, and the image of a strip mall took its place. She imagined she was sitting within the future home of a nail spa because no strip mall could be a bona fide strip mall without a nail spa. She imagined a payday loan shop in the spot of Clara Jenkins' house.

Alice went inside, stripped out of her pink waitress uniform, and took a long bath in the claw-foot tub using dishwashing liquid to make bubbles, enough to drip over the side. What did it matter if the water seeped through the floorboards? They were going to demolish the house in a month. A shower, not like the quick, horrid ones she remembered in gym class, but the slow, luxurious kind where cleansing cascades of water flowed over beautiful, sexy women in commercials would have been preferable. The house didn't possess a shower though, only an old cast iron claw-foot tub. Nor was she beautiful or sexy. She had grown pudgy from too many fries at MAC'S. The weight could be lost easy enough, but changing her hair color was not an option. Her particular shade of freckles might clash with anything other than the cinnamon-colored waves she usually tied back into a ponytail.

While soaking in the tub, she thought about the headache she would have in the morning because of the wine. After the headache subsided, she would search for an apartment in the city along with a new life, and as a part of that new life, she would turn in her resignation and uniform to MAC'S BURGERS. She might even search for her father. Other than her father and the actor, how many Jack Blacks could there be?

2

Tom

When people asked him what he did, his first reaction was to shrink back in shame. He was thirty and delivered pizzas. To make matters worse, he tried to explain as if the words *I deliver pizzas* wasn't already enough. But he never got to the explanation. If he did, he found he was talking to himself because the cute blonde or brunette in the tight outfit already had her back to him, chatting up the next guy. The same went for guys, not that he was of that persuasion. He surmised neither sex saw the allure of the pizza delivery guy of porn fame. It was all so cliché, what with cell phones and all. In fact, the appeal probably went out with large satellite dish televisions or rotary phones. He looked around. He had to be one of the few people in the bar who knew how to use a rotary phone. His parents still had one in their home, and they kept the large satellite dish to the bitter end because his dad was a connoisseur of Russian spy novels and didn't trust digital boxes. Despite his parents being professors, they remained low-tech.

Maybe he should just cut to the chase, approach a woman

and say, "I'm a loser." Didn't women want honesty first and foremost?

Plus, if that wasn't bad enough, he was shy, the type of guy who only dreamed about approaching women in any situation, least of all a bar. He was single, not married, no girlfriend, not dating—period. Single wasn't really so bad, but single because you were divorced was. His brief marriage bordered on a nightmarish illusion.

A divorced guy in a bar trying to pick up women was also something out of a horror film for him. After the first question of *what do you do,* the second was, "Are you seeing anyone?" Due to those lines of interrogation, he didn't frequent bars. Tonight was an exception. Only one pizza delivery and his boss told him to go home early.

"You could have a concussion," his boss said. "You should go to the doctor."

He couldn't afford to go to the doctor. Pizza delivery didn't offer great health insurance. Besides, he was fine. The girl had only swung the baseball bat once, barely nicking the back of his head. He would have a knot tomorrow, probably a headache. A beer would help. He splurged on a dark draft.

After one drink as that was all he could afford on his minimum wage salary and scanty tips, he made his way to the bus stop, not fearing a mugging. Any mugger worth a grain of salt instinctively knew who wasn't worth their time. He climbed aboard the bus with *his people.* He accepted long ago the *type* that rode the bus were *his* people.

As he stepped on the bus, he exchanged the putrid air of the city with its garbage stacked up and down the sidewalks for the next morning's early pickup for the stale air of the bus. He didn't even want to think what went on inside a bus to make the air worse than the smell of New York City's garbage lining the sidewalks, waiting to be picked up. One of the first things he saw was the pumpkin spice air freshener dangling from the rearview mirror. It had lost both its spiciness and orangeness. The aroma it emitted bordered on skunk, but since it mingled so well with the usual stench, no one noticed. It was only September. Holidays started earlier every year. He made minimal eye contact with the driver and moved through the aisle, avoiding eye contact with the passengers.

The bus driver was a woman. Her hips in the tight, thin blue uniform—thin because he was sure the city didn't want to spring for a denser thread count—spilled over the seat. The driver prior to her, a male, also had hips that overflowed the seat. It came from sitting for extended periods of time. The same with office jobs.

He hadn't seen this particular bus driver before. She seemed more pleasant than her predecessor, the driver who had a habit of grunting with every stop. Tom almost laughed out loud thinking of her doing the same. It was the beer. It had been so long since he had indulged in alcohol. Perhaps if he would make eye contact, she might smile.

After Halloween, she would change the air freshener. He expected to see a Christmas tree or Nativity scene taking the place of the pumpkin. Thanksgiving would be bypassed altogether. He assumed she shelled out her own money for this extravagance. He could hardly see the city paying for such items in light of the threadbare uniforms.

There were a limited number of types who rode the inner-city bus. He tried to define his own type but often felt like the ghost on the bus, the one no one else saw, the only normal one of the lot, the one who rode the bus temporarily, the one briefly down on his luck. He lived his life in a *state of temporary*.

It had been two years since his car, held together by duct tape, refused to budge from the no-parking zone. At least he'd made it to the apartment building where the pizza was to be delivered. Now, he was driving the company car. The boss said it was not permanent, but it had gone on for two years. Once a month, Jimmy, his boss, looked up from his paperwork and asked, "Still no car?" Jimmy nodded his head to let Tom know it was okay, but the pathetic look he gave him said it wasn't.

He tried to be casual as he looked around at the other passengers. He didn't want to get the look, the calculating stare that said they knew you weren't one of them, the kind that came in movies when your cover was blown—you weren't one of the body snatchers.

A woman with a headscarf, not realizing headscarves went out of vogue after Jackie Kennedy, clutched a cheap vinyl purse, not even a knockoff. She looked out the window most of the time but every so often eyed the others suspiciously, perhaps him the most, before squeezing her bag tightly to her side.

The teenage kid in the back with one half of his head shaved donned a muscle shirt with some metal band Tom had never heard of. Tom's tastes were more in the line of rock or pop. The muscle shirt exposed the tattoos running from his neck down his arm. He bopped on the torn faux leather seat to the deep bass coming from his headphones. The beat reverberated throughout the whole bus, yet he was oblivious. He imagined the kid was going through a period of rebellion. He had done the same. He looked like a Bruce. Bruce Wayne, he thought. He would step off the bus where he would be greeted by his chauffeur, Alfred, and return to his mansion.

"I trust you've had your bit of fun for the night," Alfred might say to him. Alfred would cringe at the tattoos while not being able to turn his head away from the half-man, half-woman ink art. "I *do* hope that washes off," he would add. He would make no mention of the hair. What was the point? Hair would grow back.

The old man, midway back, blurted out political stuff, most

of it incoherent. Tom was thankful no one seemed interested. If opposing political paths were to cross, someone might pull out a gun. More than likely, Tom was the only one on the bus without one. The woman hugged her purse tighter. He could almost see the outline of a firearm popping through.

A young girl who clearly saw herself a step above Bruce Wayne stared intently at her cell phone. Occasionally, she laughed out loud while rapidly punching her thumbs on the tiny screen. Her phone dinged several times a minute. The girl would have been a typical teenager if it hadn't been for the baby by her side, one of those fake ones you're given in class to learn about parenthood. It cried. At first, she ignored it, but her facial expression gave way to annoyance. She picked it up and beat it against the seat, but the crying continued. She removed the battery, stuffed it into her backpack, and returned to her texting. No one on the bus said anything, but by the clenching of teeth and open mouths, they were appalled, even Bruce Wayne. Tom had seen her on the bus before and knew her stop. He worried she might miss it since she was so absorbed in her phone. *If he were to remind her, would she think him a pervert? Probably.*

The one on the bus he admired the most was the man two seats in front of him. He snored away. Tom found it hard to relax on a bus himself. The man was possibly in his mid-sixties, near retirement. He would hate for the scary guy who sat across from him to end his chance of collecting his pension. There was always the one scary guy on the bus, the one who could end it for everyone. *Shouldn't bus passengers be screened the way airplane passengers are?* But then, there would be no passengers.

Tom was next to the last one off. He thanked the woman bus driver whose name he didn't know. She looked at him, puzzled, but smiled.

It was two blocks to his apartment. He had to stop at the

corner grocery along the way. Frozen dinners were on sale. All the pizza he could eat for free grew tiring after a while. Also, he needed to pick up cat food and cat litter. That reminded him it was past feeding time for his two cats, Simon and Garfunkel. They might be worried.

3

Alice

---

lthough it wasn't located in hell, from her new bedroom window she had a view of it. This had been one of the cons of the apartment. She looked out to see uniform red bricks almost within arm's reach if she could have stuck her arm out, but windows that had been painted shut prohibited her from doing so. She twisted her head in every conceivable angle, trying to imagine how masons could work in such close proximity to another building and how scaffolding could fit between the two, but doing so was making her claustro-phobic. Fortunately, the former tenant left behind curtains.

The view from the main living area was a typical Brooklyn view. She looked down at the street. There was a pizza shop called IT'S ALL ABOUT THE CRUST. There was a sign next to the child-like painting of the pizza on the window that announced it was under new management. That was never a good sign. Maybe they needed something more than crust, perhaps toppings. Beside it was a shoe repair shop. Who got their shoes repaired nowadays? It had a closed sign in the window and was dark with one of those black gates in front with a padlock. Who would steal used shoes? A Chinese restaurant offering both dine-in and take-out meals was busy. Fire erupted from the dragon's mouth spelling out DRAGON'S DEN. *Cute.*

Alice had written the Chinese restaurant on the pro side of her list. There were no bars on her block, another pro. It was one of the requirements for the street she was to live on. Nor were there any homeless living in the vicinity. She had nothing against homeless people, quite the opposite. She had too much empathy and could see herself joining them in the near future because every time she passed someone with their hand out, she would feel obligated to go above and beyond.

There were an array of unique individuals of different ethnicities in the neighborhood as well as in her new apartment building. The landlord was openly gay and welcomed all kinds of diversity when it came to the residents, another pro. One of the first things the landlord did after Alice signed the lease was to introduce her to Freddie, an openly gay man with two cats he treated more like roommates than pets. Pets were allowed, no doubt to deter rodents. The building was old, a con, but not a deal breaker.

The landlord told her when a new apartment opened up, he favored younger renters since there was no elevator. Alice was on the sixth floor, also a pro. Climbing six flights of stairs would be the exercise needed to shed those extra pounds she had put on as a result of all those fries she ate at MAC'S BURGERS.

The pros won out, and she signed Alice Black across the bottom line of the lease. She had heard signing a lease, or a mortgage, was a nerve-racking experience. She found it liberating even though prices had soared during her sabbatical away from the city. Living in Brooklyn was expensive but less so than in Manhattan.

Picking this particular building had been an arduous process. She visited eleven other apartment buildings but kept coming back to this one—three times, no less. It was during these times she discovered how varied the tenants were. The lady who lived on the floor below her, across from Freddie, dressed like a gypsy. Alice swore she heard the occasional sound of tambourines coming from her apartment. A woman of obvious Greek heritage loved to cook. The aroma of lentils drifted from her apartment daily. Then there was the painter, at least Alice thought he was a painter from his attire. He wore one of those French berets and carried what looked to be canvases wrapped in cloth in and out of the building. She surmised he painted with acrylics since there was no smell of oils or turpentine. A young couple—seemingly newlyweds as they couldn't keep their hands off each other— inhabited the third floor. They were an anomaly. Other than herself, most residents appeared to be older and retired.

Alice looked out her living room window. Faded lights peeked through gaps in curtains in all but one window, the one directly across from her where the curtains were pulled back displaying a balding, shirtless man in sweats peering into his refrigerator. From his expression, she deduced there was not much of a selection. She quickly closed her own curtains lest he should look over and see her.

EVEN THOUGH ALICE had lived most of her life in Queens, living in Brooklyn after living in rural West Virginia for five years, would take some adjustment. It *had* crossed her mind to hop on the first bus after her mother's death and head back to West Virginia. Wasn't it Thomas Wolfe who said you couldn't go back home again? In her heart, she considered West Virginia home.

Besides, the time she spent with Doug had run its course. She looked out the window and onto the street at the wide variety of people traversing the pavement. Most would think her mad to want to return to the rustic lifestyle she endured—no, make that cherished—in West Virginia. The backwoods she inhabited was all but devoid of the amenities most people demanded. Part of the road consisted of a creek bed, impassable during heavy rains. There were no electric lines running in. Gasoline generators produced what electric they needed, and they were only used in times it was deemed necessary. An outhouse, at first, was the only toilet except for bushes, and bathing was done using both well and spring water from a nearby lake, along with downpours of rain. Okay, she had to admit, it did have its drawbacks, but in her mind and mostly her heart, there were zillions of reasons she preferred that rustic back-country life.

Her new apartment didn't have the pastoral landscape she so relished in West Virginia. She had been cut off from civilization, but it was certainly steps above the house she left behind in Queens, a darkened tomb absent of technology with blinds drawn to the outside world without the bucolic setting. Both were lost in time in their own ways.

In high school, most of the students were using cell phones when she left. After her five-year absence, she returned to more sophisticated cell phones, tablets, and flat-screen televisions, not that it mattered. None of those things existed in her mother's house.

Having a job when she returned would have been nice, but upon seeing her mother again, she realized taking care of her would be a full-time job. It was obvious leaving her mother for any length of time would have been akin to twisting a knife into her mom's chest and hastening her demise. So, they both eked by on her mother's social security checks.

Alice's routine consisted of accompanying her mother on the bus to her doctor visits with an occasional trip to the local library to use their computer, searching Web MD to teach her how to better cope with her mother's various illnesses and slew of prescriptions with all their side effects and contraindications. When there was time, she searched for alternative treatments, but there was little time as her mother questioned her every move.

She was afraid Alice would run off again. Also, her mother refused to indulge in holistic treatments, something she deemed as nonsense. No, what her doctors said was written in stone. And what they said was never good.

If she could have made a diagnosis concerning her mother's condition, Alice would have labeled it as *detachment*—a total disconnect from anything that made life worth living. Alice reasoned if the mind or heart felt it had nothing worth living for, the body eventually followed suit. Alice only regretted her mother didn't see her daughter as enough of a reason to keep living. Alice was determined not to become a replica of her mother.

ALICE KNEW she would have to look for a job before the money ran out. It would not be waitressing or flipping burgers. She calculated rent, utilities, food, and all expenditures she could think of. She reasoned if she were responsible, and she was, she could hold out for possibly three years with the money she cleared from the sale of her mother's house along with its furnishings, depending on her frugality. Frugality had been written into her DNA. Also, making lists and planning had been ingrained into her somewhere along the way.

Alice was either blessed or cursed with an analytical mind, thus her designation as the official bookkeeper at The Farm. It was only ever called The Farm because no one had ever come up with a more suitable name for it. There were plenty bantered around, but no serious vote was ever taken. Any type of discussion usually led to smoking weed after which everyone was too chilled out to care. Pot was the most abundant crop on The Farm followed by zucchini, kale, apples, tomatoes, potatoes, and cabbage—all organic. The Farm followed a strict rule of every crop being organic. Even the pot was organic.

The house proceeds didn't bring her near market value, what it might have brought if someone were actually going to live in it rather than being torn down for a strip mall. She, along with the other residents, chipped in for a classified ad and on the following Saturday, moved furniture and knick-knacks, along with other unneeded items, out onto the front lawn, forming one large block-long yard sale. Yard sale enthusiasts, junk dealers, some passersby, and a handful of antique dealers and collectors showed up early, scrutinizing the mix for that one-in-a-million find.

Alice had moved practically the whole interior of the house outside. At first, there wasn't much interest. What her mother deemed treasure was most people's junk. To pass the time, she sat on the porch steps and read. By noon, her take for the block-long rummage sale had been scant until one well-kept elderly woman in oversized glasses, dressed in bold colors with an over-sized designer bag to her side, happened upon an old cardboard box of Hummel figurines. She clasped both hands to her chest and shrieked in joy upon pulling one of the Hummel-filled boxes —there were five boxes in all—from under the table of miscella-neous bric-à-brac. She turned to her friend, a younger and sleekly dressed woman who wore a subdued gray suit, her blonde hair pulled back tightly in a bun. Alice hid her face behind the pages of her book, pretending to be absorbed in its contents while straining to hear what they were saying.

"These are worth a fortune," the older woman said to the younger woman.

Alice's mother once told her she owned every Hummel ever made. The Hummels had belonged to Alice's grandmother, or so her mother told her. In fact, Alice had not met one single grand-parent or the mysterious aunt her brother had stayed with. Nor would Jack Jr. enlighten her the few times she asked. Alice's roots were buried as deeply as those of the oak tree, its canopy over the women inspecting the box's contents. Either that or her ancestors were too far away to visit, maybe on some distant planet. Alice often thought she sprouted from a family of misfits placed on Earth by an alien as some sort of experiment. The experiment had gone so terribly awry that no one had ever returned for them. Perhaps her father had gone mad or had gone off on his own trying to find the ones who abandoned them. Alice had made up so many theories in her mind over the years to explain her father's absence; how could it hurt if one more about aliens was added to the list?

Alice kept up the pretense of reading while taking in every word of the conversation she could make out. *Seven thousand?* Did she hear correctly? As in dollars? Seven thousand for one of those dusty little porcelain representations of a perfect child? Alice listened as staggering amounts were bantered back and forth between the older woman and the other who Alice deduced was the woman's personal assistant. She almost screamed in delight but managed to muffle any sound by pulling the book up next to her lips.

Austere thriftiness was second nature to Alice. She grew up poor and returned to poor when she moved back. Living on The Farm, even with its stringent conditions in comparison, was easy. And then after that came living on a waitress's wage. If only she and her mother had known about those Hummels before. Her mother could have had a bit of luxury during her final days. She mustn't think of that now. It was the past.

Alice set her book down on the grass and rushed over. "Oh, I am so sorry. I have no idea how those boxes got out here. Those boys I hired to carry all this stuff out for me brought them out by mistake. I certainly didn't mean to sell these. They're quite valuable, you know. Actually, there is a collector I'm supposed to call, but I haven't had the heart to part with them. They belonged to my grandmother."

Alice felt ashamed for telling lies, but they kept spilling out of her mouth like those yellow jackets leaving their nest, the one

Doug disturbed while driving the tractor over the field. She had taken the brunt of the stings, her own fault for following so close behind the tractor. Luckily, she wasn't allergic. Lies might be a different story. She wrinkled her nose to stave off an itch.

She looked at one of the Hummel figurines. The saintly little girl pointed to a heart, and Alice thought, *Easy for you to judge. You don't have to pay rent or buy food or any sort of technology because you don't live in this world. But, I do.*

Alice looked back at the woman, hoping her nose had not grown longer during the conversation. Again, she resisted the urge to scratch it.

The woman looked at her assistant, who with her eyes seemed to be giving some kind of approval, and then back at Alice. "I will give you $15,000 for the whole lot."

Alice could tell the woman suspected she was bluffing. Maybe her nose *had* grown. Only one counter maneuver, she told herself. Under no circumstances did she want the woman to walk away empty-handed. "No, no," she said with her hands gripped firmly on one of the boxes, starting to move it toward the house. "You don't understand. These belonged to my grandmother." That part wasn't a lie as far as Alice knew, but the almost tear she struggled to produce was. It was taking every ounce of reserve on her part not to jump for joy.

The woman gave a sigh and said, "$17,000. Not a penny more."

Alice shrugged. "I don't know." She looked down at the perfect little children. She paused in case the woman might up the bid, but after a quarter of a minute, which seemed like an eternity with nothing happening, Alice panicked and said, "I do have to move, and that will certainly defray some of the costs. It's a deal. Grandmother, please forgive me." Did she see the woman rolling her eyes from the corner of her own eye? Didn't matter. The woman was already reaching for her checkbook. She knew when to fold. Doug had also taught her that during those poker games she, Laura, Chris, Kyle, Renea, and Doug played while they huddled in front of the fireplace during the winters.

Alice ended up selling the remainder of her mother's possessions for a pittance to a junk dealer who showed up at the last moment. There was no way she was going to haul any of it back into the house. Hiring guys to move it outside for her had also been a lie.

ALICE LOOKED around her new apartment at her meager surroundings devoid of furniture.

The main pro in deciding upon this particular apartment was that it was the cheapest one. The extra savings meant she could take a year to find herself, or even three in the best case scenario.

Alice peeked through the small opening of the curtains at the man, now with a sweatshirt on, sitting at a narrow kitchen table shoved against the wall. He was eating from cardboard Chinese take-out containers, no doubt from downstairs.

She considered her surroundings and concluded achieving self-actualization in the city would be futile. If she hadn't achieved it in the wild, why did she think she would achieve it in the city? And she certainly wasn't going to attain it if she resorted to watching her neighbors. She drew the curtains tightly and retreated the few steps it took to reach her bedroom.

Where did she go from here? Should she try to find her brother? He was more than likely out west somewhere. At least that was his plan when Alice last spoke to him, which was at their mother's graveside service where only he and Alice were in attendance. Seeing Jack Jr. again might complicate matters. After all, it was him who encouraged her to go off with Doug.

"Get away while you can," he had said.

She couldn't deny going to West Virginia with Doug had been the best time of her life, but what kind of older brother tells his younger sister to go off and join a commune with a Columbia student three credits shy of a law degree, otherwise known as a vagabond pothead? Shouldn't he have encouraged her to apply to colleges? And why hadn't her mother suggested she get a degree even if it only meant some type of bookkeeping job? What kind of dysfunctional family did she hail from? Of course, she knew her family was not in the normal range, but now it was clearly dawning on her how absurd and dismal her family truly was.

She sat cross-legged on her sleeping bag, the one she brought back with her from The Farm and concluded that all of this analyzing was getting her nowhere. She must get on with more practical matters. She would go furniture shopping tomorrow.

4

Tom

He sat on his bed and strummed his guitar, a twelve-string with the distinguishing mark of a cigarette burn. He had gotten it cheap from a guy selling most of his worldly possessions. Tom recognized all the signs of eviction, having been there himself. And more than likely, the burn spot came from weed and not a cigarette. The guy, covered in tattoos with hair down to his shoulders, neither had the look or smell of a smoker of cigarettes but looked the part of a partaker of pot. Tom deemed himself lucky to pass by just as the guy was putting the guitar out on the sidewalk along with a couch, some end tables, lamps, and a few other items. There was no case.

Tom was only able to purchase the guitar because of the one-hundred-dollar birthday check he had just cashed from Mark and Jennifer. Luckily for him, the guy selling the guitar was selling it in broad daylight where there were plenty of people around. If it had been nighttime and near a bar, a mugger would have instinctually known by his positive demeanor he had money on him. The guitar was meant to be his.

Simon and Garfunkel snuggled around his legs. They liked

"Here Comes the Sun," or so he told himself, one of the few songs he could decently play.

He looked around at his tiny apartment, most of its furnishings having been supplied by his parents on one of their rare visits to see him. Sometimes they offered plane fare for Thanksgiving or Christmas. Sometimes he took them up on it, but he usually declined. Telling people in a bar that you were a loser was easier than seeing it reflected back to you on your family's faces.

He had a college degree in business, and this was where he was in life. Why he majored in business, he didn't know. He'd always been better with his hands. Somewhere along the line, someone must have urged him to do so. Business was a joke. Money slipped through his hands like water. Another reason he didn't go home much was seeing the look of worry on his parents' faces.

He was the youngest of three siblings, the one still finding himself. Both brothers were college professors. Mark taught business, John taught biology, and their wives taught as well, all at the same university, Georgia State. Out of pity or a sense of what they thought he needed the most, his parents and brothers, or their wives, sent him cards with checks at Christmas and on his birthday.

He was the lone man out, absent from most family functions. On Thanksgiving, his mother sent the whole ensemble of traditional fare for one: turkey, dressing, gravy, sweet potato casserole, and pumpkin pie. It would arrive in Styrofoam, packed in dry ice, complete with cooking directions.

The one brief period he moved back to Atlanta, three years ago for a total of nine months, he had Thanksgiving with John's family and Christmas with Mark's. They always loaded him up with leftovers, all his tiny fridge could handle. On Halloween, he was presented with fair-trade chocolates from Mark, the oldest brother, as it was the only kind his wife, Jennifer, a yoga mom and health-food fanatic, allowed in the house. John's wife, Carol, was the opposite, overweight and a food junkie. In a little over one week's time, he would be bombarded with chocolate from the local food co-op where Jennifer shopped along with half-eaten bags of malted milk balls, tiny Snicker bars, and Hershey Kisses, all closeout deals from the local Walmart where Carol shopped.

Carol and Jennifer had different ideas concerning most things. The one issue they came together on was Sarah, Tom's former wife. Another reason he begged off family dinner invitations, other than the eternal question of whether he was still delivering pizzas, was that Sarah's name was almost a given to come up. His parents, who were present at every family gathering, cringed at the mention of her name.

Before Sarah was mentioned, someone would always ask, "How are the cats doing, Tom?" By the cats, they meant, Simon and Garfunkel. It was as if the word *cats* triggered his failure of a marriage to Sarah, similar to Pavlov's dogs.

He had taken the liberty of renaming the cats after Sarah left him. There were so many cats, he didn't even know what particular names she had given them. He only knew it had to be something cheesy and mundane such as Paws, Miss Kitty, or Boots. He just happened to be working out the fingering on his guitar for "Sounds of Silence" when both cats were playing around his feet.

Sarah, a collector of feral cats, made it her life's mission to snatch up all cats freely roaming the city, perfectly content and happy fat cats, and housebreak them. They usually ended up nervous and disheveled after her touch. Or perhaps Tom was confusing the cats' demeanor with his own turmoil during his marriage to Sarah. He honestly couldn't remember a time it was ever good. One matter of discord between them, and there were many, was that the vet and cat food bills some months were more than what they paid for rent. Sarah's answer to the situation was that Tom should have two jobs. Thus the pizza delivery job at night after his day job as an accountant at a laminate replacement cabinet shop that had ended up going defunct. His days branched into a plethora of part-time day jobs ranging from shoe salesman in a mall to a cable guy, always with nighttime pizza delivery. At the time of their divorce, only the two cats, Simon and Garfunkel, remained. She left them with him. Most cats tended to disappear after being fixed, vaccinated, and declawed.

"Such disgusting creatures," Jennifer remarked. Jennifer abhorred any kind of pet because she said they should all be free but made an exception for the pet turtle her son kept in his room as long as his nephew was completely responsible for Spot. Carol was a dog person, one of those dog rescuers, which begged the question with Carol, "If you care so much about animals, why not all animals?" Jennifer was referring to the dead piece of cow on Carol's plate.

Tom could see Jennifer's point. But more so, the vegan/omnivore dilemma which inevitably came up during family dinners moved the conversation away from Sarah and pizza delivery. Tom couldn't deny how appreciative he was that when he lived in Atlanta there was always a free meal to be had at his brothers'—grilling out at John and Carol's, or quinoa, which he never knew existed, with vegetables at Mark and Jennifer's. After moving back to New York, Tom contented himself with watching his nieces and nephews growing up via Facebook. On birthdays, he sent cards, absent of content other than a poignant verse or funny limerick. He was sure their parents explained Tom was the poor uncle, but being bright kids, they already surmised that.

They ranged from middle schoolers to teenagers. On the rare occasions Tom *did* visit his brothers, he only saw them when they stuck their heads out of their rooms to say the obligatory *hello*. They rarely ventured out of their rooms, and who could blame them? Their rooms were equipped with every electronic device known to man.

5

Alice

A lice woke up early, turned on the coffeemaker and slid two slices of bread under the oven broiler. She had thought to buy a teapot and coffee maker on her first outing in search of essential things such a bread, butter, peanut butter, jam, potatoes, tea bags, canned soup, juice, and soft drinks—things she could easily prepare with her one skillet and one pot on the stove. However, a toaster she completely forgot. The stove came with the apartment. How long it would last was debatable. There was an art to closing the door which teetered on rusted hinges. The refrigerator had also seen better days.

She spent all of yesterday scrubbing down the entire apartment, concentrating heavily on removing the stale smell permeating from the vegetable crisper in the refrigerator. The thermometer was set on the highest possible temperature, so she moved it to the coldest. She scrubbed so hard to remove the grease that had collected around the dials of the stovetop that she removed some of the numbers. She reached for her small notepad on the counter and made a note to pick up a black magic marker. Hopefully, it would suffice in replacing the numbers she had removed along with the built-up grease.

While intermittently munching on her breakfast, she took her tape measure and calculated the exact dimensions of every room: living room, kitchen, bedroom, and bathroom.

Living on The Farm had taught her certain things. Planting seeds with the right amount of space between them and knowing when and what to plant couldn't be too different from planning interior design in a small living space. She measured the hall even though it was barely big enough to maneuver in. While trying to calculate how a chest of drawers would turn the corner into the bedroom, she fidgeted with a strand of hair that had fallen loose from her ponytail. It occurred to her she had forgotten to purchase shampoo. In defeat, she slid her back down the wall until her butt was on the floor with her legs extended in front of her. If she stretched her toes forward, she came within a hair of touching the opposite wall. She took in a heavy breath and let it out. These are all small things, she told herself. They will work out. Things always worked out on The Farm. Baking soda. She remembered Renea taught them how to use baking soda when they had run out of shampoo. Then she thought of IKEA. Laura once told her she had furnished her whole off-campus apartment with it. Both Renea and Laura had been like older sisters to her on The Farm. She remembered her saying the furniture came in kits, something you constructed yourself, the way her father put together her bicycle when she was five. That was the last summer she saw him.

IKEA was a radical idea for her. Her mother lived in a Victorian house and expressed Victorian ideals and abhorred most things modern as if reaching back to the past would return her husband to her. Alice said out loud, "I must become modern." To become modern, self-actualized, and away from any remnant influence of her mother had become her mantra.

She took her notebook and a ruler and drew out a scaled-down floor plan. On another page, she listed all the essentials she would need, the larger items.

1. Small kitchen table with two chairs. (That is all she could see fitting. She only needed one, but she had to be optimistic.)
2. Bed frame along with a mattress and box springs
3. Bedding
4. Bedside table
5. Lamp
6. Small, narrow chest of drawers
7. Couch and chair, or small sectional couch
8. Coffee table
9. A bookcase (She missed the book discussions they held at The Farm.)
10. Small desk

She looked over her list. Yes, this would be plenty, maybe *too* much, on her first shopping outing.

Electronics would have to be the next thing. If she were to become modern, she would have to replace her flip phone, the one she needed for the few times she was out running errands during her mother's illness and then later for MAC'S BURGERS in case Mac needed her for overtime. She felt like some antiquated fossil every time she removed it from her purse.

First the furniture, she told herself. She would delve slowly into the world of electronics, maybe even online dating to find someone to warm the extra kitchen chair. It was times like these she wished she had a female friend to share this new venture with, one she could confide in should anything come to pass to confide. Freddie, downstairs with the cats, had been her nearest thing to a friend. She had literally been living under the proverbial rock while Freddie flamboyantly hovered above it.

She placed her Styrofoam cup and plate into the sink, reprimanding herself for having purchased something so bad for the environment. What would they think back on The Farm? She looked around for a place to put the two bites of toast she didn't eat. She picked up her list and added waste can.

She made her way around the corner to the bathroom, slipped out of her pajamas, and stepped into the shower, her first one in her new apartment. She ran her fingers down the white subway-like tiles, the ones she had wiped down with disinfectant and cleanser until they looked new. Everything was a marvel to her. She fought the urge to linger too long under the hot water. She reached out for a towel only to remember she had none, another thing that had fallen between the cracks, like the shampoo and waste can. She gave a slight sigh which turned into a muffled scream, wondering how she could be so stupid. Looking around, she picked up her pajamas from the floor, used them to dry herself, and slipped on her robe.

She went back to her list again and added towels along with one set of dishes and silverware. Why had she not even brought some of these simple items from her mother's house? Oh, yes, she reminded herself, a new life meant leaving everything about that existence behind, even the Hummel figurines, which if she had owned a computer and properly did her research, she may have found were even more valuable than what the lady so eagerly gave her for them. She remembered her mother stating her grandmother had every one ever made, and she kept them in mint condition. Self-actualization meant not being greedy, she reminded herself.

Wearing jeans, a sweatshirt and minimal make-up—only face powder—she bounded down the six flights of stairs, off to explore where she might find an IKEA store. After acquiring apartment essentials, she intended to explore the world of hydrating, rejuvenating, and makeup, along with the thick tapered eyebrows everyone seemed to have these days.

When Alice arrived at the store, she gasped. The sign read: 364,000 SQUARE FEET OF SHOPPING. This might require several days.

6

Meeting Doug

A lice met Doug during the last semester of her senior year in high school at THE JAVA BEAN FACTORY, a quirky nonchain coffee shop, painted orange both on the outside and the inside. She had tagged along with Kayla and Meghan, girls whose social status fell between the cool crowd and the nerdy lower echelon. Alice hovered somewhere in the void, not truly fitting into any category.

KAYLA AND MEGHAN reminded Alice of conjoined twins. Kayla was a people fixer, mostly a fixer of Meghan who followed her blindly. Kayla, a year younger, started kindergarten a year early for two reasons. One, her birthday fell right on the cutoff. Two, according to Kayla's mom, she was extra bright though Alice saw no evidence of it.

When Kayla tired of fixing Meghan's life, she zoomed in on Alice's. "God only knows Alice needs some guidance," were the exact words Alice overheard Kayla say to Meghan. "God only knows so and so needs some guidance" were the words Kayla's mother used a lot. Alice knew because once she slept over at Kayla's—only once. Mrs. Morgan used the phrase several times during dinner about this or that person while Mr. Morgan repeated, "Yes, dear," between asking for the chicken and the mashed potatoes to be passed.

Alice's mother never let her go back when she found out Kayla's mother bombarded her with questions. Her mother had been against it from the start, but Alice had begged and begged and even cried until her mother gave in. There was even a faint light in her mother's usually flat eyes when Alice hugged her and said, "Mom, you're the best."

It turned out to be Alice's first and only sleepover.

"What does your mother do?" Mrs. Morgan asked. Meghan stood beside her, her eyes bulging out toward Alice with a half-frightened expression, studying her like she had been through this drill before, wanting to see if Alice fared any better with the oral pop quiz. She should have warned Alice.

"She keeps house and cooks, I guess. She worked at MACY'S DEPARTMENT STORE before I was born."

"Your father must make a lot of money," Mrs. Morgan replied with a slight tilt to her head and judgmental eye. Alice wore only secondhand clothes, and she fidgeted nervously, suspecting Mrs. Morgan, who perused her up and down, knew.

"Maybe he did. I don't know. He left when I was six." Why she said that, she didn't know. Her mother warned her about saying things like that. She said people wouldn't understand. She realized her mom was right when Mrs. Morgan took a step back and raised her eyebrow. Did Mrs. Morgan question all of Kayla's friends this way?

Maybe if her mother had instructed her on social etiquette, the same way she had taught her to write her name over and over before kindergarten, she might have been better prepared to answer the questions.

Alice quickly added. "I was only six. I barely remember my father."

Just then, Mr. Morgan came through the front door, distracting Mrs. Morgan from her line of questioning. "Well then, you girls make sure you come back downstairs at seven and don't forget to wash your hands," Mrs. Morgan said.

Mrs. Morgan must have been boning up on her interrogation skills while peeling the potatoes because when they did all sit down at the table, a whole new slew of questions ensued.

"Your mother never remarried?" Mrs. Morgan asked.

"No." Alice didn't know what else to say.

"Not even a boyfriend?"

"No."

Alice took a bite of green beans, chewing them slowly. She had never even considered the thought of her mother having a boyfriend. Maybe he might take her mother out to dinner and a movie, maybe even take her along too. A whole new realm of possibilities entered Alice's mind, a perfect idyllic world, one in which Alice wouldn't have to buy her clothes at a secondhand store and where her mother would smile, even laugh. Her new stepfather, they would marry, might even drop her off and pick her up at school, a thing she would be proud of and not be embarrassed by like the other kids. Without thinking, almost spitting out a mouthful of green beans, she blurted out, "Do you know of anyone?"

Before Mrs. Morgan could say a word, Mr. Morgan looked at his wife sternly and shook his head.

After that night, Alice steered clear of Kayla for several weeks, sitting at the lunch table with Brandy and Karla, the school's nerds. Their main topic of conversation was how disgusting cafeteria pizza was and how they looked forward to tater tots' day. Brandy's or Karla's parents would have been thrilled if either of them brought a friend home with them from school. But rather than go through the ordeal of begging her mother once again, Alice, for days on end, became a loner, walking amongst the popular and unpopular through the school halls like a ghost.

When the days of being invisible became too much for her, she flitted back and forth between the two factions, the nerds and the second-in-command, the name she had given them, since like The Farm they bore no designation. The cool crowd was not an option.

THE THREE OF them sat quietly at THE JAVA BEAN FACTORY, slurping on their drinks. It was Kayla who said, "Alice, you really ought to get out from under that dreary mother of yours after graduation. I mean, who in this day and age doesn't have televisions and computers in their home?" Kayla, who had clearly been designated with a cool girl name, had somehow missed the mark and fell short of her parents' expectations for her. Junior college and an office job were on her horizon.

Alice corrected Kayla, "We do have a television."

"But didn't you say it has rabbit ears?" Kayla asked.

"What's rabbit ears?" Meghan asked. Alice ignored her, thinking about the time she had to explain the standard issue black rotary phone supplied by the telephone company still in their house.

Doug, a table away, drinking a Frappuccino without a straw because he professed them to be bad for the environment, took this as an opening to introduce himself. "Technology will be the demise of us all. I'm Doug, by the way."

The three of them almost jumped out of their seats. Boys never talked to them, least of all a college student. Doug was clearly a college student. He looked the part. In fact, he went to Columbia. His given name was Oliver Douglas Barton. The name of Oliver came from his grandfather, a judge, and

Douglas from his father, a lawyer. He preferred to be called Doug.

The fact this blue-eyed hunk behind the wire-rimmed glasses was even looking their way sent the three girls at the table into swoons. Later on, Alice revised her initial opinion of Doug. Hunk material he wasn't, but rather, he was five years their senior with both the breeding and demeanor of someone ready to step into the movers and shakers of society; in other words, he was someone who could talk circles around a group of high-school seniors who were a step or two below the cool kids. He probably wouldn't have stood a chance with one of the cheer-leaders or Megan Lawson, not to be confused with the Meghan in their own group—a popular name that year—who was both a cheerleader and on the school council. That Megan went for jocks, and a jock, Doug wasn't.

Doug took a special interest in Alice, not romantic but rather pragmatic. The only thing he really wanted was to shake loose the chains he felt tightening around his neck by the expectations of his father who was a senior member of a well-established law firm in New York as was his father before him who was now a judge. Doug was itching to ditch the whole law career for some-thing less tedious, less monotonous, less challenging, and some-thing that would radically defy his father whom he had a less than stable relationship with. He saw the similarities in Alice's own parental woes and seized upon them.

"I'm headed somewhere remote to get away from this monstrous gobble-you-up machine of a city. What about you, Alice? Will you join me?"

Alice smiled demurely, shrugging it off as a joke, a calcu-lated flirtatious gesture. Having never been flirted with, she was at a loss of how to react and momentarily looked away before turning her head down to her ice water, not being able to afford any of the drinks the other girls were consuming.

Telling her mother she needed to go to the library to study,

Alice, without Kayla or Meghan, met Doug at THE JAVA BEAN FACTORY after that for the duration of her senior year. He bought her drinks using a credit card. The rendezvous put both rebellious and romantic ideas into her head. She was ripe for both although Doug had never made one gesture toward anything of a sexual nature. The romantic inclinations were all of her own design.

"West Virginia? But what's in West Virginia?" she asked.

"Wild, beautiful, rugged land. I have a few others who are interested."

"Interested in what?" she asked nonchalantly, trying not to sound too naïve. She and Doug had been having conversations leading up to this for a month, but somehow, the reality of him ever going through with anything seemed somewhere up in the clouds, in the never-come-to-pass dream world. And he already had a *few*? What did that mean? Had he been talking to other girls? A shiver of jealousy coursed through her body.

"I really need to get home," she said, shoving her unfinished strawless drink aside. If she had spent her own money, she would have been making a ridiculous slurping noise, totally unladylike, the noise small kids made to get every last sip, but since it was on Doug's dime, of which he seemed to have plenty, she felt full.

He reached for her arm. It was the first time he had ever touched her. His touch was gentle. A vibration ran through her whole body. She had a teenage crush on this older male. There was no denying it.

"Please think about it, Alice. We want to leave within the month. You would be the youngest. The rest are college students. But they are all good people. Good people who want to live off the land."

The youngest? He thought of her as a child. No, that couldn't be. He was asking her to join him to live in a commune in some remote part of another state. She had never been out of the city. The thought both thrilled and scared her.

Alice walked away, squeezing her book bag to her chest, attempting to control the nervousness she feared was showing in her body. Like Kayla, she thought junior college might be in her future. If not that, a waitressing job. She had no special talents, and she knew nothing about the land. She grew up in Queens. The only land she knew about was a somewhat larger back yard than most.

IT HAD BEEN a week since Alice talked to her brother. She waited near the street, hoping to spy him in the garage. The bay door was open, and she knew, eventually, he would come out to take a smoke.

He was wearing the gray oil-and-grease stained uniform with the red cloth embroidered company emblem on the shirt pocket. She watched him pull out his pack of cigarettes.

"Jack!" she yelled.

He lit up before gingerly strolling over. "What's up?" he asked after lighting up and placing his lighter back in his pocket.

"I graduate in a couple of weeks."

"Yeah, I know," he said. "Got plans?"

"Not really. I did think of possibly getting a two-year degree at a junior college, but I would have to get a job to pay for it."

"And stay at home?" he asked with a smirk on his face.

"There is another option."

"Oh?" he said, blowing out a stream of smoke from the side of his mouth.

"There's this guy." She hesitated. She saw Jack's lips pull up into a smile.

The smile vanished when he asked, "You're not pregnant, are you?"

"No, Jack, it's not like that at all. He goes to Columbia."

Jack's eyes grew wide. He stepped back, holding his

cigarette off to the side while looking Alice up and down as if re-evaluating his plain-Jane younger sister.

"Jack, he's never even kissed me."

He seemed disappointed.

"He's not gay, is he?"

"No, well, I don't think so."

"So what did you call me out here for? Make it quick. I have to get back to that radiator job."

"Well, he wants me to go away with him, not just him, but with a group of other college students." She paused. "West Virginia."

"West Virginia?" he took another step back. He couldn't have been more surprised than if she said she *was* pregnant and having Doug's quintuplets.

He threw his nub of a cigarette to the ground. "I wanna meet this guy."

"Really?"

"Yes, really."

Alice smiled. That had been the most concern he had ever shown her. Maybe the myth of the big brother protection was actually true.

"You set up a meeting. I have to get back to work now."

She walked away with a satisfaction on her face and a new spring to her step. The sky couldn't have been bluer or the line of grass between the street and the sidewalk greener.

7

Tom

The judge was a woman, not resembling Judge Judy, but a stately, serious, slightly irritated, heron-like figure of an African-American woman who looked like she ate only salads, never pizza, a woman who might give three privileged white kids punishment to the full extent of the law.

Tom's head had hurt for a whole week. He was sure she would throw the book at the girl who hit him with the baseball bat that night in the cul-de-sac when he was mugged for two pizzas and eighteen dollars. After all, both the girls and the guy had pled guilty. His only reason for being there was a formality.

This might even fall into RIPLEY'S BELIEVE IT OR NOT under stupid criminals if there was such a category. He would be listed as the thirty-year-old loser who delivered pizzas, the one who was stupid enough to take his eyes off them for a moment, long enough for the swing that wouldn't even make it on a T-ball team.

The bailiff called his name, and he made his way up to the witness stand, placing his hand on the Bible, promising to tell the whole truth and nothing but the truth.

"Mr. Walker," the judge said, "please tell us your version of what happened on the night in question."

He cleared his throat. "We got a call for three pizzas to be delivered about a quarter of a mile away. We didn't have the ingredients for one of the pizzas. My boss, Jimmy, said to call the customer back and let her know and ask her if she wanted a substitution. No one answered. I told my boss it wasn't far, that I'd go ahead and deliver the two pizzas we already had made up.

"I found the address, but the house was dark. It was at the end of a cul-de-sac. But, I saw a couple of girls off to the side, next to a row of trees. They were waving at me. I thought they didn't want their parents to know they were getting pizzas. It was a little suspicious, but stuff like that happens with kids all the time. I got out of the car with the pizzas, facing them the whole time. It's part of the rules. I told them about the one pizza, and that I only brought two. I only turned my head to the side for a split second to look at the slip to tell them how much they owed before pulling the pizzas out of the hot bag. It was then I felt the blow to the side of my head. I said, what the f... sorry, Your Honor."

She smiled. "Proceed, Mr. Walker."

"A boy wearing a ski mask came from behind the row of trees. He said he had a knife. He told me to hand the one girl without the bat the pizzas and what money I had. I didn't see the knife, but I handed the other girl the pizzas and pulled eighteen dollars from my pocket and handed it to her. They all ran to a car that was parked about fifty feet in front of me. I got in my own car, turned on the lights to see their license plate, and called it in."

"And a police car was in the vicinity and followed the suspects and watched them enter an apartment. The two officers knocked on the door. They reported a girl opened it, revealing a living room that looked as it had been hit by a tornado. Two open pizza boxes lay on the coffee table, revealing half-eaten pizzas along with too many beer cans to count," the judge said.

"Yes, ma'am," Tom responded.

"No, Mr. Walker, that was a general statement to the court. Since you were not at the apartment, you could hardly testify to that."

"Yes, ma'am," Tom said, thinking he could add himself to the list of stupid witnesses.

The judge looked over her glasses at the defendant. "Mr. Jones, since this is not the first time you have been in my court, and since you have admitted to carrying a weapon, you will serve one year in prison, no probation." She then cast her gaze upon the two girls and called them by name. "Since you have no priors, the court reprimands you with six months' community service and six months' probation."

Tom wanted to say what the f... again but restrained himself. Instead, he placed his hand over the pea-sized knot remaining on his head. He walked out of the court determined to find another job, one that didn't involve pizza.

IT WAS four o'clock in the afternoon when he walked out of the courtroom. He didn't want the bar scene but something to relax with, something cheerful. He walked a few blocks and came upon a brightly painted coffee shop like something out of a cartoon, an open invitation to those who wanted to escape life for a while. He ordered a plain black coffee and a blueberry scone which would have to be his dinner. He looked over at the bulletin board. He singled out the notice that said, MAKE INQUIRIES IF YOU WOULD LIKE TO PERFORM ON SATURDAY NIGHTS. He wished.

Something about the place seemed familiar. Then he remembered. It was when he first came to New York. He was here, a few tables down if he remembered correctly. There was a college

dude chatting up a group of high-school girls. One girl in particular caught his attention, the one he thought was the cutest. She
had the most fantastic shade of red hair and the prettiest blue
eyes. The college guy was urging her to go off and join some
commune with him. *Wonder if she did.* He did the math in his
head. That was around seven years ago. He finished his scone
and coffee and made his way to the bus stop, thinking he needed
a different life. It would be a long, cold, and he hoped not lonely,
winter.

Alice

She spent an entire day walking the treadmill of a store, arriving one hour after opening and leaving only minutes before closing. This should have exhausted her, but she was pumped. There was something about the smell and look of bed linens and textured pillows, especially the ones with buttons, along with the bright colors of pots, pans, and small kitchen appliances that exhilarated her. All the colors and plethora of gadgets were steps above the drab interior of her mother's house with its beat-up aluminum cookware and starched white doilies covering the dark, heavily polished tables —the polish being the off-brand her mother purchased from the DOLLAR GENERAL STORE—devoid of family pictures, instead displaying the idealized life of porcelain Hummel figurines.

Alice prided herself on being practical. So for her shopping trip, she wore stretch jeans, an oversized sweatshirt, a stretchy tee underneath, and her well-worn sneakers. She could hear Doug now, "Alice, you're still wearing those?" No one had ever accused her of being fashionable. The sexiest outfit she ever owned was the tight-fitting, short pink dress bearing the logo of MAC'S BURGERS. She also prided herself on being comfortable, and she had abandoned bras while on The Farm. They were totally impractical on a rural hillside when it came to bending, hoeing, and the like. Nor were they utilitarian after she returned from The Farm to take care of her mother.

Tight-fitting camisoles, substituting as back braces, had become her norm during the early days of her return. Besides cooking the meals, she helped her mother move about the house, mostly up and down the stairs. Later when her mother was bedridden, her duties as a nurse included lugging up trays of food that went untouched, changing bedpans, and doing her best to change sheets while her mother was still in the bed, the way hospice had taught her. In looking back, she didn't know how she had endured. Alice was far from nurse material; she had even screamed once at The Farm when Doug showed up with blood running down his arm. It turned out to be only scratches from a briar patch.

The only thing about her that wasn't pumped was her feet. In her waitress days, Alice wore standard-issue nursing shoes. This she learned from Eleanor, the older waitress who worked at MAC'S BURGERS. Eleanor's legs still looked good for her age, but the legs of the woman whose place Alice filled looked like 3-D roadmaps with small mountain ridges, even under support hose. Today, Alice could have used those shoes, but sadly, they were a part of the bulk load she sold during the final hour of the yard sale.

Her feet ached from hiking on the concrete aisles of IKEA. Her soles longed for nature's carpet, soft grass. During her first month at MAC'S, she came home to a foot bath of Epsom salts. Afterword, she'd nestled her feet inside thick woolen socks even in the heat of summer, another trick she learned from Eleanor.

She looked down at the permanently stained, tattered sneakers. She tried to imagine her bare feet against the soft soil of a newly hoed garden, and in her mind, she was almost there until a woman in three-inch leopard heels walked past her. While most women gravitated toward shoes, they had never been Alice's thing and certainly not on The Farm. She never understood the seduction of spiked heels in a display window, a woman's version of a peep show, or the wild frenzy of women she had to shuffle through amid boxes strewn across the floor of the shoe department with bustling young salespersons, usually all male, as she made her way to the leftover closeout rack for the most comfortable, cheapest pair of sneakers she could find.

She needed a break—a pause to rest her weary arches and to reflect, to check off her list, tabulate the purchases she had made and what she yet needed, and how much she was going over her budget. Plus, she was ravenous.

It was so smart of IKEA to provide a cafeteria. *Good marketing.* Don't give a customer the chance to leave the store. From farm to table, keep it all contained, the same way they planned the garden and farm activities, strategizing for the most productive yield as Doug called it. All successful businesses did it he'd said. But The Farm had never developed into a business. It scraped by.

Brad and Ellie, the overzealous sales associates who waited on her, highly recommended the Swedish meatballs. While partaking of the recommended dish for lunch, she almost put her fork down when she overheard one lady swear they still used horse meat. Instead, her fork lingered in midair until the other woman assured her they didn't.

Alice had no idea what they were talking about. So much had happened in the world during the time she had shut herself away from it. Her mother often said, "The world is going to hell in a handbasket." Alice didn't know how a handbasket entered into it, but she had to agree.

It was a good thing Doug was still back in West Virginia. So many days she longed to be back there herself, but she had a responsibility to her mother, and after that, there was the sale of the house. Besides, she hadn't heard one word from Doug since her return. So many times she had picked up pen and paper to write Doug, but the cons of doing so outweighed the pros. The bottom line was she was sure he had moved on, and like Thomas Wolfe said, "You can't go home again." The past was the past.

ALICE RETIRED to her sleeping bag, hoping to get a good night's sleep in preparation for all of the assembling she would be doing when her furniture arrived the next day. It would be like Christmas morning when she was small. She purposely left the blind in the bedroom slightly raised. The city lights peeking through the narrow slit between the buildings illuminated the large IKEA shopping bags, the ones she was able to lug home from the store. They stood erect against the bare wall, the trophies of her first major shopping safari.

In her exuberance and truly thinking Brad and Ellie had become her new friends, she invited them to come help with the assembly, offering Chinese takeout in return. They politely turned her down and assured her she could handle it. What must they have thought?

Although IKEA provided a convenient Allen wrench, she purchased a screwdriver and battery-operated drill which she thought would come in handy for future projects. The drill was also against the wall. She had the foresight to test it upon returning home. Home, yes, she was beginning to think of her new apartment as home. While there was a certain peace and serenity to The Farm, the place she *once* called home, there was also a longing to rejoin society—or in her case, join for the first time—since growing up the way she did didn't really epitomize society.

IT HAD BEEN A LONG NIGHT, what with waking up several times and anticipating the arrival of her furniture. "Yes, Virginia, there *is* a Santa Claus."

She had just disposed of the empty cartons of Kung Pao Chicken and rice she had for lunch and was getting ready to crack open her fortune cookie when the delivery men arrived. Steve and Brad—not the same Brad who worked in the store— wearing their special back braces, were kind enough to set each box in the room where it belonged. As they were leaving, it occurred to her she had no box knife with which to open the boxes. She called after them down the six-flight stairwell, but there was no answer. She ran back in her apartment to the window and opened the blind to see the truck pulling away.

"What now?" she asked out loud. Her Christmas morning joy had turned sour.

She opened her package of silverware for four. Four was the smallest set the cutlery came in. Delighted the knives bore a slight perforation, she stabbed at one of the box corners, jabbing the knife with such force it missed and gouged her opposite thumb. She jumped, screaming in pain and holding her thumb, which only showed a trickle of blood. And of course, she had no BAND-AIDS. She stepped into the kitchen, holding her thumb under cold running water while staring at the new dishcloths lying on the counter, still tied in raffia. She would not defile them with her blood. It could be a bad omen. The unopened fortune cookie lay beside the dishtowels. Putting pressure on her thumb until she was sure the bleeding had stopped, she let go and picked up the cookie, broke it, and pulled out the fortune.

Creativity in precarious situations will prevail.

She picked up the knife again for a second go at the box, but it occurred to her that restaurants have box knives. She grabbed her key and bounded down the steps, holding the tiny strip of paper in her hand along with the knife that had wounded her.

DRAGON'S DEN was ripe with customers at thirty minutes past noon.

After what seemed like half an hour performing pantomime in front of the older man who seemed to be running the place, the one who displayed every known facial expression from downright fear to laughter, she wrung her hands, one holding her apartment key and fortune, the other holding the knife in desperation. It was then that a young girl entered the kitchen where Alice stood with the older man. They exchanged something in Chinese that Alice didn't understand, but the old man rolled his eyes toward her, indicating to Alice that he was telling the young girl she was a lunatic.

The black-haired, black-eyed girl in stretch jeans and a tunic top, donning a small backpack, turned her way, speaking perfect English. "I'm Chen. My uncle is ready to call the police. What's your story?"

"My story? We would be here all day for that. What I need is a box knife."

The girl eyed her suspiciously.

"I mean. I want to borrow one. You see, I ordered furniture for my apartment. Across the street on the sixth floor." Alice pointed across the street. "IKEA. I can't open the boxes."

"IKEA, IKEA," the girl squealed. "I have Ikea in my college dorm."

Everyone on the planet must own IKEA, Alice thought. The girl's facial expression changed back to serious. "We can't just give you a box knife. Who is to say you're not a raving lunatic? But I suppose if you meant to do us harm you wouldn't have come over here with only a dinner knife." The girl looked at her uncle and back at Alice. "My uncle says you're crazy." Her uncle stood there, nodding his head even though Alice was sure he didn't understand one word of what they were saying, except for perhaps crazy.

Alice extended the small piece of paper toward the girl. Chen took it, squinting her eyes at Alice before looking down at the fortune. "Are you not right? You believe these things? And what is this?" She eyed the red stain on the paper. "Blood?"

"I cut my thumb trying to open the boxes with this knife," Alice exclaimed.

Chen looked back at the paper and read out loud, "*Creativity in precarious situations will prevail.*" She handed Alice back the thin strip of paper. "This whole situation is *precarious*, wouldn't you say?"

"I assure you I'm perfectly all right. I gave you my business earlier. I'm your neighbor across the street. I figure being across the street, I might eat over here a lot. I used to work in a restaurant. I know you have box knives. I only need a little help. That's all."

"You actually held down a job?" Chen questioned, raising her eyebrows.

Alice was somewhere between despair and tears. Alice asked herself what Doug would do. "That rice looked and tasted a little funny. Was it from yesterday? I hope I don't get food poisoning."

The girl said something to her uncle in Chinese, walked to the back through a door, and returned holding a box knife. She said something to her uncle and turned to Alice. "Come on. I'll go with you and will open your boxes myself. If I'm not back in ten minutes, my uncle is calling the police."

Alice smiled.

"Would you please put that knife down to your side?" Chen said.

Alice obeyed and followed Chen, who was in total command of the situation, across the street and up the six flights of steps.

"Which one?" Chen asked.

Alice took her key and put it in the lock of the door that said 602.

While Chen cut through boxes, Alice apologized for being so foolish. She explained about leaving for The Farm with Doug right after high school and being cut off from the world for five years. Why she was telling all this to Chen, she didn't know.

Right before the ten minutes were up, Chen whipped out her cell and phoned her uncle, or at least Alice concluded it was her uncle.

"So what happened on this farm?" Chen asked.

After an hour and a pot of tea, Chen sat in awe. "I'm majoring in psychology with a minor in journalism. Your story could be my psychology class term paper. Actually, this could lead to a book." Chen spoke fast in perfect English with only a few notable instances of her accent coming into play when she got excited. The possibility of Alice's farm experience becoming a book was one such instance.

Alice hesitated. "Oh, I don't know. It's one thing to casually tell someone what happened, but to have it recorded, I don't know…"

"I wouldn't use real names."

"Let me think about it."

"Okay, well here, let me text you my cell information." Chen moved her two fingers with rapid dexterity.

"Text me?"

"Yes, where's your cell?"

"I don't have one."

"What?"

"I plan on getting one, along with a flat-screen television and computer. My first," Alice added.

A wide grin broke across Chen's face. "Do you know the first thing about buying those?"

"Well, no. But, they were really helpful at IKEA, so I'm sure…"

Chen cut her off. "No, girl. You will need an expert to accompany you when you make those purchases."

"Are you an expert?"

"I'm Chinese, well, my family is from China. Technically,

I'm Chinese-American. But, where do you think electronics come from?"

"China," Alice answered. Doug had certainly ranted enough about it.

"How about Saturday?" Chen asked.

"Saturday?"

"Yeah, we'll go shopping together."

"Well, I suppose. I could certainly use some advice."

"Say ten o'clock?" Chen asked.

"Sure," Alice said. It wasn't as though she had any kind of schedule to adhere to.

"Meet me in front of the restaurant. They don't open until eleven, but my uncle is always there by ten."

"Okay," Alice said.

"I'll leave you to your furniture then," Chen said as she walked toward the door with her box knife.

"Chen," Alice called out.

Chen turned. "Yes?"

"I'm sorry I said the rice tasted funny. It didn't. Your food is great."

Chen smiled.

ALICE GLIDED through her tiny apartment, reveling in pride and a sense of accomplishment in her new surroundings, her new home, while smiling at her ingenuity in putting together a whole apartment of furniture. She not only constructed a whole new environment of living space, but she had made a new friend, Chen. At least she hoped she had.

She walked around her new space, admiring the beige and burnt umber comforter across her bed adorned with no less than seven pillows, all of which had bamboo buttons. She rubbed her hand over the sleek white chest that set the two white pillows on the bed off. The two white nightstands matched although why she needed two she didn't know, but she preferred to be optimistic. She wondered what Doug would think but instead, ended up imagining him being sound asleep. They were on the same time zone, and it was nine-thirty. They were usually in bed by nine most nights at The Farm.

She had yet to deposit her all white dishes into the cabinets. Both Brad and Ellie had strongly steered her away from the multi-colored ones, suggesting white was both elegant and timeless. Brad, in his early twenties, was both flamboyant and cheery and oozed expertise in design. Her new white dishes sat stacked on the white laminate table with its two matching chairs at the end. Tomorrow, she would wash them along with her set of glasses and figure out how to best position her stainless-steel toaster on the small counter space.

The living room was no less a wonder with a beige sectional and white throw pillows, a colorful throw, and a standard black coffee table. Brad suggested she go with black to offset all the white. "Plus, most flat-screen televisions come in black," he said. She had told him she intended to buy one. And the desk where her new laptop would go—because Ellie said she must go with a laptop—fit perfectly next to the window. Alice only hoped the guy across the way would close his blinds occasionally.

Alice considered herself fortunate to have had so much help in the vast expanse of a store. After telling Brad her story of living on The Farm for five years and then caring for her mom for one, it wasn't long until two other sales associates, Ellie and Carmen, gathered around her, helping her with every decision, making sure she didn't leave the store without any item they felt she needed. It was after lunch that she lost Carmen, lured away by another customer, but Brad and Ellie stuck with her until the end. It was like she won the IKEA lottery, only she didn't because she almost went into shock when the total was rung up. And she might have passed out if Brad had not been by her side the whole time. She looked around. Was it common to have a sales associate accompany you to the register? She looked around again. It clearly wasn't even though she had signed up to be part of the IKEA family with a new credit card to arrive in the mail in a few days. IKEA Family—did this make Brad and Ellie her cousins or something of that nature? Would she see them on family get-togethers? She had never been to a family get-together in her life, one of the sad reasons Brad and Ellie insisted she sign up. Alice sighed. How had she become such a chatterbox?

She made another pass through her small home to delight in the beauty, which helped to counteract the stress of the final tabulation at the cash register. She took one look at the drab curtains the previous renter had left behind, shaking her head, realizing how bad they looked in comparison to her new furniture.

She was now down from three years to two-and-a-half without having to worry about a job. She suspected the purchase of electronics would bring her down to two. Out loud, she said, "Thank you, Hummel figurines," before setting out her new plush beige towel, discarding her clothes into her new wicker hamper, grabbing her new loofa, and stepping into the shower. Her mother would be appalled at such extravagance.

9

Leaving The Farm

A lice lay in her perfect bed, not able to fall asleep. Why did she bring up The Farm to Chen? The Farm seemed to be on her mind almost constantly, even amid this new phase of life she was entering. Not once had her mother asked about The Farm. When Alice did try to talk about it, her mother looked away, disinterested.

So many times during her mother's illness and then at MAC'S BURGERS, Alice thought this was not the way life was supposed to be for someone her age. A day's work at playing nurse and waiting on customers at a burger joint had drained her differently than a day's work at the The Farm. The Farm was a clean, wholesome release. She could look out the window and see a myriad of stars and feel a sense of accomplishment as she drifted off, even more so when a bountiful crop of tomatoes or beans was celebrated with sticky, sweaty lovemaking to the point of passing out, sometimes not in their bed, but in their own private spot near the lake where the full majesty of the nightly spectacle of celestial bodies formed a giant canopy above them and the sounds of tree frogs and katydids lulled them into a deep sleep. Alice had felt so small and so magnificent at the same time. She felt none of that after a day of waitressing, not even after a day of good tips.

She could have lived the rest of her life out on The Farm, but on the day Kyle handed her an envelope from Clara Jenkins, she knew it wasn't to be. Clara, it turned out, had learned of her whereabouts from Jack Jr. The envelope from the nearest post office had been addressed to her with a general delivery address.

Kyle and Laura were The Farm's liaisons. They went to the nearest towns for farmers' markets, setting up wares, the seasonal crops, jams and jellies, and honey from their bees. On other occasions, usually once a month, they made a monthly visit into the nearest town for supplies. The town with a population of 1,800 boasted a seed-and-hardware store, a Piggly Wiggly, a consignment shop, a bank, a local diner called Bucky's, a Dairy Queen, and a post office.

Alice wrote Jack numerous times to reassure him she was fine and that nothing nefarious was going on. She omitted the growing and smoking of pot. She imagined her brother laughing at the fact his little sister partook in an occasional reefer. It was hardly nefarious—criminal perhaps but not wicked. Doug cautioned her about what to write. "Don't think for one minute there isn't talk about some commune or cult types who come out of the backwoods from time to time. I wouldn't be surprised at all if our mail wasn't being read."

For someone who studied law at Columbia, Doug had little trust in the government or the judicial system, even less in people in general, especially the locals who labeled them the hippies who occupied the old Crosby place. Doug had a word to describe almost everyone. For the natives living beyond the borders of their farm, it was the *locals*, and it was their farm now in a manner of speaking since Doug owned the deed even though it would forever be known as the Crosby farm.

Doug's one word to describe Alice was naïve. It was a statement, nothing accusatory, nothing that would cause a fight. A fight on The Farm was almost unheard of. What was there to fight over? When to plant, when to harvest? That was all decided by nature. The stresses on a farm weren't the same as in a city where technology abounded, and people had time on their hands. And when nerves did become a little frayed, a patch of green weed intermingled amid zucchini plants took care of it.

When they weren't dead exhausted from farm work, the topics of conversation were conspiracy theories. Alice had been the last holdout in accepting them to be true, but Doug could certainly make a case which made her wonder if he shouldn't be in a New York courtroom instead of on a hillside in West Virginia. But Doug was adamant he would never practice law.

Alice eventually, after pondering all the evidence although circumstantial, accepted the theories as true. Every time she had walked past where the Twin Towers used to be, she got a sick feeling in the pit of her stomach. During one of their late-night conspiracy-theory sessions, Doug had made a strong case of 911 being an inside job.

Jack Jr. wrote back a total of two times if you could classify a Christmas card as a letter. But she knew her brother was still around the city somewhere when she received Clara's letter. It was obvious Clara did too although in the letter, Clara swore to Alice she never told her mother. It would break her heart if she did, she said, Jack Jr. being so close and not once visiting. No, Clara's letter had a single purpose, that of telling Alice her mother was in dire condition, and as her only daughter, if she had any kind of heart, she must come home immediately.

She slept with Doug one final time. Their relationship did eventually blossom. It more or less fell under the category of Adam and Eve, not that they were the only people of the opposite sex on the planet, but in their own little world, they were the only couple not paired. Alice didn't define it as love. Nor did Doug. Not in the conventional sense. It was the main reason she didn't write after returning to her mother.

Perhaps it was the intense labor in getting The Farm underway and the abandoned ramshackle house they inhabited up to snuff or maybe just becoming more mature caused the schoolgirl crush to wear off. Their relationship was comfortable, something to fall back on after a long day working in the garden or tending to the cows they raised for milk or chopping enough wood or canning enough food to tide them over during the winter months.

It was during that first winter the sexes paired off, officially. She once asked Doug if he had planned on an equal number of females to males. He laughed once again at Alice's naïvety, his way of saying yes.

Even though it wasn't romantic love, it *was* love, maybe more so than the standard definition of goosebumps and stomach butterflies followed by a big wedding and all the stress that came afterward. It was the kind where their hands touched as they spit on seeds and placed them in the ground.

Laura said spitting on the seeds gave them their own chemical composition and what sprouted from them guarded those who spit on them against illness. Laura also recommended working barefoot in the garden. She called it earthing. Laura was a fount of wisdom when it came to stuff like that. Alice didn't remember one illness while there, not even a cold.

By the third year, there was one birth. Kyle and Renea had a little girl, April. She was thus named being that April was the month she was born in, along with the new calf that also came a week later. Kyle and Renea were the other couple aside from her and Doug and Chris and Laura. Doug's original plan was to have twelve, but the others got cold feet at the last moment. Alice was glad. Twelve under the same roof with one outhouse would have made everyone feel like penned rabbits.

Why she didn't conceive, she didn't know. She and Doug rarely used protection. She reasoned it was the experiment—the one where her family was placed on earth, the one her father couldn't cope with. There was to be no more dysfunction. Either she was sterile or Doug was, maybe the both of them. She and Doug were dysfunction's prodigy.

Farming was rewarding, but it was also hard, not for the weak of heart. It was only out of stubbornness toward his father that Doug persisted, and now he was left without a mate. Doug drove her into town in the old pickup truck shared by members of The Farm. She wore the same off-white dress she had worn when they first came to The Farm. After five years, having come into her womanhood, she properly filled it out. There were tears in both of their eyes as she boarded the bus. Doug made no mention of her ever returning, another reason she couldn't bring herself to write.

10

Tom

He slid the completed job application under the small opening in the window. He'd fudged a little, but most of it was right. He knew to some degree how to operate heavy equipment. He had driven a tractor at age fifteen on his uncle's farm in Georgia. He could heavy lift with the rest of them although pizzas didn't quality as heavy lifting, but he had helped enough people move. During college, he'd had a plethora of part-time jobs that should surely qualify him for something: manager of a shoe store, cable guy, a door-to-door salesman, landscaping, along with some odd construction jobs here and there.

All the jobs were interesting in their own ways, but the world of shoes was like stepping into a cult, a parallel universe—one he dreaded entering each day. There was the stock room from hell with boxes of mismatched shoes, never in the right place when you were looking for a particular pair, the size seven the customer requested when upon seeing their bare feet he knew were a size eight, and he would have to make another trip to the back and return juggling more boxes. It was a given the customer would see more shoes to try during his absence. There were the woeful stories about their corns, bunions, sprains, and past breaks. For some reason, customers confused him with their podiatrist. Stinky feet was the least of it. It was either all hell breaking loose with ten customers coming at him at once during the time he was supposed to have his break or excruciatingly boring. It was during the slow times he stood in the doorway, staring out from the invisible bars of his cell, and watched conditioned consumers or the early morning mall walkers pass by, all the while trying not to lose his faith in humanity.

Although, he learned a lot about people working in a mall shoe store as a door-to-door salesman, he sucked. At least with the shoes, sales were assured.

The construction jobs were his favorites. He had a knack for working with his hands and learning how things worked. He enjoyed most aspects of it, which could be anything from running wires through a house to connecting waterlines or air-conditioning ducts in tight crawl spaces, the part most guys dreaded. Usually, being the skinniest guy on the crew, this job fell to him.

The jobs he left off his résumé were inconsequential such as babysitting in both junior high and high school along with driving a truck at age sixteen, carrying workers who were probably illegal aliens for a suspect company. He wrote at the end of the application that he was open to new experiences, which possibly implied something to the receptionist he didn't intend.

"When can you start?" the bleach blonde with too much eye makeup and fire-engine red lips asked.

"Anytime," he told her.

"Your number's on here?" She looked down at the application.

His writing wasn't the best in the world, but he double-checked to make sure everything was legible before slipping the paper through the slot.

"Yes," Tom said, smiling. It was a staged smile, and she probably knew it, but oh well.

She smiled back more than a woman her age should. It reminded him of one woman, pushing sixty, who came every two weeks on Saturday like clockwork to the shoe store. She insisted on being fitted by one of the male shoe salesmen, usually him. She went from shoe store to shoe store, every one of them in the mall with male employees, rarely ever purchasing. The unmentionables that most shoe salesmen were privy to when fitting women wearing short skirts were absent on this particular woman. She would leave one store, only to be announced by the last salesman helping her of her eminent arrival at the next store and on up the line. Tom couldn't see how this experience would fit on his résumé. Nor could he see how the similar cable guy experiences he encountered would get him anywhere in any respectable form of business.

He had been sending out résumés and filling out applications for a solid week with no bites, but today he felt lucky.

The lady called the next morning. "Can you be at a job site in Queens in two hours? There is a construction crew there waiting on some permits to demolish a row of houses in preparation for a strip mall."

He almost shouted yes over the phone but showed restraint.

She gave him the address. "See Benny when you get there," she said.

11

Alice

With taking care of her mother and working at MAC'S, Alice had never actually experienced free time. But free time was what she had until her anticipated shopping spree with Chen scheduled for Saturday.

Alice spent one whole day walking through the galleries of THE METROPOLITAN MUSEUM OF ART and still only skimmed the surface. She had been to this museum before as well as THE MODERN MUSEUM OF ART and THE GUGGENHEIM on school field trips. While her appreciation at the time lagged somewhere behind that of the art students in the group, she was definitely seeing the paintings through new eyes now, especially Van Gogh. His pastoral scenes of fields and hay made her long to return to The Farm—that combined with looking at a program of upcoming exhibits, one about conspiracy theories and art coming in January, and for a split second, thinking she glimpsed Doug out of the corner of her eye.

The man who had similar features wore a designer suit but was absent of the long unkempt hair and wire-rimmed glasses she was so accustomed to seeing on Doug. He turned down another corridor so abruptly, she couldn't be sure. Still, the thought of glimpsing him sent an electrical surge through her body. She shrugged it off to the peasant scenes of farming and the program about the upcoming conspiracy exhibit. They *only* reminded her of Doug. And the woman he was with wasn't his type at all: blonde, sophisticated, looking like she leaped off a billboard for Prada. How many times had Doug told her *she* was *his* type? She spied her reflection in a glass panel. Plain was Doug's type?

It had been a long day. Her feet ached. She needed to get home. It would be a long walk back to Brooklyn with aching feet, but riding the subway was one of her least favorite things about New York.

The previous day she had spent within the confines of Brooklyn, exploring little shops, the most miraculous of which was one not much bigger than her apartment, a shop called NATURE'S BLUSH.

It was like entering a different dimension. The brash sounds of the street were replaced with serene tones and reverberations resembling the music at the end of the movie *Bill and Ted's Excellent Adventure,* the music that in the future would bring mankind into harmony. Even though Alice had no proper working television at her mother's home, she did occasionally see older movies with Kayla and Meghan because she couldn't afford the newer ones.

The aroma of the shop ganged up on her like some otherworldly presence, not in a hostile way, but as something soothing, bathing not only her nostrils but her whole body. Totally alien, but nice aliens, the ones who were going to swoop down on earth and solve all of its woes, probably not the same aliens who must have placed *her* here. Alice breathed in the essence, trying not to choke. It was one of those things one had to adjust to slowly, like adapting to the atmosphere and gravity of another planet. Entering another world was the closest thing she could compare the experience to.

A middle-aged woman levitated up behind her, or so it seemed since her long tie-dyed dress and Birkenstocks hardly made a sound, telepathically conveying, *Namaste, how may I be of service*? Before The Farm, Alice might have giggled in ignorance or run out of the store, but some of what she saw was familiar, minus the artistic packaging, almost all of which bore the word organic.

"Is there anything I can help you with?" she asked.

Alice wanted to ask her if she'd already asked that but didn't. "No, I'm only looking. Exploring the shops of Brooklyn."

"Oh, are you new here? You don't look or sound like a tourist."

"No, I moved from Queens to Brooklyn."

"Oh, I see."

Did she really see? No one could be that telepathic except for a deity. Alice saw a small pewter statue, part man, part elephant, on the shelf in front of her. She could recite what most herbs and vitamins were used for, but all she knew about the elephant man was that he hailed from India.

"I'm Iris." An apt name, Alice thought, the color purple being one of the higher chakras. "I see you have noticed our little Ganesha."

Alice picked him up for closer examination. "Yes, but I'm not familiar with what he represents. I know all the gods of India represent something."

"Ganesha is a widely revered god there. He removes obstacles, is the patron of arts and sciences, and the deva of intellect and wisdom."

Alice placed Ganesha back on the shelf. "I guess at the moment I don't have many obstacles. I did, but they are behind me."

Iris raised her eyebrows and smiled. Maybe she wasn't so telepathic. "It's rare to find someone who doesn't have obstacles or doesn't foresee any in the future."

The door dinged as another customer walked in. "Look around, and if you have any questions, just ask," Iris said, making her way over to the woman who entered with a seriousness of purpose or multiple purposes. Alice looked over to see the woman had picked up a hand-held cart and had already placed two items in it.

It wasn't long until a thirty-something woman with her hair tied back in a ponytail, wearing yoga tights and a light jacket over a running bra came through the door. She bent over to pick up a bottle of something out of the refrigerated compartment. Alice noticed the name Kombucha on the bottle she picked up along with the sheerness of the yoga tights as she bent over. She was either wearing no underwear or a G-string. Alice admired her daring.

After both customers made their purchases and left, Alice had only advanced to the third aisle of the store.

"Are you sure there is nothing I can help you with? You are reading those labels as if you are studying for an exam." Once again, Iris was upon her in a flash.

"No, it's just, I'm familiar with a lot of these. We used herbs on The Farm. "

"The farm?" Iris asked.

Why did she even mention that? Before long, if she didn't keep her mouth shut, everyone in the city would know about The Farm. Well, Brad, Ellie, Carmen, Chen, and Iris weren't everyone in the city.

"What's behind the curtain?" Alice abruptly asked to change the subject. It was obvious the low-key music was coming from behind the curtain. "Is there a wizard back there?"

Iris laughed. "No wizard, only me. That is for when I have help in the store. It's a massage room. I give massages and practice various forms of energy work, mostly Reiki."

"Oh," Alice said.

"But tell me about this farm," Iris said.

Maybe it was the music or the incense coming from the back mixing with the enticing odors of every nonpharmaceutical cure known to man on this side of the curtain that set her mouth spinning about Laura and about how she was a fount of knowledge about every plant that grew from the ground, no doubt why Doug had lured her to The Farm. She told Iris they also had Kombucha, but they made theirs in a large vat with what Laura called a scobi mushroom.

Another customer walked through the door. Iris reached into her smock pocket and held out her card. "I could use someone with your knowledge in the shop. If you're looking for a job, we should talk."

Alice stumbled around, not knowing what to say.

"Just think about it," Iris said before walking away.

Alice walked down the street, taking a backward glance at the shop. Its front although blue, reminded her of THE JAVA BEAN FACTORY where she had met Doug. Both were small, unassuming businesses with a good atmosphere. The dress code for a health food store would be easy enough. No bras, spiked heels, or no tight-fitting waitress uniforms was a plus. Maybe she could find some tie-dye at a second-hand shop.

IT WAS FINALLY SATURDAY. Alice had been dressed since eight, anticipating her day out with Chen. A television, cell phone, and computer couldn't come soon enough. Staring at the blank walls at night was getting boring. She could only appreciate the marvels of her new furniture so much. Why she hadn't thought of paintings, posters, or something while out shopping, she didn't know.

Alice looked at her watch. She had one hour before she was to meet Chen at her uncle's restaurant. She lay across her couch and stared at the ceiling.

12

Alice and Chen

E lectronics shopping with Chen was not what she expected. It was short and sweet. Chen had done her homework.

"There is no need to go through the unnecessary formality of computer stores with their nerdy everyday, bad-hair employees. Shopping online bypasses all of that," Chen said with an air of authority, and Chen reeked of authority.

In Alice's apartment, Chen removed her sleek pinkish-toned laptop from her backpack after finding something she called a hotspot with her phone. She signed in and showed Alice the different options of computers and flat screens. She went over her own recommendations, heavily suggesting refurbished ones on a site called eBay.

"It will save you money," she said. "And if something should go wrong, my brother is a whiz when it comes to electronics."

There was the *bid* option or the *buy now* one. Chen said to go with *buy now*. She didn't see how Alice could go without the amenities of technology for a day longer without exploding.

For the phone, they went to a store dealing only in phones. The employees all looked to be straight out of high school.

People took numbers, a system that might have been implemented in the women's shoe department because the crowd reminded Alice of the same madness, except half of the people in there were in a perplexed complaining mood rather than in the ecstasy of a new shoe purchase.

After an hour, Chen had guided Alice through all the rigors of the purchase of a cell phone with a two-year contract, the thought of which made Alice slightly nauseous. Chen told her it was the price one had to pay for living in the real world. In Alice's mind, what Chen referred to as the real world was up for debate. Henry David Thoreau and John Muir, the two people Doug most liked to quote, would rush back to their graves if they could see the world now.

"Aren't you excited?" Chen asked as they walked out of the store. Alice was carrying the extra layered paper bag with the fancy draw-string handle, which held the empty box the phone had come in. In actuality, the phone was already set up and secured in Alice's purse. The whole thing was a rather lengthy and ceremonious process with the sales clerk congratulating her. What next? Would shoe clerks be handing out certificates of glamor with shoe purchases?

"Yes," Alice said rather matter-of-factly, not the gleeful response Chen was looking for. Chen had already added her own number to Alice's favorites. The only other number Alice might put there was the one for NATURE'S BLUSH if she decided to take the job. After reflecting on the reality of the business world, she could hardly see adding Brad's or Ellie's number. She could hear Brad's response if she were to go back to IKEA, search him out, and ask for his number. "Aw, aren't you so sweet?" he might say before politely pushing her away and calling security. "I'm afraid we have a legitimate country bumpkin here," he would whisper to the guard. Doug was clearly right about her naïveté.

The sound of Chen's voice interrupted her musings. "We have to get you set up with some apps." Chen came to an abrupt halt in front of STARBUCKS. Since the autumn day was unseasonably warm, they sat outside at a table although the green umbrellas had already been withdrawn. "Okay, let me see your phone again."

Alice dug out the phone housed in the sky-blue case Chen insisted on since the color matched Alice's eyes. "First app, STARBUCKS." She moved her two thumbs in rapid succession over the screen, and said, "There. Now you need to add some money and sign up for their rewards' program." She handed Alice back her phone.

The knot in Alice's stomach tightened. Technology seemed to have a never-ending price tag. Alice sighed.

"Don't worry. You can add what you want. Ten dollars is fine."

The knot lessened a little.

"Here." Chen reached for Alice's phone a second time. "Let me show you." She touched the app. "You can put your own thumbprint in later. I thought until you get the hang of it, though..." She trailed off as she moved her thumbs over the screen again. She held the phone up momentarily. "I've added FACEBOOK too. Good picture. And I'm your first friend."

Alice thought, *My only friend.* "Where did you get my picture?" Alice asked.

"I just took it. See?" Chen took another.

Alice cringed. "It's too close-up, don't you think?"

"No worries. We'll add an app to fix any flaws."

"How much are these apps?" Alice shrieked.

"No worries. Most are free."

But she *was* worrying. Digging potatoes from the ground, hoping for a good yield to last through the winter, was far less stressful.

"You need to put your credit card in your phone."

"But..."

"You only get charged for what you type in. Quit worrying. We won't do automatic reload."

Chen guided her through the process.

"Now what?" Alice asked.

"We go inside the store and order, or we could order from our phones and pick it up at the counter."

"If you don't mind, I still prefer a friendly face even if the smile is fake."

Not being a connoisseur of coffee, except for black, and getting dizzy-headed from the endless selections and sizes she couldn't comprehend because she was used to MAC'S BURGERS' selections of small, medium, large, and super mac, Alice went with Chen's suggestion—a green tea frap with a single shot of white mocha and extra whip because they were celebrating her new phone and first STARBUCKS' purchase. Chen rattled off the order so fast it made her head spin. The only thing Alice contributed, other than saying her name to be written on the cup, was holding up the line by waving her phone numerous times in front of the red beam, or so she thought, until the barista—an awfully fancy name, Alice thought—smiled with what Alice deduced was sincere empathy, holding up the contraption in front of her phone like an adept umpire catching the ball after a strike.

No sooner had they picked up their drinks at the counter and secured the only two vacant seats did a banner roll across the screen of Alice's phone, stating her balance was three dollars and thirty-three cents. She gasped. The apps may have been free but using them was like feeding money into a slot machine.

"So maybe we can go back to your place, and you can tell me more about this farm?" Chen asked. Alice had already gotten to know Chen's insistent nature well enough to know there would be no wiggling out of it.

13

The Farm

C hen pulled a notebook and pen from her backpack, shed her shoes, and settled in on Alice's new sofa, drawing her knees up to act as her desk.

Alice lay on her back on the floor, staring up at the white ceiling, imagining it as a movie screen where she might project images of The Farm.

She turned her head in Chen's direction. "What do you want to know?"

"Start at the beginning," Chen said, pen in hand.

Alice turned her gaze back toward the ceiling and thought for a moment before speaking. "I had so many emotions flooding through me when I knew for sure I was leaving with Doug— mostly excitement. There was a bit of guilt, but when I reflect back, not much. I mean, I was eighteen. I was so ready to get out from under my mother's thumb.

"My mother was still in bed at six a.m. when I snuck out of the house. I took all the things I thought I might need and stuffed them into my mother's suitcase. I took the sheets and pillow from my bed, carrying them separately. I didn't feel guilty about taking the suitcase. It was only gathering cobwebs in the back of her closet. It wasn't like she was going to be taking a trip. She hardly left the house. Anyway, I was so careful, tiptoeing around. My biggest fear was her waking up before I snuck out of the house.

"It was like Christmas Eve when I was young. I hardly got any sleep. All that anticipation of what the next day would bring.

"I was waiting on the front steps of the house when they pulled up. Laura and Chris sat in the back of Doug's black Suburban, a gift from his father for his high school graduation. Doug had already racked up plenty of miles on it. We squeezed my measly belongings in, and I sat up front with him. Said it was an opportunity for me to see the countryside, seeing as I was the only one who had never been out of the city.

"We were wedged in like pickles in a jar. Every square inch of the vehicle had been utilized, including the top luggage rack, and had a purpose in transporting us to our new life.

"I was both nervous and excited, but no less than the others were. I wore my off-white dress, the one I had worn for my high school graduation, and my new sneakers. The dress was big on me, being secondhand and all. I felt awkward at first when I saw everyone else wearing jeans."

"Did you have on the same shoes you wear now?" Chen interrupted.

"Yes," Alice replied with an eye roll before continuing. "No one made a comment or seemed to care. I only felt uncomfortable for a moment. What was going on was bigger than clothing. The feelings inside the vehicle reminded me of a revival meeting I went to once with my mother. Everyone was revved up. Doug was going on about all the stuff we were going to do, and we were all chiming amens, not literally, of course. When I think back on it, the atmosphere reminded me of the Beach Boys song, "Good Vibrations."

"Anyway, we were off to live the dream. Doug talked about

the others who would be joining us, eight more, but I'm jumping ahead."

———

THE METALLIC GRAY of the cityscape changed to hues of faint green countryside as they entered Pennsylvania. Trees were just beginning to bud. Alice noticed a certain symmetry came into play upon crossing the border. Not long into the journey, Alice found what might be considered a front yard in Queens was about the width of a ditch line in Pennsylvania. In New York, it was all about the real estate, the square footage, how close it was to the subway or if it had a view of Central Park. As they got farther away from the city, she discovered every house had its own Central Park. It didn't make sense to her at all why after leaving the city, the property values declined.

The road stretched on. Multiple lanes narrowed to two, and houses became sparser. To both the left and right were rows of fence lines, and behind them, groups of cows huddled together in one spot as if they were plotting something or philosophizing about the stupidity of humans. They came upon an Amish buggy. Despite the evergrowing line of vehicles piled up behind them and the buggy, there were no horns blaring, only a polite acceptance and reverence for those who chose this unhurried pace of life.

After a while, Doug passed. When he did, the driver of the buggy, a bearded man with a black hat, blue shirt, and suspenders which held up black pants, nodded. There was no mustache, just a beard. Was the absence of a mustache commonplace or unique with this one Amish man? Alice wanted to ask, but didn't. Maybe it didn't have to do with the tenets of their faith at all, but rather it was a matter of practicality having to do with prevention—preventing mashed potatoes and gravy from getting stuck there. Being farmers, they were sure to grow lots of potatoes. All four of them waved back. As they did, Alice rolled down her window to hear the clop of horseshoes on the pavement.

Alice thought of the Orthodox Jews she often saw walking the streets back in the city. The attire was similar, but try as they might to stand out, New York had assimilated them as their own, making them look stiff and formal as they walked the sidewalks at an urgent pace with some serious single-minded purpose. Seriousness and singularity of purpose was the main way you could tell a true New Yorker from a tourist other than the *I love New York* t-shirts and hats the out-of-towners wore.

The man holding the reins, bopping ever so slightly on the seat, looked comfortable with whatever the world had to throw at him. The woman beside him sat just as at ease in a simple dark-blue dress. A heavily starched bonnet cast a shadow over her face. The pleasant face that peeked from the austere starched headdress gave them a genuine shy smile as they passed.

"They can ride in automobiles but can't own them," Chris said. "The same with phones," he added.

"The sexes aren't equal," Laura said. She had lived in Kentucky in her youth, not far from an Amish community. "My family bought some furniture from them. They're friendly, but at the same time, keep to themselves. They have some strange customs."

"Like what?" Alice asked.

"They have this thing called Rumspringa. Teenagers are given two years to live outside the community and explore different lifestyles."

"Like?" Alice asked.

"Anything. If they want to try sex or drugs, they can. Dress differently. Their parents give them the funds to do it."

"And then what?"

"They mostly go off to a big city but rarely ever stray from their own group. Nine times out of ten they return back to their community."

"Like a trip to Vegas," Doug piped in.

"What?" Alice asked.

Doug reached over and put on arm around Alice's shoulder then withdrew it back to the steering wheel as he passed a semi making its way up a hill. "You are *naïve*, aren't you? You know what goes on in Vegas stays in Vegas. Anyway, they live simple, happy lives devoid of what we consider *necessities* such as computers, televisions, cell phones, and automobiles."

"Like the automobile we're traveling in, and all this stuff we have crammed in the back and strapped to the roof to take us to our new simpler life?" Alice asked.

"Touché, Alice," Laura said.

The terrain became more mountainous as they came upon a bold green sign: WELCOME TO WEST VIRGINIA, WILD AND WONDERFUL. The landscape *was* wild in comparison to what Alice had left behind in New York. They maneuvered the roller-coaster ride of the interstate in awe of the stretches of majestic mountains and just as sickened by their demise.

"Mountaintop removal," Doug said, frowning.

During the journey, Alice went through a myriad of emotions: contentment in breathing in this man she hardly knew, her body only inches away from his, not quite knowing her place; embarrassment at the familiarity between Laura and Chris; and butterflies in her stomach at being chosen for this adventure.

At no part of the journey did she have regrets, well, except for one, leaving her mother with only a note. She promised to write, but she didn't know if she would keep that promise. Nor did she give her mother an address since she didn't know the exact address, and even if she did, she wouldn't have given it to her. She wasn't sure how her mother would feel other than abandoned.

Never once had her mother asked what she wanted to do with

her life. It was almost a given she would get some low-paying job and stay by her side, caring for her until she grew into an old maid, hardly distinguishable from her mother. She pushed the guilt down. It was easy enough with the constant unfurling of newness before her. She felt like Dorothy leaving Kansas. It took a tornado for Dorothy to embark upon self-discovery. It took a total stranger, an off-beat college guy with wild ideas, for her. Doug was Professor Marvel, and she was Dorothy, only Doug never encouraged her to return home, only to leave home. "All birds must leave the nest," he'd said.

The Wizard of Oz, her favorite movie, was perhaps a sign of what was to come. She couldn't remember one year of missing the annual replay on television. Luckily, it was broadcast on the one station remaining after the rabbit ears broke, the one that broadcast her mother's favorite soap operas.

The four were in constant conversation until the final hour of the journey. Both tiredness and subdued acceptance of what they had signed up for set in during that final hour. It had been a long drive, eleven hours total, the longest stretch through the mountains of West Virginia. The trip should have been only a little over eight hours, but there were numerous stops for stretching, grabbing something to eat, and last-minute supplies.

"It's rough," Doug cautioned as they left a gravel road and crossed the creek onto a dirt road. Doug had made the trip before by plane, flying into Charleston's airport and renting a car.

After several miles of roadway marked only by worn tire tracks with a foot of grass on both sides and between that made a grating sound underneath the truck bed as they passed over it, they came upon a two-story frame house. Peeling chips of paint indicated the house had once been white, and at another time, a light shade of blue. A barn with traces of red paint stood off in the distance.

Nothing could have prepared Alice for the shock. She *had been* naïve but maybe no more than Chris or Laura, whose mouths had dropped open in complete surprise. In contrast, Doug displayed a broad grin.

A large oak, wider than the one at her old address, was sprouting its new foliage—foliage that would provide a canopy of shade in front of the house. A worn tire hung from a frayed piece of rope tied to the lowest branch. There was still a patch of bare ground where children's feet must have pushed from, beckoning those children to return.

The sun was making its trek behind the hills. It might have been better had they gotten there after dark, but she wasn't certain. She, Laura, and Chris sat frozen inside the vehicle. Doug stood, stretching beside the driver's door, still smiling. He turned his gaze from the direction of the house back to them.

"It's not that bad. We'll fix it up," he said.

"In a week?" Laura exclaimed.

Chris made the next move, departing the vehicle. "Well, let's take the tour and get settled in before it gets too dark."

Alice and Laura gave each other looks of skepticism before making their way out of the black Suburban. They followed Doug up a stone path leading to a porch housing an old wringer washing machine and a swing suspended by rusty chains to the point of nearly touching the ceiling. Alice wanted to ask why it was up high, but more pressing matters caused her to dismiss it for the moment.

"Where is the bathroom?" she asked.

As the four of them stood on the porch, surprisingly of solid construction—Chris had given it a few stomps to test it—she turned to Laura who undoubtedly wanted to know the same thing.

"Have you heard of an outhouse?" Doug asked.

This can't last, she thought. She told herself to think of it as an elaborate camping trip. It was late spring. If they had arrived nearer to Halloween, she would have told herself to look at it as a night's adventure in a spooky old house, something high-school kids might do, but not sophisticated college kids.

"BUT IT DID LAST," Chen said. Chen had abandoned her note-taking and had squeezed her arms around her knees in anticipation of what was to come.

"Yes, for five years. Hard to believe," Alice said.

"IT'S IN THE BACK," Doug said. Doug knew the house and the land. He owned it more or less by default. It was deeded over by his father as a tax ploy to Doug, something Alice didn't understand.

"Here, let me get the toilet paper from the car. We did get some on our last stop, didn't we, Doug?" Chris asked, laughing nervously. Chris liked to joke, but at that particular moment, his humor was falling flat.

Both Doug and Chris came from wealthy parents who gave their sons everything. Both harbored some sort of ill feeling toward this. Later, Alice would discover Doug collected people like this for his little project, the way he might collect members of a jury.

Laura's story wasn't so obvious, but Alice was sure she had one. During the trip, she kept silent regarding her upbringing. Alice knew she was from Kentucky. She still retained the accent. Maybe her parents were only a few hours away, right across the border. Unlike Doug and Chris, she wasn't from a wealthy family. She went to Columbia on a scholarship and had completed her degree in botany. On the trip, she talked a lot about herbs and what was common in the mountainous region they were going to. One suitcase, the heaviest of the lot, was dedicated to books on the subject along with jars, presses, mortars and pestles, and something she called carrier oils. It was carefully placed in the back behind the seats rather than on the luggage rack on the roof.

Alice and Laura walked behind the house to see a small building approximately one hundred feet from the house. A moon was carved into the upper part of the door. Laura, with one of the several flashlights they brought, entered first. "It's a two-seater. Won't you come in with me? I don't want to be in here alone. It's kind of creepy," she said, holding the door open.

The showers after gym class were always a source of shame and embarrassment for Alice. She had learned to hold her eyes down and be quick, perfecting the placement of her towel outside the open shower so only one edge got wet. She practiced more physical fitness in the undressing and hiding of her body than she did out on the field while playing volleyball.

Stepping into the two-seater toilet with Laura was her first act into total acceptance of her body with all of its flaws and imperfections as well as its beauty. The second thing would be the nude swims in the nearby lake.

"An old Sears catalog," Alice exclaimed. "I guess someone used to read and wish while out here."

"That was only part of it," Laura said, laughing.

CHEN'S EYES grew as large as they could get. "I have only ever swum nude one time. It was at a party. Almost everyone was drunk, and it was in a pool. I don't think I could swim in a lake." She hesitated, which was unlike Chen's usual direct approach. "Weren't there creatures in the water?"

"By creatures, I'm going to assume you mean water moccasins."

"Yes."

"Those as well as frogs, bugs, catfish, and cattails."

Chen's eyebrows rose.

"You get used to them. I was more worried about undressing in front of the others. Laura had a perfect body as did Chris. It was the first time I saw an actual penis. Of course, I accidentally saw my brother's a few times. I was small, and it was natural. We only had one bathroom. Seeing the penises of two men who were in their early twenties was totally different."

"Is swimming in the nude how you and Doug started up?" she asked.

"No. In fact, he didn't seem the least bit interested in my body. I think he saw me as an underdeveloped, skinny teenager. Anyway, the first time was awkward, swimming in the nude, that is. At the same time, swimming in the lake like that was some of my freest moments on earth. Later, stripping and swimming in forty- to fifty-degree water in the moonlight, was even more freeing."

Chen reached for the throw, pulled her shoulders in, and hugged her knees even tighter. "Just the thought of that sends shivers through my body. How on earth…?"

"You get used to it. Mind over matter. Doug was adamant we try it, but it was Laura's idea. She said it would build our immune system. She told us all about studies that had been done. Thomas Jefferson bathed his feet in ice water for ten minutes first thing in the morning."

"When you say Doug was adamant, was he like some kind of cult leader?"

Alice laughed. "No, nothing like that. Oh, Doug had his quirks, but I have to say he was one of the kindest men I've ever known, not that I really had known any men at all. Seeing him that day at the coffee shop was fate."

"He was your father figure."

"Maybe. I guess. I never thought of it that way. He was older, of course, but not that much older."

"What about the house and the others? You said there were more coming."

"One other brave couple came."

BY THE TIME Laura and Alice returned from the outhouse, Chris and Doug were inside. They entered, brushing cobwebs from their shoulders. The front room was large, and the furniture was still there: a lumpy old beige couch, an upholstered flowered rocking chair (it would come in handy later), and a coffee table. A rock fireplace took up almost one whole side of the room.

"Not to worry, we have plenty of firewood for one season. After that, we're on our own. We'll have to clean out the chimney," Doug said.

"What's that crunching?" Alice asked.

"Yeah, I feel it, too," Laura said. She shined the flashlight on the wooden floorboards.

"Oh my gosh. Dead bugs and animal droppings!" Alice exclaimed.

"Mice," Chris said. "We have a lot of cleaning ahead of us."

Doug claimed a room on the first floor as his bedroom, the one next to the kitchen. Entering the kitchen was like stepping into a *Little House on the Prairie* scene. A wooden table covered in dust, surrounded by four chairs, sat in the middle of the room. The cook stove was heated by wood. A large white sink, its pipes hidden by a worn curtain, faced a window.

"Look, we have running water," Doug said, attempting to play up the place. He turned on the faucet, and sure enough, out came water. "It's fed by a spring, some of the purest water you will find. Won't find that back in the city."

"Do you think there is a possibility of running that to an indoor toilet somehow?" Laura asked.

Doug must have thought the question rhetorical because he didn't answer.

There were no built-in cabinets but rather one lone hutch, housing crocks and old dishes, some of which were cracked. Chris took one out, examining it. "I bet these would bring a fortune on eBay."

"Maybe later, but for now, we'll be using them," Doug said.

"Why do you suppose the people who lived here left everything behind?" Laura asked.

"Ooh, maybe their ghosts are here," Chris said.

Doug's face went kind of ashen, but he made no comment.

A door from the kitchen led to the outside. Doug opened it, revealing an outer screen door barely hanging on. A straight path, now overgrown and part of the one Alice and Laura traversed earlier, led straight to the outhouse. Off to the side, something Laura and Alice had missed, was a rock structure built into the ground. They found rotted potatoes and apples and shelves of food in jars with rusted lids.

"Some could still be edible," Doug said.

Another door led into a small room housing a larger table, a fancier dark-wood veneered one with six chairs. Another hutch displayed fancier china. The table was moved into the kitchen even though there was barely room so that room could serve as a bedroom. Upstairs there were two more rooms with iron beds and worn, stained mattresses and an attic above that. Alice and Laura laid their sleeping bags over the mattresses. Both Doug and Chris laid their bedrolls onto the floor of the rooms downstairs.

The next morning, the sun entering the dingy windows shed new light, although subdued, on their situation. Mouse turds abounded throughout the house, but the good news was the mice appeared to have abandoned the house from lack of food.

"They'll be back," Chris said.

"We have to get cats," Laura said.

Over the course of the summer, they brought in two cats, an orange tabby and a striped gray female. Chris said orange tabbies were always male.

"And let them multiply," Chris said. And they did. By the time Alice left, there were sixteen cats, all feral, some more friendly than others, all living off moles, rodents, and whatever bugs they could find, sometimes, to Alice's dismay, even butterflies. Alice found out, contrary to myth, when a cat tears off the wing of a butterfly, it doesn't grow back. They had thought about getting a dog, but considering the expense of dog food and the fact they were so secluded with the unlikelihood of strangers venturing their way, they voted against it.

The next morning, after scrubbing down the kitchen table and chairs, they feasted on camp-style eggs, toast, and coffee heated by a Bunsen burner.

They walked down to the barn and discovered a '65 model Ford tractor along with various equipment that attached to it and an old Ford pickup truck. The upper section of the barn was filled with hay bales.

"We'll need those for the milk cows," Doug said. Doug had everything planned out, or so he thought. He didn't anticipate the engine in his Suburban going bad during their first winter there.

During that first week, all four of them scrubbed until their hands and knees were raw, trying to make the place inviting for the eight yet to come.

———

"I COULD HEAR it in Doug's voice and see it in his eyes. He was scared they would chicken out."

"But, they did come, didn't they?" Chen asked.

"Yes, but they were two weeks later than expected. And there were only two of them, Kyle and Renea. It was the first time I ever saw Doug angry. But it didn't last. There was too much work to do.

"Kyle and Renea had rented a van to haul in extra supplies. The nearest place to return the van was an hour and a half away. Cell reception was scanty, one of the things Doug didn't enter into the equation. He kept the phone charged using his Suburban at first. The light of a cell tower was barely visible off in the distance.

"I could say the realities of what we had gotten ourselves into settled in quickly. No words were spoken, but we knew on our first night there."

"The conditions sound so horrible. What made you stay?"

"I'm not sure. I would have to say it was stubbornness on Doug's part. Chris and Laura were totally committed to the project. I think Kyle and Renea found it a challenge, something they could tell their grandchildren, not their own, because I didn't expect them to stay together."

"Did they?"

"They were still there when I left, along with their two-year-old, April. They left from time to time to visit family. Most of their trips were for doctor visits we discovered. Renea announced she was five months pregnant after one of the trips. We thought they would desert us for sure, but about a month after April was born, they returned in a new four-wheel drive."

"How did they leave if the engine was out in the Suburban?"

"Chris, aka Mr. Fix-It. He couldn't do anything with computerized vehicles, but he had that old pickup and tractor running like new. He took Kyle and Renea to the nearest bus stop on several different occasions. At first, they never talked about where they went, but I think they took minivacations to cheap roadside hotels with bathtubs and showers where hot water poured out instantaneously without having to heat it on the wood-burning stove. I once saw a STARBUCKS' cup in the car. It's amazing how many things we take for granted. I give our ances-tors lots of credit."

"Did you ever want to leave?"

"I couldn't see going back to live with my mother. But more than anything, the peace, I suppose, kept me there. Oh, the house wasn't much the way it was, but in its day, I think it had been something grand, and I could see it being that way again. Every day there was something new. Each time the sun came up over the hills, it was different, a new splendor to behold. It was the perfect picture postcard, the one you wish you could step into, and I had actually physically stepped into it. And at night the stars were so clear. On some nights, fireflies lit up the sky as well, sparkling and dancing in and out of the trees, sometimes up so high they appeared to be among the stars. All I can say is it was magical." Alice laughed. "Laura said in Kentucky, they call them lightning bugs. Of course, Doug had to say they could be tiny UFOs." Alice took a deep breath. "More than anything, I felt I belonged—to the hills, to the soil, and to the people I was sharing the house with. They were the family I had always longed for. How could I leave? I cried on the day I did, but... I'm jumping ahead, again.

"We each had our function. Chris could fix things. And he and Laura both loved gardening. I suppose it was one of the reasons they fit so well together. Renea saw it as some behav-ioral study. Her minor was in sociology. Kyle was a psychology major. Even though they came down together, they didn't end up as a couple until a few months after arriving. They kept us in check when our nerves became raw, and believe me, they did from time to time. But other than Renea's interest in human behavior under primitive conditions she could cook, can, and do all of that stuff people only heard their grandmothers talking about. She worked at a reenactment village during her summers. Said she learned a lot from it. I never knew my own grandparents, but my mother still retained some of the skills, that is, before she became sick after my father left."

"You never said what exactly was wrong with your mother," Chen said.

"Oh, that would be a whole other term paper or book for you."

"I could never do that, leave the city and live in the wilderness. We should get some takeout from my uncle's. We can eat while you tell me more."

Chen pressed the number she had on speed dial and spoke the order in Chinese. Alice wanted to ask Chen if she ever ate anything other than Chinese, but the memories of The Farm had cast a spell over her she didn't want to break.

14

Priscilla Black

F rom what Alice could remember of her mother before her father went away, Priscilla Black was once normal. Alice, like any girl under the age of six, was under the illusion her parents made the sun and the moon, and all was right with the world. There were usual family things: baking cookies, licking the batter straight from the bowl, shopping for a frilly dress, a new doll under the Christmas tree, her father putting the bicycle together for her, and the smell of sawdust on him as he came from his woodworking projects in the shed.

One of Alice's better memories of her mother was born of an accident. She had wrecked her bike and scraped her knee. Her mother said, "Alice, how in the world do you wreck a bicycle with training wheels?" It was one of the happier memories. Her mother smiled the whole time she put antiseptic on Alice's knee, the red stuff that stung. She placed a BAND-AID over it. "Now, all better," she said and kissed her.

She remembered her mother fixing lunches for her dad in the mornings before he went off to work. He kissed both her mother and her goodbye and told Jack Jr. to be good.

Alice's original intent was to start totally fresh in her new apartment, but at the last moment, she had second thoughts. She rubbed the palm of her hand over the beat-up metal lunch bucket that still contained the thermos with the faint odor of lingering coffee. She hoped rubbing the piece of metal might evoke a vaporous cloud to appear out of the minute gap in the rusted hinge from which a genie would materialize and grant her three forgotten memories. Ironically, inside were the three faded pictures of her father.

She also hauled her mother's monstrous solid walnut three-tiered jewelry box from Queens to Brooklyn. Other than her mother's wedding rings, an eighteen-karat white gold band with a matching engagement ring with a baguette-cut sapphire and diamond, the rest of the jewelry was inconsequential. She sold it all during the yard sale, except for the wedding rings and a string of fake pearls she had remembered her mother letting her wear. As hard as she tried, Alice couldn't remember the rings on her mother's finger.

Besides the fold-out tiers, there were two rather large drawers, one holding the deed to the house and her mother's social security papers. Upon opening the other drawer, Alice cried when she found all of her report cards, perfect attendance certificates, and drawings and cards she had made as a child, things she had no idea her mother had kept until after her death. Strangely, there was nothing of Jack Jr's. in it.

Jack Jr. was an anomaly. Alice often wondered if she and her brother were dropped off by two different species of aliens. They were so different. Her mother had commented often enough about their distinctly separate personalities. When she was small, Alice thought it had to do with her being a girl and Jack Jr. being a boy, but upon reflection later on, she knew there was more to it than that. On Thanksgiving, Jack Jr. would fight anyone for the drumstick while Alice had no preference as to which part of the turkey she was served. On Christmas morning, he ripped through his presents with the speed of a race car driver while she carefully removed the bow and peeled the paper with precision from beneath the SCOTCH tape. And there was the Halloween when he ate his own candy and all of hers. Jack Jr.'s aura was one solid cloud of ruckus whereas Alice's own aura matched her own invisibility.

When Jack Jr. brought his friends over, they retreated to the shed, using it as a clubhouse, forbidding her to enter. Their mother always seemed to be yelling at him for something. While Alice craved her mother's attention, Jack Jr., not wanting it, possessed it during most of her mother's waking hours. She told him not to run through the house, which he ignored. He ignored most things their mother said. "A handful, Jack Jr. is," she remembered her mother saying while holding her hands up in despair.

Seemingly overnight, things changed. Police officers showed up at their door with Jack Jr. They looked grim, more than grim, and her mother was crying. She rarely saw her parents hold hands, but her dad was squeezing her mother's hand tight, not in the same way that Clara Jenkins later would squeeze hers. Jack Jr. sat on the floor beside them, looking angry. It was something about Jack Jr., something they didn't want her to hear because they sent her to her room.

The voices of the two men in blue were muffled. It was dinner time when Alice heard the door slam, but there were no aromas drifting up the stairway. Alice's stomach growled, but she was frozen in place on her bed. It wasn't long until she heard yelling, her father and Jack Jr. Another door slammed, this time the back door. She just knew they were going to the shed. Her father once switched Jack Jr. good out there. She figured the same was about to happen. Her stomach still growled, but she heard no pots or pans banging in the kitchen.

Alice didn't know how much time had elapsed. She only knew it was dark outside and still January. Her birthday had been last week. Her mother made a chocolate cake because chocolate was her favorite. It had vanilla frosting covered in rainbow sprinkles with six candles her father helped her blow out. That was when her mother still made cakes. They told her to make a wish but not to tell. If she told, it wouldn't come true. She wished everyone would quit yelling at Jack Jr.

Most kids Alice's age were already in kindergarten, but Alice's mother thought it better they wait another year. Alice wasn't sure why. Maybe it was because she was small for her age or because she was so quiet her parents thought her slow. Maybe they feared she would be like her brother who had difficulty in school. It could be because she still used training wheels on her bicycle. She would start kindergarten in September, which in her mind was an awfully long time away, and it was. A lot of things transpired after that fateful night in January until September.

She had almost drifted to sleep when her mother finally brought up a glass of milk and a peanut butter sandwich on a plate, watched her eat it in silence then helped her into her pajamas, and told her to go to sleep. Her father trailed in a few moments later to kiss her good night. He was so distracted, he had forgotten to read her a bedtime story until she reminded him. He pulled "Goodnight Moon" from the shelf. Alice couldn't understand why there were tears in his eyes as he read. She didn't think "Goodnight Moon" was a particularly sad book.

It was the last time she saw her father. Nor was Jack Jr. anywhere around the next morning when she woke.

For the longest time, she thought it was her fault—the birthday wish came true. Jack Jr. was no longer there to be yelled at, nor was her father around to yell *at* him.

The next few days were chaotic. Women from her mother's church appeared frequently at their house, bringing casseroles and such. It was if someone had died. After reflection, Alice guessed that was the case since her mother had taken to her bed and was never the same again.

It was during this time Clara came into their lives. There was something about Clara she didn't like. Being so young, she couldn't give it a proper definition, but Clara's presence repelled her, and the feeling never got any better, even when things became more settled. Maybe she associated Clara with all the strangeness that happened after her father's and brother's disappearances—the strangeness and disappearances no one explained to her.

"What's wrong with Mama?" she asked.

Clara gave her the pitying look that was to be her trademark and told her she was too young to understand. In time she would, and when that time came, her mother would explain everything. But her mother never did.

For a while, it seemed as though her mother was trying to do normal things, but they never came off as normal at all. Before kindergarten, she sat Alice down, telling her how it important it was to learn to write her name. Her mother wrote it and told her to copy it. When she protested, her mother said, "Shush, now. Write what I'm showing you and read it out loud." So she did. Over and over again, she wrote and repeated Alice Black. She was one of the few students in kindergarten who already knew how to write her own name in print and the only one able to write her name in cursive. The teacher gave her a gold star for it.

With each passing day, her mother retreated more into her own world. For eleven years, Alice endured. Some days were brighter than others. There were occasions Alice saw a spark of life come back into her mother, but then something would trigger the depression to set in again. Sometimes, the melancholy hit after Alice asked questions, so Alice learned to be invisible around her mother.

15

The Apartment

I t had been a week since Alice had seen Chen. Several times she thought about calling, but she knew Chen was busy with classes.

Chen's younger brother also worked at the restaurant. Chang, although he preferred Charlie, came over and helped her set up her flat-screen TV. Even though she could have walked across the street, by design, Alice called in food deliveries from DRAGON'S DEN during the hours when she knew Charlie worked. He usually ended up staying much longer than he should, fiddling with her electronic devices, introducing her to new apps, and answering her technical questions.

Charlie had also helped her set up her new computer. He even put a picture of the Appalachian Mountains as a screensaver on it for her.

One of her favorite apps was GOOGLE EARTH. She immediately went to The Farm. It looked the same. She could even see Doug's black Suburban parked nearby. If Doug had known they were being photographed, he would have gone on a rampage with his favorite thing—late-night conspiracy-theory discussions. She saved its coordinates. She looked up where she and her mother had lived. The house still stood, along with all the others on the street. It had to have been torn down by now. The map probably hadn't been updated. Charlie had said things weren't up to the minute on there, except if you were in the government. "They can spot a dime on the sidewalk, zoom in, and read it," he said. It sounded like something Doug would say.

On other days, she found herself exploring the world, the pyramids in Egypt, Paris, and Venice—all the places she would someday like to travel to, places Doug had told her about. She had never even been on a plane.

When she did finally feel brave enough, she typed Jack Black into the search bar. After going through twenty pages of nothing but various articles about the actor, she found only nonsensical things, nothing that would lead her to her father. She tried typing in Jack Black, not the actor, and got the same results. It was useless. She typed in her mother's name, Priscilla Black. Facebook profiles came up. These were definitely not her mother. She found her mother's obituary. It was short and sweet, merely stating that she and Jack Jr. had survived her in death and that her mother had once worked at MACY'S DEPARTMENT STORE. It was the only thing she could think to tell the lady at the funeral home.

One thing led to another, exploring this or that on the internet, which she discovered led to the weirdest advertisements popping up on her Facebook page, the one listing her two friends, Chen Wang and Charlie Wang. She filled in all the information she could think of on the "about" section of her page, not being too opinionated or political as Doug had said it would attract all the creeps. Just to show she was a normal American citizen, she shared some cat pictures.

When she wasn't idling away her time on the internet, she was sitting or lying on the couch in front of her flat-screen TV, only thirty-two inches, watching NETFLIX. Even that size overwhelmed her apartment. She made a list in her notebook of all the movies she had missed out on, researching them first on the internet.

Sometimes she ordered Chinese takeout and ate it while watching NETFLIX, trying to hone her chopstick skills. She hoped to become proficient before seeing Chen on the weekend.

On other days, she ordered pizza from across the street. On the in-between days, she went with canned soup and peanut butter sandwiches, always giving herself unheeded advice about eating better.

She calculated her hours spent using her phone, the television, and the computer, and found she was paying nearly $7.50 per day for their use. She estimated the phone would be the highest if she were to make a chart and tabulate them separately. If she could cut back on sleep, she would get more on the dollar. But she didn't know how that was going to happen. She watched three episodes straight of *Breaking Bad*, telling herself she would go to bed at midnight, but then kept telling herself one more until she saw the sunlight from the corner of her eye seeping in through the cracks in the window shade. She had become a junkie. If only Doug could see her now.

She thought about Doug a lot and talked about him so much that it caused Chen to repeat he was the replacement for her dad. She didn't like to admit that, but deep down, she knew it was true.

Everyone who worked at DRAGON'S DEN had by default, a new computer word she learned, become family, even the ones who spoke no English. Who would have thought after the infamous box knife incident that would happen? They had even invited her for Thanksgiving dinner.

ON SATURDAY, Alice opened her door to see Chen's mouth almost on the floor as she stepped across the threshold. If Alice had been as adept at using her phone as Chen was, she might have taken a picture capturing the look on Chen's face, but her phone was never in the right place at the right time. Even if it was, she fumbled so, losing that millisecond she needed to snap the right picture. Chen's phone was usually in her hand, or if it wasn't, she could pull it into view and snap a shot as quick as a gunslinger on an old Western.

Chen looked around in disgust at the discarded pizza and Chinese take-out boxes and unwashed dishes. During her intermittent internet searching and binge-watching Netflix, Alice had only washed dishes on an as-needed basis.

"My dorm room looks better than this. Have you even combed your hair today?" Chen sounded like a mother reprimanding her teenage daughter.

Of course, she had, or she thought she had. Come to think of it, she had only taken three showers, or was it two, in a week's time. She did remember brushing her teeth this morning after a heavy dose of black coffee.

"Have you been out of this apartment at all?"

She wanted to say yes but replied, in a weak voice, a flat, "No." It was all she could verbalize. Having spent all week in front of screens, conversation had not been a priority, and her vocal cords had gone into atrophy.

"Go take a shower and put on something nice. We have to get you out into the world."

Out in the world to Chen was actually inside, exploring endless racks of clothing, shoe displays, and cute accessories. Before closing the door to the bathroom, she saw Chen picking up her apartment the way a mother might.

She came from her bedroom wearing the only clean top and pair of jeans she had because she had also neglected to visit the laundry downstairs.

Chen said, "We'll grab a STARBUCKS." STARBUCKS or shopping was Chen's answer to most everything.

16

Nature's Blush

I t was mid-November. Her small apartment with its pristine furnishings, flat-screen television, and laptop computer sitting on the desk she intended to use for the paperwork of an independent, responsible adult sat vacant most of the time. There was no paperwork as she paid all her bills on her phone, and her laptop usually was somewhere on the sofa or on her bed or on her kitchen table as she drank her morning coffee and ate her piece of toast.

While she was doing none of the things she intended—meditating, yoga, or reading inspiring literature—she was at least making her bed and picking the apartment up, after getting over the newness of NETFLIX and the internet. The bathroom tile was even becoming less exciting, and on some days, she longed for a bathtub.

She stared at her empty bookcase, the one she had ordered online from IKEA. The thought of going to the store had crossed her mind, but she felt she, Brad, and Ellie needed to move on. Good inspirational books were what she needed to fill the bookcase. She needed help. Iris's words came back to her, "Is there anything I can help you with?"

There was plenty of stuff she needed help with. There was that self-actualization thing she had intended, the one technology and possessions blotted out, along with the worry of paying for them. Yes, she would go back to NATURE'S BLUSH.

Alice put on her new tights and oversized blue top, the one Chen said looked so good with her eyes and cinnamon-colored hair and remembered how nerve-racking looking in an actual store for clothes was, new ones, ones that no one else had left their aura on. Having Chen with her made it fun and took away some of the anxiety of dipping into her wallet further. The prices in Manhattan were outrageous, Chen had said. Of course, Alice knew that. For that reason, they went to TJ MAXX, which was like Christmas morning, the ones when her father was still home, with all the boxes, hangers, and abandoned articles of clothing she had to step over, like the discarded wrapping paper Jack Jr. so eagerly tore off. It was all rather marvelous to her, but Chen found it disgusting. "They could use some more help in this store."

Alice wore her sneakers, the only shoes she had other than the farm shoes Doug had gotten for her. She had left those back at The Farm. Chen had tried to get her into a more stylish pair but could see that was one place where Alice drew the line. Besides, a new pair of shoes would put her way over budget. She wore her hat, the one she had knitted herself while watching YOUTUBE videos on how to knit. Chen had given her the idea. Chen was knitting scarfs for everyone on her Christmas list. Chen was currently the only one on Alice's Christmas list, and as of yet, she had no idea what to get her. The thought of a massage at NATURE'S BLUSH crossed Alice's mind, something to relieve the stress. However, unlike herself, Chen seemed to thrive on stress. Taking it away might remove a part of her personality.

Chen had a big family. And, like Chen, they rode the waves of stress like skilled surfers. She guessed it came with the restaurant business. They shouted back and forth to each other in

Chinese while chopping vegetables with rapid precision and banging stainless steel spatulas against the largest woks she had ever seen. The whole family looked like chickens running around with their heads cut off, but Alice had to admit what seemed like chaos on the outside had the inner workings of a perfectly synchronized dance. And they still managed to smile when placing food in front of the customers, even when the young girl who wanted to learn how to use chopsticks asked for help. She was eating Won Ton Soup.

Chen sometimes helped out at the restaurant. How she found the time for handmade gifts with waiting tables, taking classes, and working on her paper, Alice didn't know, but Chen was a ball of energy.

The term paper about The Farm was due before Christmas break, and Chen constantly scribbled any tidbits Alice gave her in her notebook, although Alice was running out of things to say. Chen said, "No worries, I'll fill in the missing parts myself."

That did kind of worry Alice, and when she said so, Chen promised to change the names. When Alice expressed further misgivings, Chen promised to let her read it before presenting it to her professor, the one Chen had a serious crush on.

Alice grabbed her purse and bounded down the stairs.

"ALICE!"

"You remember my name?"

"Of course, I do," Iris said. "Given any thought to that job offer?" She was opening boxes and placing items on the shelves.

"It's still open?" She tried to hide her excitement.

"If you want it. I hoped you would be back in. You know how it is. If you hold the intention firmly in your heart, it happens."

Actually, no, Alice didn't know. She had held the intention in her heart that her father would return for eleven years, and that never happened.

"I had a girl work in here for a couple of weeks. She was a little out there. In la-la land if you know what I mean. While it may look like the kind of place for that, I really need someone level-headed and knowledgeable. You appear to be both."

Iris finished placing the last item from the box on the shelf— B vitamins. She picked up the box, carrying it toward the back. "Let's go in back and get you started on the paperwork."

AFTER A WEEK, Alice was handling almost everything in the store, including the ordering and restocking. This freed Iris to do what she loved best, give massages and perform Reiki. She said people needed it most during the holiday season. Also, during the winter months, rich housewives went through a depression. During the spring and summer, the massage and Reiki part of the business would slow down.

Alice implemented ideas for the store, ideas Iris had thought of but never had the time or the proper help to take care of herself. She made herbal gift baskets right in the front of the store, not in the back like most shops might do, but up front by the window where passersby, especially men, might come in for that last-minute gift. Men were the easiest to please. Women usually wanted certain things in the baskets but sometimes would go with something else if there was a slight discount. This meant certain items not selling well were thrown in. Of course, the customers were none the wiser, or if they were, the discount took care of it.

Chen stopped by Alice's apartment on Saturday nights and sometimes by the store during the day if she had Saturday night plans.

"Ooh, girl, you smell so good," Chen remarked more than

once. It was because of that she made up her mind to make Chen one of the gift baskets, one with her special signature touch, which was what she told all of the customers, but with Chen, she really meant it.

17

Tom

During the first few days of his new job, despite every muscle aching, exhaustion won out and transported him into a deep sleep. By morning, he was always renewed. He bounced out of bed with a sense of purpose he hadn't felt in a long time. Sure, the job could be manually taxing and sometimes repetitive, but he was working with his hands, sometimes even problem solving, but most of all learning. With each shovel of dirt, he fantasized about putting the skills he was learning to use for his own construction projects. Tom had dreams of building his own house one day or at least fixing one up.

On some days, he operated the lighter equipment, but on most days, it was merely hard work. He was one of several in charge of cleaning and preparing the construction site. For starters, that meant the removal of the houses, then flattening out the area. For that, the bulldozers would do most of the work. Tom had hoped to be able to operate the heavy equipment, but there was a hierarchy. Burt, one of the older men on the crew, who took him under his wing, told him his turn would come. Tom mostly unloaded and loaded materials and tended to the machines. They had a mechanic for that, but when the foreman saw he had a knack for it, Tom sometimes stepped in. Later, after the ground was made ready, Tom would move on to reading plans and specifications, mixing concrete, pouring concrete, and assisting carpenters, operating engineers, and other construction site workers.

TOM REALIZED the boss wasn't yelling at him, not directly, but it felt like the blunt blow of the baseball bat all over again with all the cussing and ranting. Tom had been the one to unearth the bones, the ones appearing under the remnants of where a building had once stood, probably a yard shed of some kind.

"I thought Halloween was over," Burt, the burly fellow he had shared a beer or two with since beginning the job, said.

"Maybe they're only animal bones," Tom said, trying to be optimistic. Sadly, they looked human. Tom had enough exposure through his brother, John, who taught biology, to recognize human bones when he saw them. The skull was barely sticking through the dirt, but it looked human enough. And the ribcage definitely looked human.

All work was halted, and the site where the bones were found was cordoned off with rope and a tarp.

The newest man on the job. Why did it have to be him whose shovel hit the skeleton? If these men didn't work, the ones who weren't union didn't get paid, and one of those nonunion men was him.

"So what do we do now?" Tom asked Burt who sat beside him on the bar stool as they drank their mugs of beer in the middle of the afternoon. Most of the men went to bars following the early dismissal.

"Wait. It's all we can do. They track down who owned the property. If they're human bones, it might be a long wait. Might be evidence in an unsolved investigation or mark the location of a long-abandoned cemetery."

"Has this ever happened before?" Tom asked, taking a sip of his beer.

Burt laughed. "In New York? What do you think?"

Burt took a big gulp and did a double take on Tom before saying, "Oh, don't look so glum. It doesn't actually happen that much. And it was only one skeleton. We'll probably be back to work before Thanksgiving."

"I was hoping to have some spending money before Christmas."

Burt slapped him on the back, almost knocking the beer out of his hand. "Don't worry. It'll be fine. The boss will more than likely move most of the crew to another job."

Tom knew as the lowest man on the totem pole that wouldn't include him.

"BONES, YOU SAY?" John said.

"Yes," Tom replied.

"Could be animal bones. Not that easy to distinguish between animal and human bones with the untrained eye."

John paused, took a moment. Tom could hear Carol in the background. "On the phone with Tom," he yelled

"Tell him I said hello," she yelled back.

"Carol says hello."

"Tell her the same," Tom said.

"Hm, back to the bones. If the skeleton is intact, and you can determine that the bones are from an animal, you can rebury or move the bones to another location. But if they are only fragments, well…"

"Well, what?" Tom asked.

"They'll be harder to identify. Could be a bear. Their paws

resemble human hands. A pig's tibia can look like a human tibia. You'll need an expert to determine the origin. Do you know if they called in a coroner or nonforensic archaeology expert?"

"No," Tom said.

"If it turns out to be an archaeological site, well, that's a whole new ball of wax. You might not go back to work for months."

"Months?"

"Has anyone from Columbia University been called in?"

"John, I'm really not in the loop on that, the lowest man on the totem pole, remember? I was just hoping to keep this job and not go back to delivering pizzas."

"You can always come back down to Georgia. Why do you want to stay up there anyway? It's so cold." He paused. "Oh, yeah, Sarah's down here. It's not like you're going to run into her."

"I like it here, well, for the most part. I'd rather be out in the country somewhere but can't see that happening anytime soon. I thought maybe…" Tom paused.

"What?"

"Well, this job pays really well. I might save up, buy a small place somewhere out in the country, build my own home. Maybe somewhere in North Georgia. Or find some rickety old house I could fix up."

"And live like a hermit?"

"There's nothing wrong with that."

"You and Dad are the ones with all the smarts when it comes to fixing things. Me, I barely know a saw from a hammer. Well, that's an exaggeration, but you know how Carol always has you repairing things when you're here. Why don't you look at this time off as an opportunity and come down for Thanksgiving? My car is due for an oil change." He laughed.

"Maybe I will. Depends on what they say about this job."

"If it turns out to be something that looks like it might be a significant discovery, you can kiss that strip mall goodbye. It'll turn into an archaeological resource site. They'll be looking for artifacts for years to come."

"There were Native American tribes around this area, weren't there?"

"I think so. If that's the case, they have to determine the tribe the bones came from and contact them."

"Then what," Tom asked.

"Then it's up to a tribal council as to what happens next."

Tom sighed. "Thanks, John. I'll let you know what happens about the bones and my plans for Thanksgiving."

"You take care now."

"You too."

Tom picked up his guitar and gave a heavy sigh as Simon and Garfunkel brushed by his feet.

18

Thanksgiving

DRAGON'S DEN closed from 2 p.m. to 4 p.m. so the whole Wang family could enjoy Thanksgiving dinner. Including Alice, there were twenty-one people from one baby up to the eldest couple somewhere in their eighties. Charlie had lined the tables up into one long row to accommodate everyone with Chen's uncle at the head. There was the classic stuff like turkey, sweet potatoes, and assortments of pumpkiny things: soup, pie, rolls, tarts. Also, there were the traditional Chinese foods as well: dumplings and flavors like sesame, hoisin, and ginger.

The clicking of chopsticks, the clatter of cutlery, the clanging of wine glasses and various toasts—some in Chinese, some in English—filled the air. They even drank to her, opening the bottle of wine she contributed. A roar of laughter erupted as a result of something Chen's uncle said. Chen interpreted it as they might want to hide the corkscrew from her. Alice laughed along with them. If it hadn't been for the box knife incident, Alice wouldn't be sitting with them feeling like she belonged somewhere.

THERE WERE ONLY two other times she had truly felt like she belonged to a family. One was when she was small, when Thanksgiving meant her whole family was together. The morning started with the MACY'S Day Parade on the small television set before the rabbit ears broke and the picture became fuzzy. Her father carved the turkey followed by her brother lunging forward like a ravenous lion to beat anyone else to the drumsticks, and she and her dad would pull the wishbone and gorge themselves on pumpkin pie and whipped cream. The second time was at The Farm.

How could she have omitted to tell Chen about Thanksgiving at The Farm? It was comical and would definitely add zest to Chen's paper. It started the day before with Doug, Chris, and Kyle hunting a wild turkey. Funny how, on that particular day, the turkeys were nowhere to be seen when on any other day they would have paraded across the lawn, flapping their wings and making their rapid gurgling sounds. Animals sensed when something was up.

The guys did eventually find the turkeys' hiding place. The three of them came strutting back like cavemen, holding what must have been the scrawniest bird of the lot. But by the looks on their faces, you would have thought they had killed a wooly mammoth. The saddest part of all was the bird wasn't even dead, well, not sad for the bird. Doug tried handing it to Renea, probably thinking since she had worked at a pioneer reenactment camp during her summers, she would be experienced in the next stage of what to do. She let out a big squeal which caused Doug to lose his grasp on it. The turkey did its best to hobble away because it couldn't fly since one whole side of its wing was gone. It seemed like fate since no one had the heart to chase after it and actually kill it.

"I hereby pardon Tom Turkey," Chris said, all serious and presidential like.

"Oh, we've given him a name now? And so original," Laura said, rolling her eyes.

"Seems only fitting, seeing as we mutilated him for life," Doug said.

"I think Tom is a female. Female birds are smaller," Renea said.

"So what do we do now?" Alice asked, watching their dinner walk away. Her stomach rumbled.

"The diner in town is serving Thanksgiving dinner. They had a sign up during my supply run earlier this week," Kyle offered. Kyle didn't have to say BUCKY'S DINER since it was the only diner in town. The only other eating establishment was DAIRY QUEEN, plus it would be closed.

"Do you think we need reservations?" Chris asked with his usual dry sense of humor.

Everyone looked at him, shaking their heads partly in disgust as if saying *Could we not put more of a damper on this situation?* Laura rolled her eyes again.

The six of them crowded into Doug's Suburban, still operational. The sign on BUCKY'S door said CASH ONLY. Kyle had the foresight to tell them in advance, and they went to the bank's ATM before navigating the potholes of the gravel parking lot of the diner, inhabited mostly by pickup trucks.

All heads turned and conversation ceased when they walked in, and it was after a moment of confusion that Renea said, "I believe we seat ourselves."

The only sound, other than the shuffle of their coats and footsteps until they seated themselves in a back booth, came from the jukebox—Elvis Presley singing "How Great Thou Art."

Roomy booths were made from weathered barn wood. Rustic wood seemed to be BUCKY'S theme. The seats felt slick and smooth, almost petrified, from all the buttocks that had slid across their surfaces over the years. Wallpaper made from ochre-colored vintage newspaper ads displayed contraptions no longer in existence and cure-all medicines with ridiculously low prices. It was divided every so often by more rustic barn wood. It was all part of the ambiance. The most modern thing about the place was the jukebox.

After they shed their coats and sat down, the locals went back to their eating and conversations more than likely about the party of six *not from around here*. Elvis came to the end of his song. Another gospel song followed.

The middle-aged woman with the jet-black hair and painted-on eyebrows to match came to take their order—not the brassy blonde older woman who stared at them like a deer blinded by headlights when they first walked through the door.

They gave the woman—whose name they learned was Betty from one of the regulars shouting it out—their drink orders. There were no menus since it was Thanksgiving, and they were only serving typical holiday fare: turkey, stuffing, mashed pota-toes, giblet gravy, sweet potatoes, green beans, cranberry sauce which looked as if it came straight from the can—it still had the ridge indentations—cold store-bought rolls with a more than adequate supply of butter, and a choice of pumpkin or coconut cream pie. Betty gave them two options: a single serving or all-you-could-eat, the latter including a piece of both pies. At only two dollars more, which included the drinks and refills, they all opted for the all-you-could-eat alternative. The waitress brought out their drinks in red plastic tumblers, followed shortly by beige plastic plates heaped with turkey and all the trimmings.

Betty brought the handwritten check to the table. Even though you were supposed to pay at the register, Doug handed Betty a hundred-dollar bill and told her to keep the change, a hefty tip by BUCKY'S DINER standards.

They weren't sure if the locals, those who were hard-pressed not to see Doug's generosity, morphed into friend or foe. Betty might have been tempted to throw in something extra if Doug would have given her a sign.

As they were donning their coats, Doug said, "I'm totally stuffed. I say we make this an annual thing." She imagined them all at BUCKY'S today and smiled.

THE CHATTER and twang of Chinese became louder near the end of the meal. Chen told Alice their specific dialect was Cantonese, and the different dialects and languages were as plentiful in China as they were in India, which Alice knew nothing about.

While gathering up the plates, she thought of Jack Jr. and wondered if his Thanksgiving was happy. Maybe he was sitting down to Thanksgiving dinner with a wife and kids, but he had never even mentioned a girlfriend to her during their brief talks at the garage.

After the meal, Alice was invited into the inner sanctum of DRAGON'S DEN, the kitchen, where she helped clean up so they could reopen for customers in half an hour. Alice had never felt so included while standing alongside Chen, rubbing steel wool cleaning pads against the stainless-steel woks. Even Chen's uncle shot her a smile. Charlie's job was to realign the tables and remove all evidence of the wine since DRAGON'S DEN didn't have a liquor license.

"TO TOM," they all repeated around the table as they clanked glasses of champagne.

"It's not often we have the whole family together," Tom's father said.

"Dad said you found a skeleton," Clark said. John's son, like his father, had an interest in science, in particular, archeology.

"Yep, the reason I'm not working and am here for Thanksgiving."

"Did you take pictures?" Clark asked.

"No, I had a shovel in my hand, not a cell phone."

"Shit, I would like to have seen it."

"Clark!" his mother exclaimed. "Not at the table."

"Sorry, Mom."

At eighteen, Clark was the oldest of the kids. His sister, Jean, was ten, having come from an unplanned pregnancy. And then there were the twins, Robert and Wynn, Mark and Jennifer's kids who were twelve and had been delivered via C-section as Jennifer's tight yoga body couldn't handle natural childbirth, nor could she probably have been bothered with the time of birth not being written down in her planner.

The kids giggled at Clark's profanity. Although Tom hadn't seen the kids in ages, he knew Robert and Wynn had potty mouths. He had heard them while they were playing video games.

Mark moved back from the table. "I'm stuffed."

Their mom offered to help Carol with the dishes, but Carol said, "That's what we have a dishwasher for, Mom"

Carol always called his parents Mom and Dad, while he had never heard Jennifer ever call them anything but Robert and Doris. Robert was named after his dad, and Wynn was named after Jennifer's dad.

"There's no way all those dishes can fit in that dishwasher," his mom said.

"So we'll do them in two different cycles. Who's ready for pumpkin pie?" Carol shouted out.

Everyone said yes, except for Jennifer who had brought her own dessert, some kind of vegan custard with currants, apples, and

almond milk. Jennifer brought her own food to most family functions and brought enough for the others, but it always ended up
untouched by anyone other than herself, and she ended up taking it
back in the containers she had brought it in. She turned a blind eye
to what Mark and her kids ate when they were elsewhere, but she
had a strict policy of no animal products in her house.

Jennifer didn't offer to help with the dishes. She didn't touch
pots and pans infected with carnivore substances. She even
cringed at the thought of sitting on John and Carol's leather
furniture. So when Tom's dad suggested they all go into the
living room and eat their desserts, Jennifer sat cross-legged on
the floor, eating her custard dessert along with her herbal tea, one
of the few things Carol had in her cupboard that Jennifer
approved of. Also, since she didn't condone violence, which she
swore football was, she read a book while everyone else shouted
at the oversized screen that gave them the illusion they were
sitting on the ten-yard line.

Tom's family wasn't the kind who went around the table
saying what they were thankful for. If they had been, he would
have said he was thankful to have found the construction job,
albeit short-lived. He was also thankful finding the bones was a
big part of the conversation, so much so, that not once was
Sarah, his ex-wife, mentioned.

19

Bones

lice was knee-deep in boxes, stocking shelves when a man in a suit asked to see her.

"Hello, Miss Black?"

"Yes?" she asked, confused.

"I'm Detective Johnson. I need to ask you some questions. Just routine."

"Alice, why don't you and the detective go to the back?" Iris suggested.

The presence of the man sent dread through her. Alice had developed a distaste for cops, particularly those in uniform, after the night things went so awry when they brought Jack Jr. home. Intellectually, she knew it was perfectly unfounded. Still, she was relieved this one was wearing a suit.

All the reasons he could be there went through her mind as they walked the several steps behind the curtain where Sanskrit chants were playing and incense permeated the air. Even though Iris had a live-and-let-live attitude, Alice knew she would be curious and would be only a few feet beyond the curtain. Alice led him farther back, past the massage table where a door led into a small office, the one where she ordered supplies, the one where Iris had asked her to fill out information such as her social security number and address—all the red tape needed to get a paycheck. Sadly, when she came to the part about next of kin to be contacted in case of an accident, she had no one, not knowing Jack Jr.'s address, and she was sure by this time, Doug had moved on, plus the fact he was so far away and almost unreachable. She put down Chen's name and address.

Maybe something happened to Doug, and he wanted to get word to her. Or she was being arrested for the pot she smoked on The Farm. Such bad timing to get arrested. She was finally getting her life back on track. She usually took her pot in the form of brownies. Was that still illegal?

She so wished Doug were here. He would know what to do. Maybe she should talk to an attorney first? Doug's proclamation of her naiveté came back to her.

"It was only brownies," she blurted out.

A slight grin arose on the detective's lips.

"That's not why I'm here. Miss Black, you recently moved from 123 Tucker Avenue, Queens?"

Her heart leaped. After all these years, had her father returned? Or had something happened to Jack Jr.?

"Yes," she said.

"We are going to need a DNA sample then," the detective said.

"DNA?" Alice must have turned white.

"Am I being arrested?"

The detective still had the grin on his face.

"No, not at all. It's merely procedure when we find bones."

"Bones? Whose bones?"

"That's what we are trying to determine."

"My father's bones?" she blurted out.

"Your father?" The detective momentarily acted surprised but regained his composure. "Why would you ask if they are the bones of your father?"

"My father disappeared when I was six."

His eyebrows raised. "Miss Black, what was your father's name?"

"Jack. Jack Black."

He took a small pad from his pocket and wrote it down. "We show your mother, Priscilla Black, as deceased and you inheriting the house. Is that correct?"

"Yes."

He handed her his card and asked that she come to the Queens' police station to see him the following day so they could take a DNA sample. Alice took his card and nodded her head.

Alice was still in the back, looking at Detective Johnson's card, when she heard the ding of the door, letting her know he had left the store.

Alice was still standing in the same spot with his card in her hand when she felt a hand on her shoulder. "What was that about?" Iris asked.

"They found bones on the property where I grew up. They want a DNA sample."

20

Dna

On the Tuesday after Thanksgiving, Alice stood watching the falling snow dissolve into the sidewalk while she waited for the bus that would take her to Queens. Iris insisted that she take the whole day off. Yesterday, tears flowed as soon as she told Iris what had transpired and how her worst fear was that they could be her dad's bones. Iris's reaction was to immediately reach out to her and pull her into a hug. At closing time, she insisted on giving Alice a deep tissue massage. "You need a release," she'd said.

Iris had her own problems, not that she confided in Alice, but sometimes, Alice heard bits and pieces of phone conversations. Iris was forty-four, divorced, and had a twenty-year-old son living somewhere in California. Alice was fairly certain from the one-sided conversations she overheard Iris having with her ex that the son was a drug addict. Alice could also tell from various snippets that her ex worked in the movie business, a behind-the-scenes person. Iris didn't need to add a troubled employee to her woes.

"Everything is stored in our bodies," Iris said as she kneaded her palms and elbows deeply into Alice's skin. "You're so tight here. Are you worried about money? We store money concerns in our lower back," she said.

Iris sometimes complained about her own back, and Alice knew she worried about money. Iris was a single woman who owned her own business in a high-rent district of Brooklyn. Alice was always thinking of new ideas to help—to expand the business, much the way they did on The Farm to increase their yield and get them through another winter. Alice was always the one who brought the most innovative ideas to the table. She was a firm believer in not putting all your eggs in one basket. It applied in most areas of life.

"Some," Alice almost slobbered out, her drool hitting the paper towels that lined the slit her face popped through on the massage table.

"You shouldn't be." It was a simple statement, not some Buddhist philosophy she was so used to hearing Iris recite.

Iris finished her massage, following up with Reiki. Another fifteen minutes must have passed as Alice drifted off. The sound of Iris's voice brought her back. "I sometimes get messages during Reiki sessions. I'm getting, *all will soon be resolved.*"

The message was rather vague like a fortune cookie and a little like Professor Marvel looking through Dorothy's purse while she had her eyes shut, except Iris didn't need to snoop. Alice had inadvertently spilled her guts about her father during Iris's embrace. Still, Alice thanked her and said she would see her on Wednesday. Iris hugged her again before she walked out onto the street—the long cold lonely street, the one she trudged down in her worn sneakers that were getting wetter by the minute. She planned on buying boots soon. She let the sting of city air slap her in the face as she made her way back to her apartment.

There were days she almost said out loud how much she missed The Farm. The stars shined so brightly there. She could really use one of those frigid swims under the stars.

Alice wished she had someone to talk to about this, Doug mainly, but she didn't even know Doug's cell phone number. She should have written it down before she left but never thought to since at The Farm the others had all but abandoned using them. Plus, she didn't possess one of her own at the time.

A part of her didn't want to know about her father. It had to be something horrible, so horrible it changed her mother forevermore. Alice had always heard, *The truth shall set you free*, but now that she was falling into some semblance of a normal life, it might be easier just to let the truth slide on past her.

———

"I'M HERE to see Detective Johnson. I have an appointment," she told the man at the front desk.

The uniformed older officer behind the window barely took his eyes off the computer as he asked, "Name?"

"Alice. Alice Black."

"Take a seat." He pointed to a row of rather stiff-looking chairs against the wall. What Alice judged as unsavory characters occupied two of the seats. Alice had never been in a police station before. It reminded her of the old *Barney Miller* shows her mom used to watch reruns of. The officer picked up the phone, she assumed to call Detective Johnson. She took the seat farthest back, leaving two chairs between her and the woman who could have been a prostitute or drug addict or an actress playing the part of one or the other. Her mixture of orange, purple, and black hair covered one part of her face with its caked-on makeup. Her tight skirt exposed bare legs that had to be freezing, and she was sitting directly under the vent.

The guy in the black leather jacket, a seat down from the woman, looked shady. Suddenly, a horrible thought came to her. He reminded her of Jack Jr. He pulled a pack of cigarettes from his pocket. The officer behind the window called out, "Hey, no smoking in here."

"Miss Black." She looked up to see Detective Johnson. He was smiling; hopefully, that was a good sign.

Detective Johnson looked to be in his late forties, clean cut, a tinge of gray starting around the temples in his thick black hair. He held out his arm with an open palm, motioning Alice to walk ahead of him. The detective was a gentleman, another good sign.

"Please sit," he said, pointing to the seat beside his desk.

Desks with stacks of paperwork were shoved up against each other with only narrow walking aisles. Several men in white shirts with loose-fitting ties and their jackets hung over the backs of their chairs along with a few in uniforms were pecking away at keyboards. Others were coming and going or conferring with each other. Alice observed a lot of pecking and a lot of talking with a curse word thrown in here and there. A woman came over.

"Alice, this is Miss Snyder. She will take a sample of your DNA."

Miss Snyder, who was rather pointed and angular and wearing a dark suit, said a quick hello and proceeded to open the case she was carrying. She took out a pair of the tight clear gloves, the ones so prevalent in hospitals and doctors' offices, and stretched them over her hands. There were no rings. Then she removed a vial and a long swabbing stick and said, "Please open your mouth for me."

She scraped Alice's jaw with the stick, placed the sample in the vial, sealed it, removed her gloves, threw them in the trash can beside the desk, and said, "That's it." She closed the small metal briefcase and walked away.

"Wasn't so bad, was it?" Detective Johnson asked.

In her mind, she could see Doug shaking his head. *No, except now they had her on file, and her DNA would be stored in West Virginia where the X-Files were along with all the other alien DNA.*

"No, I guess not," Alice said. "Is that it?"

"I need you to sign this paper for me." He shoved it toward her along with a pen.

Alice went five years without once writing her name. Signing her name had almost been a daily occurrence since moving back to the city. She was constantly signing Medicare and Medicaid forms regarding her mother, employment forms with MAC'S BURGERS, all the papers with the sale of the house, and with every purchase, a signature, usually with a stylus, along with her cell phone number was required. Doug had always said we were signing our lives away. It was just dawning on her what he meant by that.

She shoved the signed form back over toward Detective Johnson. "Will you let me know what you find out about the bones?"

"If it's a DNA match, I'll be calling you, but I ran a search for a Jack Black and found nothing—no missing person's report or anything else. So I seriously doubt if those bones have anything to do with your father." He smiled.

Alice didn't know if that was good or bad news. "When will you be able to tell me something?"

"Should know something within a couple of days."

Alice got up and started to walk out but turned. "You don't know anything about my brother Jack Jr., do you?"

"Alice, you are full of surprises. Are you telling me you think the bones might be your brother's now?"

"Oh, no, not at all. It's just I haven't seen my brother since my mother's funeral. I thought you might know his whereabouts."

"No, but if there is a DNA match, I'm sure we will be locating him."

SHE TOOK the bus to the stop nearest to where she used to live. The house that once so repelled her was now drawing her in like a magnet. She stood across the street, trying to identify the spot where her house once stood, but she couldn't pinpoint its exact location nor could she identify where Clara Jenkins' house used to be. The whole area was encased in the orange-webbed fencing so prevalent in construction areas with signs saying KEEP OUT. Not one brick remained of the eleven houses. Nor was there a single twig left from the line of oak trees that once stood in front of the houses.

Tears rolled down her cheeks as she walked her old route to school and stopped at the auto repair shop, hoping her brother might come out and ask her how it went in West Virginia and if she was happy to be back. He would pull out his cell phone and show her pictures of his wife and kids who she would be an aunt to and invite her over for dinner. "Oh, and I quit smoking," he would say.

Instead, a heavyset man, wearing the same oil-stained uniform with the company emblem across the pocket, came out. "Anything I can help you with, ma'am?"

"Did you know my brother, Jack? He used to work here."

"No," he said.

She continued on, walking past her old school, thinking she might look up Kayla and Meghan on FACEBOOK. Why she hadn't thought of it before, she didn't know. But they would both probably be married now and have different last names. She could look up Mr. and Mrs. Morgan. Chen said a lot of older people were on FACEBOOK. Chen said INSTAGRAM was where it was happening. Or maybe she wouldn't bother looking any of them up. They were her past. Chen always emphasized the future while Iris stressed the importance of the present.

As she stepped onto the bus, the snow picked up. There was plenty of daylight left, and she wanted to make one more stop.

21

Clara Jenkins

T he receptionist at the assisted living home said they had moved Clara to a different facility, one more suited for her special needs. "I'm afraid we can't give out any more information," the woman had said. It wasn't necessary. Alice knew her son worked in real estate. Clara had bragged about him often enough when she wasn't spreading the gossip of the neighborhood. The fact he had married a doctor, a pediatrician, was what Clara boasted about the most.

Alice remembered Ted Jenkins's face staring back at her from the billboards in the neighborhood. The billboards had JENKINS REAL ESTATE—LET US WELCOME YOU INTO YOUR NEW HOME in big bold letters. If the name of his business hadn't been so pronounced, Alice might have mistaken the ad to be for a dentist since his teeth were so white, or for a hair gel model. Every shiny strand of hair was sculpted into place.

Alice heard the dismal sigh emitted from the receptionist across the phone line when she told her she wasn't calling about real estate but about Clara Jenkins.

"Oh, I see," the receptionist said. "Well, considering her age…"

"No, no," Alice quickly said. "Clara was a friend of my mother's, and I would like to talk to her."

"Mr. Jenkins will be showing houses until after lunch. If you want to give me your name and number, I will leave him a message."

There was nothing to do but return to her apartment.

When Ted Jenkins returned her phone call later that night, not from his office but from his cell, he told her his mother would most likely be incoherent. She was most days. The fact he returned her call at all surprised Alice. She picked up on the curiosity in his voice.

"I've been researching my family history and thought my mother might have talked to your mother about her parents. I never knew my grandparents," she said, which was no lie, but the main reason she wanted to talk to Clara was to see if she might shed any light on what happened with her father, being her mother's best friend and all, and then there was the matter of the bones dug up in their backyard. She doubted Ted Jenkins knew about the bones.

"You can visit her, but I don't think it will do you any good." He gave her the name of the care center and the address. Alice heard a child in the background as he was hanging up. Clara had never mentioned a grandchild. Maybe it was born after Clara moved.

ALICE WASN'T sure what she hoped to achieve by visiting Clara Jenkins.

The smell, the stench of death waiting patiently on the side-lines—grim reapers waiting to swoop in and pluck the residents one by one—attacked her as soon as she entered the nursing home. It was the smell of her mother in the final days. Only in here, it was multiplied many times over.

A nurse brought Clara out in a wheelchair, stopping just short of where Alice stood. "Are you a relative of Clara's?" the nurse asked.

"No, but she was my mother's best friend."

"That is so nice. And you've come to check on her? Is your mother with you?"

"No, I'm afraid my mother is dead."

"Oh, I'm so sorry." The nurse tilted her head in a momentary acknowledgment of sympathy, more like an involuntary twitch that came with the turf. The nurse looked down at Clara, adjusting the brakes on the chair. "Are you okay, sweetheart?" she asked Clara.

Clara remained mute.

"It is so nice that Clara has a friend to come visit her. My name is Nancy. And yours?"

"Alice."

"The poor thing, Alzheimer's. We have so many here. Clara's disease isn't that advanced yet. She has good days and bad days. I'm afraid today is one of her bad days, the poor thing. On some days, her mind comes back as clear as a whistle."

Clara looked fragile, all bent over like a pretzel. Her once plump cheeks were hollow, and her eyes reminded Alice of milky glass.

"Well, Alice, I'll be right over there if you need me," Nancy said, pointing to a thin veiny man slumped over in a chair. An orderly had just brought out a tray of food for him. The orderly removed the beige plastic lid revealing an indistinguishable slab of meat, runny mashed potatoes, slimy carrots, and red JELL-O. The JELL-O was still wobbling from the ride on the cart.

Alice stumbled for the words to say to Clara. Why, she didn't know. Any recognition of her on Clara's part was absent. It was best to get right to the point. From Clara's zombie-like gaze, Alice deduced it was going to be a short visit. Alice leaned in so close she could hear the raspy breath coming from Clara's nostrils and see the wisps of gray hairs sprouting from one side of her face lit by the sunlight coming through the French doors, beyond which lay a garden of roses whose wintry remains were blanketed by piles of mulch with bluntly chopped thorny stems protruding.

"Hi, Clara, it's Alice. Alice Black. Priscilla's daughter." If there was any recognition on Clara's part, Alice didn't see it.

"Clara, I know you and my mother talked a lot. Well, I was wondering if she ever talked about my father."

"Jack," Clara said, staring straight through her behind those opaque eyes.

Alice jerked back at the mention of her father's name. Upon first seeing Clara when the nurse wheeled her in, Alice didn't have high hopes. But she said her father's name. She had so many questions, she didn't know where to begin. She should have been more prepared, written something down. All the recent events had thrown her off-kilter.

"Where did he go, Clara? What happened?" The words spewed from her mouth in rapid succession lest Clara get off track. Alice's hands were trembling. Clara reached over and grabbed her arm, the same way she did when she was a child, when she told her to be a good girl. This time, Alice didn't try to escape her grip. It was still strong.

"White," she said.

"What?"

"White," she repeated. She looked over at the tray of food. Perhaps seeing the mashed potatoes made her hungry. The order-lies wore white. They also wore back braces. She remembered all the lifting of her mom she did. Clara looked straight through Alice and repeated the word "white" several times in a louder voice. She still gripped Alice's arm. Alice could feel her finger-nails digging into her skin.

Alice didn't know what to do. It was useless. Nancy saw what was happening and ran over. She took hold of Clara's arm, massaging the liver-spotted skin until Clara released her grip on Alice's arm. The memory of running up the stairs and doing math homework until the fingerprints faded from her skin was what Alice was thinking about as the nurse talked to Clara, using the words "sweetheart" and "dear." The hospice nurses used those words a lot with her mother. Alice was doing math problems in her head and forced herself to stop.

"Like I said, today is one of her bad days," the nurse said.

"You said on some days her mind was sharp?"

"Yes, on some days it is. Those days are getting fewer though."

"Do you think if you're on duty and her mind is clear you might call me? It really is important."

"Yes, I could do that. I'm sure she would love the company. Her son hardly ever comes in to see her."

Alice got a pen from her purse. She wrote her name and number along with the fact she would like to speak with Clara Jenkins when her mind was sharp so the nurse wouldn't forget, on the back of a NATURE'S BLUSH card and handed it to her. Nancy smiled and put it in her pocket.

On the bus, Alice thought about all the trays of food she carried up the stairs to her mother, about all the bedpans she had emptied, and about how she fought back gagging over the smell when she cleaned her mother. She had changed April's diapers, the cloth ones, at The Farm. It wasn't the same. She realized how glad she was she had returned to care for her mother and that her mother hadn't ended up in a place like the one Clara was in. Why hadn't her son moved Clara in with him?

22

Fortune Cookies

fter that first fortune at DRAGON'S DEN, Alice
considered it bad luck to throw them away. Instead,
she collected them the way some might collect coffee
mugs or teapots. Even Chen, who had scoffed at the idea of
random messages printed on tiny slips of paper having any
meaning, couldn't deny the fortune Alice received on that day
was the seed that blossomed into a friendship between them.
Maybe it was Alice's belief in the words printed on them. That is
what Iris would say.

She put every fortune she acquired into her father's metal
lunch bucket which functioned as the centerpiece of her kitchen
table. Over that hung a poster of Buddha smiling down at her on
the rare occasions she ate at the kitchen table. The poster was
one of the perks from working at NATURE'S BLUSH. It came as
part of a promo with some new Ayurvedic herbs a company was
pushing.

It had only been two days before Detective Johnson appeared
at NATURE'S BLUSH that Alice read the strip of paper from her
cookie, *A tall dark stranger will appear in your life and answer
all your questions.* The detective was neither dark nor handsome,

and he certainly hadn't answered her questions. After no word from him, Alice had called the station several times to no avail. All kinds of fears went through her mind, but Iris told her to quit worrying.

"Do you know how overworked the police in New York are?" Iris asked.

Alice knew Iris was right.

She taped that particular fortune along with the first one she ever got from Dragon's Den, *Creativity in precarious situations will prevail,* to the lid of the lunch bucket so she would see them each time she put a new one in. The first one, after all, had brought her luck. She met Chen because of that fortune and had practically been adopted as a member of Chen's family.

Alice speculated on who the tall dark stranger might be. Doug was six foot and had dark hair. He was no stranger, but then, she hadn't seen him for so long he could be construed as a stranger if she ever were to see him again. There was always the possibility of meeting someone entirely new, someone who would sweep her off her feet, a guru figure who would not only be her lover and future husband but someone who would finally help her realize the peace she sought regarding her father.

23

Skeletons Under the Shed

A lice grew up speculating about what had happened to her father, inventing one preposterous theory after another. One of her most absurd theories involved her father being abducted by aliens. The most prominent one was he suffered from amnesia and wandered off. It happened on all the soap operas her mother watched. Maybe that's why her mother was so intent on watching them. He had a whole new family somewhere with half-siblings she would never know, and he would never remember her. At least he was happy. That scenario didn't hurt as much as him having amnesia and wondering the streets of New York and sleeping on cardboard under smelly blankets in alleyways.

Once, not too long after he disappeared, she woke up screaming. He had cast her aside and adopted all the perfect little Hummels as his children. She woke up shouting, "I'll be perfect, Daddy!" Her mother rushed into her room and held her until she fell back asleep.

Or sometimes, he lay on a stretcher with his head bandaged. He so wanted to get back to her, but he couldn't remember. It was like in the movie *The Little Princess*, her favorite other than *The Wizard of Oz*.

When she started high school, the bad dreams stopped, but since Detective Johnson's appearance at NATURE'S BLUSH, they had returned. Even though it was almost December, she woke up in the middle of the night with drops of sweat running down her body. In one dream, her father's body lay in a shallow grave behind their house. He wore Khaki work pants and a red plaid shirt with his lunch bucket in his bony skeletal hand. Tufts of cinnamon hair sprung from a cracked skull.

Even when she wasn't dreaming, she awoke several times during the night, tossing and turning. All the sleep aids Iris recommended—ambient music, dabbing lavender on her temples, along with the herbal capsules she was taking—weren't working. Learning about the discovery of a skeleton under the shed where her father had once hammered and sawed, singing while he worked, was too hard to overcome without the stuff found on drugstore shelves. With eyes resembling those of a raccoon, Alice, against Iris's advice, asked a pharmacist for some over-the-counter medication to help her sleep. What he recommended, knocked her out, but still, it was usually a ghoulish nightmare that woke her up every morning right before the alarm on her phone went off.

She saw bits and pieces of her father in the dreams but never his face. The worst and most horrible of the nightmares, the one she couldn't shake, began with the sound of a drill, a modern one, coming from the shed. When she opened the door of the shed, she saw Jack Jr., not with a modern drill but with an antique hand-held one, boring it into their father's chest ever so slowly. He turned to look at her, smiled, and pulled a cigarette from his pocket. She woke up screaming.

Why had she never connected the dots? The clues had been there all along. They had been rattling around in her subconscious for years waiting to surface, the way the skeleton had been lying in wait all these years to be discovered.

1. He stayed in trouble at school.
2. How many times had he blown up at their father? When she thought about it, she could hardly ever remember a time when they weren't fighting.
3. The police brought him home the day before both he and her father disappeared.
4. There was no aunt. There never had been. He had been in reform school or prison. Could they put a thirteen-year-old in prison?
5. And then, there was the tattoo, the knife on his right forearm. A knife, not a drill, was the murder weapon. What did Doug always say? The truth is hidden in plain sight.

Jack Jr. had murdered their father in the shed and buried him there.

No, no, no. It was faulty reasoning, she told herself. How could they convict Jack Jr. of murder without a body? They are only now turning up the body. There were so many questions. She had to find answers.

Jack Jr. wasn't a bad brother. He cared enough to meet with Doug and talk to him. He was looking out for her. If he had killed their father, it was an accident. Maybe he only wounded him, and because of it, they both went away. Her brother had been a handful and an angry teenager, but he would never intentionally hurt their father.

There were so many tools in the shed. He didn't use a knife at all. He picked up a hammer and hit him over the head with it, but he didn't hit him hard enough to kill him, only enough to cause him to have amnesia. For all she knew, her father was in some hospital still in a coma after all these years. Whatever happened, it had to be Jack Jr.'s fault. That's why her mother didn't like talking about him.

Her head was spinning in circles. Why did they have to dig up that skeleton? She had just gotten her life on track. Better yet, why hadn't she stayed on The Farm? Being on The Farm was the happiest time of her life.

She looked in the bathroom mirror. She looked worn, older. Who wouldn't after the news of the skeleton? The raccoon circles hadn't entirely disappeared from around her eyes.

"Get ahold of yourself, Alice Black," she said out loud.

If she were to get any peace of mind, she would have to take matters into her own hands. It was Tuesday, a whole week since Alice had taken the DNA test, and still, there was nothing from Detective Johnson. She called Iris and asked for the morning off, explaining she needed to go back to the police station.

"Oh, Alice," she said in a pitying tone. "Have they found something?"

"No, nothing, or I haven't heard if they have, but Detective Johnson said they would know something in a few days, and he hasn't called. I have to find out."

"Okay, I understand. Take the whole day if you need it." Iris was nothing like Tony, her old boss. She was understanding and caring.

The one good thing to come from the dreams or nightmares was the unlocking of memories stored in the deep recesses of her mind or body. Iris said they were in both. Her father was a carpenter and worked in construction. Why hadn't she remembered? And he sang while working in the shed.

The morning air was brisk. Today, she opted for the subway instead of the bus even though catching it would mean a longer walk than to the bus, but she needed the fresh air, time to clear her head, prepare what she might say to Detective Johnson. There was something about the people on the bus that distracted her. There was the constant stopping and eyeing of each passenger as they stepped on or off. The subway was less personal, one massive swoop of people moving about like automatons.

ONCE AGAIN, Alice sat at the police station, third in the lineup of those seated against the wall. Today, she fit right in with her ghoulish eyes.

"Next," the desk sergeant called out.

Assuming that was her since no one else made a move, she went up to the window. "I would like to speak with Detective Johnson."

"I'm afraid Detective Johnson is out. Would you like to leave him a message?"

Alice let out a heavy sigh. Maybe she should have called although calling had done no good over the past few days. "Do you know when he'll be in?"

"Nope," the sergeant said matter-of-factly.

"No message," she said as she walked away. She glanced back over at the occupied seats. Someone had already taken the one she had vacated. They reminded her of the people waiting to hear their number called at the Social Security office.

She had gone with her mother frequently, those times her mother had to get a question answered or something settled, something the Social Security office had screwed up. Alice had always been rather blasé about the whole ordeal, thinking her mother was complaining needlessly about all the bureaucracy and red tape and stressing out over something minor. This whole unpleasant experience had made her reconsider what her mother went through. Doug had ranted about bureaucracy and red tape enough.

Doug's biggest complaint was about the DMV and what a hellish nightmare it was and how there were no special favors for anyone unless you were possibly the mayor or a congressman. He said everyone waited in line, even the Godfather, Robert De Niro. *The Godfather* was Doug's favorite movie. He said it was an accurate depiction of how the world worked. Alice said she doubted Robert De Niro even had a driver's license. He didn't need one. He had a driver, she countered. Alice didn't actually know that, but surely he did being famous and all. Doug corrected her, saying the actor not only had a driver's license, but he also had a cab license. He had gotten it during the filming of *Taxi Driver*. Doug was full of trivia like that.

Owning a vehicle in New York was a hellish nightmare, period. Driving through New York was something she never wanted to attempt. And, the cost of storing a vehicle you didn't drive was astronomical. She heard Doug quote it once.

Being the only one on The Farm who couldn't drive, Chris took her out in the old pickup truck he had brought back to life and let her practice in the fields. She got rather proficient at using a clutch and stick shift from the house to the barn, but trying for her license was a different matter altogether, and not another stress she wanted to add, especially in New York. If she had stayed in West Virginia, she might have.

She didn't remember her family owning a car. If her father had a driver's license, she could ask Detective Johnson to check if he had renewed it, but he said he found nothing on Jack Black. More than likely, a driver's license would have been the first thing he checked if he checked at all. Like Iris said, the police had a zillion things on their plate. Her fears about her father's disappearance twenty years ago was hardly a priority. If she was going to find out anything, she had to take matters into her own hands. She walked out onto the street, heading for the nearest bus stop.

She thought viewing the bones for herself might induce some shamanic vision, giving her answers or at the very least, possibly stopping the nightmares. She arrived to see a different worksite than on her previous visit. The orange webbing remained but within its boundaries were heavy equipment, bulldozers, dump trucks, and cement mixers, along with a swarm of men in hard hats. She even saw a flatbed truck loaded with cinder blocks and steel beams. Could they be that far along?

She walked across the street and called out to the man who was the closest. "Sir!"

He looked up. "Lady, you shouldn't be here," he said and motioned her away.

Determined to find answers, she didn't budge. She walked up to where he was and stood behind the barrier. "They found a skeleton here. I need to see it."

"It's not here."

"Where is it?"

"I don't know. All I know is they removed it and called us back to work."

"Oh," she said, holding her head down, unsuccessfully holding back tears.

"Oh, now, why are you crying?" he asked all perplexed.

"I used to live here, and I thought, well, it might be someone I know, and the detective was supposed to get back to me, but he didn't."

"Look, lady, I'm no cop, but I'm sure if the skeleton they found had anything to do with you, the detective would have gotten back to you."

"Yes, I guess you're right," she admitted with a frown, wiping the dribble from her nose with her jacket sleeve.

"Do you know what the skeleton was wearing?"

"Wearing? I don't know. Listen, it was Tom that found it. Let me see if I can get him for you."

She let out a sigh of relief. Finally, she was getting some-where. "Thank you."

This Tom had to be the tall dark stranger who would give her answers, possibly the man of her dreams. She stood on the curb for what seemed like an eternity although when she checked her phone, it had only been five minutes. But more time went by, and she grew impatient. She dug her beaten-up sneakers into a mud hole from the previous day's snow that had turned to rain. Why she was destroying what was left of her shoes, she didn't know. Frustration, she supposed.

She looked at her phone to see fifteen more minutes had gone by. Did all people with an ounce of authority lie and shrug off those without it? She moved her muddy sneakers in the direction of the opening she saw in the orange web barrier, the one with the signs plastered all around it saying KEEP OUT and avoided the Porta Johns which reminded her of the outhouse on The Farm.

The outhouse on The Farm had been a short-lived thing. It was during the first winter when Doug moved in upstairs with Alice that he decided to call a plumber after threats from everyone there. The guys weren't any fonder of trekking out in the dead of winter to do their business than she, Laura, or Renea were. The plumber, an older gentleman, referred to it as the Crosby place the whole time he was there running another line from the spring making what amounted to an indoor outhouse. Doug's downstairs bedroom was the logical choice for the composting toilet.

Just as she was ready to make her way through the makeshift fence, she saw a man emerge from behind a pile of dirt. He wasn't tall. At most, he was five foot eleven, maybe less, and he wasn't dark. The hair peeking out of the yellow hardhat was light brown. Plus, he had a light complexion.

"Hi, are you the lady wanting to know about the skeleton?"

"Yes."

"I'm Tom Walker. I hope you haven't been waiting long. I was on my lunch break when Burt found me."

"Burt?"

"The guy you talked to. I would shake your hand, but I'm

rather dirty as you can see. So what did you want to know about the skeleton?"

"Anything you can tell me, like what clothes was it wearing?"

"There weren't any clothes. I suppose they rotted off. It turned out to be a Native American."

"Native American?"

"Yes, from the Matinecock tribe. It was a tribe common to this area. Everyone was afraid the worksite might be shut down permanently, that the skeleton might be part of an Indian burial ground, but the guy was obviously a loner, maybe out hunting or something."

"Oh," she said.

"You look disappointed."

"No, not really. Maybe relieved."

"Why relieved?"

"It's a long story. How come Burt couldn't tell me?"

"He probably didn't know. I asked the boss. My nephew took a keen interest when I told him my shovel struck a skeleton. He plans on majoring in archaeology."

"And they're sure it was Native American?"

"As far as I know."

"When did they find out?"

"Sometime Wednesday. The Columbia University Archeology Center came and got the bones. Everyone was called back to work last Thursday."

"On Thursday," Alice exclaimed. She could feel the heat rising in her face and resisted the urge to kick her foot against the mud.

"Are you okay?"

"Yes, sorry. It's just... Nothing. Thank you so much. I'm really sorry I bothered you, especially on your lunch break."

"Oh, no. No bother."

"I'll let you get back to your lunch." She turned but could

feel his eyes on her as she walked away. He was cute. The dimples in his cheeks were to die for. If she hadn't been so worked up over the whole incident, she might have looked to see if he was wearing a ring. But then, construction guys rarely wore rings, too hazardous. It suddenly hit her. Her father didn't wear a ring. She once heard her mother and father fighting about it. Or she thought the fight had something to do about rings.

She stopped dead in her tracks in the middle of the street and turned. She couldn't help but smile when he was still looking in her direction. She yelled out, "Did the skeleton have a ring on?" *That was stupid. A Native American wouldn't be wearing a ring. Now he'll think I'm flirting.*

He laughed and walked toward her, grabbing her arm. "You need to get out of the middle of the street. It's dangerous." He let go of her on the sidewalk. "Sorry. I was afraid you were going to get yourself killed."

He looked down at the sidewalk. *Embarrassed*, Alice thought.

"As in, was he married?" Tom asked, looking back up at her.

"I suppose."

"Well, I guess he could have been, but I don't think Native Americans wore rings back then, or maybe they did. I don't know." He smiled.

"Again, sorry to interrupt your lunch," she said. He stood looking at her as if he wanted to say something. When he didn't, she said, "Thanks a lot," and turned to go.

As she walked away, she found herself muttering about Detective Johnson and how he didn't even have the common courtesy to give her this vital piece of information. He knew she had concerns about her father. She had half a mind to go back down to the police station and give him a piece of her mind, but by the time she made her way to the bus stop, she thought it probably wouldn't be the most rational move. She was sure Iris would concur.

24

Tom

T om couldn't shake the feeling he had seen her somewhere before. He racked his brain for every possible instance it could have been. Maybe it was a pizza delivery. He wanted to kick himself for not asking her name. Why? Because he was shy. Well, that was part of the reason. The other part was that he feared rejection. In his relationship with Sarah, she had been the aggressor, the one to make the first move, also the one to call it quits.

"Friday night. Wanna go out for a beer?" Burt asked.

Burt was as alone as Tom, having gotten a divorce a year ago. His kids were grown with families of their own and living in other states.

"Sure," Tom said.

THEY BOTH DUSTED a light layer of snow from their coats as they entered the long corridor, crunching the peanut shells beneath their steel-toed work boots. It was a bar frequented mainly by construction workers from all over the city, the ones who walked either bravely or stupidly—however you wanted to look at it—atop narrow steel beams of future high-rises, and the ones like Burt and Tom who were content with lower-paying jobs closer to the ground.

A dark mahogany bar curved around from the front door, forming a straight line for about twenty bar stools back, half of them filled but it was still early. On the other side, wooden tables with sturdy chairs lined the wall on which old prints concerning anything construction related hung, the most famous having been taken on September 29, 1932, in Manhattan. The construction workers were eating their lunches atop a steel beam eight-hundred feet above the ground. It was at the site of the RCA Building in Rockefeller Center. It hung in the center with other vintage black-and-white photos of some of the greats in progress: the MANHATTAN BRIDGE, the BROOKLYN BRIDGE, and other more down-to-earth masterpieces such as CENTRAL PARK. They lined every square inch of wall. The bar paid homage to every construction worker who walked through its doors, making them feel like they were a part of something big. By Tom's and most people's reckoning, they were.

Until Burt, Tom had no idea this bar even existed since there were hundreds, no thousands, throughout the five boroughs.

At both ends of the bar—dark wood beaten down by time and heavy glass mugs hitting its surface—were flat-screen televisions, both turned to a football game between the New York Giants and the Atlanta Falcons. Those engrossed in the game were shouting their admonitions to the players, coaches, and refs over the rock music coming from the jukebox in the back, the other voices, the clanging of glasses, and the breaking of peanut shells.

Tom ordered his usual, a dark draft, while Burt ordered a lighter amber.

"So what did the girl who came by the site earlier this week have to say?" Burt asked.

"She wanted to know about the bones."

"I know that. You talked to her for a long time. She was pretty, looked to be around your age." Burt grinned, took a drink, and then popped open a peanut, throwing the shell to the floor.

Tom started to say something, but just then, everyone shouted in unison, momentarily drowning everything and everyone else out in the bar when the New York Giants made a touchdown. Tom, being from Georgia and a dedicated Atlanta Falcons fan, kept his cool, neither going with the cheers of the bar crowd or against as he wanted to remain intact.

When the sound died down, he said, "Yeah, I thought she was pretty. I could kick myself for not even getting her name."

Burt smiled. "I can tell you're the introverted, reflective type. And you're shy although I don't know why—a good-looking guy like you? I mean, look at this mug. I've never had trouble getting women. Keeping them is another thing. If I had been twenty years younger, I would have gotten her name, but then probably not, since twenty years ago, I was still happily married or so I thought." Burt took another drink and gobbled down a few more peanuts. "I do know she used to live where the bones were."

"Really? She didn't tell me that."

A stream of cold air came through the bar as several more men entered, two with women hanging onto their arms. They got a table in the back.

Burt finished off his mug and ordered another. Tom was only halfway through his. He was a lightweight compared to Burt. He was a lightweight compared to most of the men he worked with.

"You know the company building the strip mall had to pull the records of who they bought the house off of in order for the police to have contacted her. I'm assuming the police contacted her or else she wouldn't know about the skeleton. After all, it was in her back yard. And if she didn't know about it through the police, and for some reason was coming around to ask about a possible dead body in her back yard, then I would for sure steer clear of her."

Tom laughed. "It was a two-hundred-year-old dead Native American, Burt."

"Just saying."

Tom took another drink. "Would the police department give me her name?"

"Highly doubtful. But I have a cousin who works at another precinct. Those guys do each other favors all the time. I could probably get her name for you for a drink. I'm easy like that." He laughed.

Just then, the crowd turned sour as the Atlanta Falcons scored a touchdown. Tom took that as a good sign.

25

Tall Dark Stranger

T hey say things come in threes.

It was a typical day at NATURE'S BLUSH. Iris was in the back with her massage appointments while Alice and Tina were working in the front. It was Tina's first day on the job. Tina, the daughter of one of Iris's friends, was the temporary help Iris hired to work through the Christmas season. There had been a new surge in business, mainly due to the gift baskets which Alice was to train Tina in making.

Number one.

Alice wasn't sure if Tina should even be considered as number one lest something more formidable come along for number three, and since there is also the saying *the third time's the charm*, Alice counted Tina as the first since Tina was the first of three things to happen in one day. Upon reflection, Alice thought she should back up and reconsider counting the discovery of the bones as the first and drop Tina from the equation. *Yes*, she told herself. *Much more appropriate.*

Number two.

There were two types of customers who came into the store: those who had a slew of health problems and were looking for some miracle cure but never kept up any kind of health regimen that might put them on the path to restoration and those who came in the store glowing, which made you think they were practicing just the right balance of herbs, juicing, yoga, meditation—something. The middle-aged woman who came in the store asking about natural skin products though Alice should have been asking her, was the latter.

Alice did her best to answer the woman without saying this or that was the fountain of youth since a health food store was forbidden to make such claims. The whole time Alice was trying to answer the woman's questions, she looked at Alice strangely, a tad disconcerting because Alice was trying to keep an eye on Tina, who was fumbling with a gift basket for an older man who was growing impatient. Tina was all bubbly and great when it came to conversing with customers, but as far as the actual nitty-gritty practicality of business was concerned, she was a train wreck.

Alice was about to say *excuse me for a moment* to the lady, when the woman asked point-blank, "You wouldn't be Priscilla's daughter, would you?"

Alice hesitated before saying, "Well, yes, my mother's name was Priscilla."

"The Priscilla that lived on Tucker Street in Queens? And your father's name is Jack?"

"Yes, the same. I'm Alice."

"Yes, Alice. I remember you from when you were, well..." The woman held her gloved-hand about two feet from the floor. "Priscilla White, I haven't seen her in years. You said *was*?"

"Yes, my mother died. But her name was Priscilla Black."

"Oh, I'm so sorry. And, I'm sorry for saying White. I never actually knew if your mother and Jack married."

"Of course they were married," Alice said.

"And you go by Black or White?"

"Black, of course."

The woman looked puzzled. "Not that it really matters," the woman said.

Alice suddenly remembered Clara Jenkins kept repeating the word 'white'. She must have turned pale or even green because the woman asked, "Are you okay?"

The bell rang, indicating another customer had walked through the door. She looked over to see Tina getting more frustrated by the minute.

"Just a moment," Alice told the lady. "I have to finish that basket for her. Please, please don't leave."

Alice hurried over to Tina and said, "Let me finish this. You ask whoever came through the door if they need help and then take care of the cash register."

In five more minutes, Alice had the man's gift basket finished up, and he made his way up to the register where Tina was ringing up the woman.

Number three.

Alice turned the corner. "You," she said, surprised.

Tom Walker smiled.

Alice stood frozen, mesmerized by his dimples until the chime on the door jolted her back to reality. Alice looked to see the back of the woman on the other side of the glass. Everything seemed to happen at once. The tinkling chimes and the sound of waterfalls coming from behind the curtain where Iris worked her magic massage fingers did nothing to ease Alice's agitated mind. In fact, there were times she wanted to silence them completely. They reminded her little of the real thing back in West Virginia.

"Sorry," she said to Tom, "I have to catch that lady."

"Why, did she steal something?"

"No, no, I need to talk to her."

"Don't worry. I'll catch her and ask her to come back."

He ran out of the store.

Within minutes, the lady was back, looking a little flustered but not so much she lost her gracious goodwill and elegance. The woman with her refined features, long black coat, and leather boots, exuded sophistication and charm. "I *was* planning on coming back when you weren't so busy."

"Oh, I'm sorry. I was afraid you wouldn't. You're right. Those were my parents. My mother died, and well, my father, I don't know. The thing is my name is Alice *Black*, not White."

"I honestly didn't know what last name your mother was going by."

"How did you know my mother?"

"I worked with her in MACY'S DEPARTMENT STORE before you were born, and after what happened with her and Jack, I came to visit her at your house. I'm sure you don't want to talk about it here." She looked over at Tom. "Is this your boyfriend?"

"No, no," Alice said. She saw Tom's face turning beet red.

"I get off in an hour. Could we possibly meet somewhere, maybe for a coffee? Maybe you could tell me about my father?"

"I have more errands to run. There is a STARBUCKS down the street. Do you want to meet there?"

"I do. Thank you so much."

The woman smiled and walked back out onto the street.

"I didn't notice before, but she was tall and dark," Alice said.

"Definitely taller than me," Tom said. "She looked kind of Greek."

"Dark hair too, but dyed," Tina said as she came around the corner.

"Can I help you with something?" Alice asked Tom. "You didn't come about the bones, did you? Wait, how did you know I worked here?"

"No, nothing about the skeleton. It still belongs to a Native American as far as I know."

"That's good to know." Alice let out a sigh. "Oh, thank you so much for running after that woman." She paused, still curious about why Tom was here. "So why are you here?"

He stumbled. "I only wanted to ask you out."

She stood silent, not because she was going to say anything but yes, but because she realized this was the first time a boy, well, a man, had asked her out. Doug was the only one of the opposite sex she had any experience with, and that hardly fell into the category of a normal courtship.

"You're not married or engaged are you?" Tom asked.

"No. But how did you… "

"Alice," Tina called. Alice looked to see Tina was with a customer.

"Just a moment." She took a step toward Tina and abruptly turned. "Don't leave," she said to Tom.

He grinned.

Why on earth did I say that? He will think I'm desperate. Chen would say asking him not to leave was really a plea to my father. Chen psychoanalyzes everything, even the colors and texture of the fabric when we're out shopping.

Alice walked over to where Tina was. The customer had moved away.

"Go out with him. He's a hunk, a little old, but a hunk for his age," Tina whispered.

"Tina, I was about to say yes when you called me. I thought you needed help."

"Oh, no. She just asked which aisle the vitamins were on."

Alice shook her head. There were times she wanted to strangle Tina, but to do that in front of the man who had just asked her out could certainly put a damper on things. In the course of the short walk back over to Tom Walker, she envisioned the crime scene in her head. Detective Johnson was dragging her away in handcuffs while she screamed, "Yes, I'll go out with you," to Tom Walker, who was looking at bath soaps. Examining bath soaps—Chen would say it was symbolic of Tom wanting to cleanse himself of her—while Iris was standing on the sidelines saying it was some past-life karma replaying itself.

"Yes," Alice said to him when she returned.

"Yes?"

He seemed surprised, but at the same time, he was still smiling. Alice wanted to say quit smiling for just a moment out of fear an extended smile might crack his dimples.

"Okay, tonight? Maybe for a cup of coffee or something?" he asked.

"Well, I'm kind of having coffee with the lady tonight. I won't sleep if I have that much coffee."

"Oh." He looked disappointed.

"But I'm sure I'll be hungry after the coffee."

The look of disappointment turned back into a smile.

"Do you like Chinese?" she asked.

"Doesn't everyone?"

"My favorite restaurant is DRAGON'S DEN. Do you know it?"

"No, sorry, but if it's your favorite, I'm sure I'll like it."

"I have one of their cards in my purse. Be right back." *At least I didn't ask him not to leave this time.*

Alice reached behind the register and pulled one of their many cards out of her purse and handed it to Tom. "Do you want to meet me there at seven? No, eight." She thought about the woman and had no idea what she would find out or how long it might take. An extra hour would give her sufficient time to get back to her apartment and freshen up, even change.

"Sure." He looked back, smiled, and waved as he went out the door.

A woman came out from behind the curtain, followed by Iris who rang her up. As soon as the lady left, Iris asked, "How's it going out here? Didn't get too busy while I was in the back, did it?"

Alice and Tina looked at each other and said, "No," in unison.

Alice looked at the clock, five minutes until quitting time. She pulled out her phone and added twenty dollars to the STAR-BUCKS' app, enough to cover buying the woman coffee and a pastry should she want one. It was the least she could do. She had to tap it in twice as she was nervous and hit the wrong numbers the first time. She should have gotten Tom's number.

How did he know where she worked? She would have to ask him tonight.

ALICE SAT AT STARBUCKS, berating herself for not getting the woman's name. Alice was almost ready to leave when the woman came through the door, what must have been all six feet of her, so slim and graceful, perfect makeup over her olive complexion, her sleek hair tied back in a stylish bun like Audrey Hepburn.

"Sorry, I'm running a little late. You know how this time of the year is in New York." The woman offered her gloved hand. "I don't think we've been properly introduced. I'm June Maxwell."

"Hi, Mrs. Maxwell," Alice said, extending her own hand.

"Oh, no. Please call me June. I held you when you were a baby. Your mother brought you into MACY'S after you were born and then a couple more times. And she always brought you at Christmas to sit on Santa Claus's lap."

"Please sit down, Mrs. Maxwell. I mean, June."

June Maxwell removed her coat, draping it across the back of the chair. She kept her gloves on. "Glad you got us a table. It's so hard to find a seat in these places."

"I'll get us some drinks."

"Oh, no, you don't have to do that."

"No, I insist."

"Something hot, then. A cup of tea will be fine. You pick."

Alice came back with a tea and coffee.

"I remember the one time you were about three. Priscilla was buying you a party dress. She stopped by MACY'S, showing you off to all the girls. You were the spitting image of your father with that beautiful cinnamon hair and those blue eyes. That's how I recognized you when I stopped by NATURE'S BLUSH. I know a lot of time has passed, but both your and your father's hair are distinctive. I knew it was a long shot, but if I hadn't asked if it were you, I would have regretted it. I'm so glad I did."

"I'm glad you did too. I've wanted to find my father for the longest time. So can you tell me about my parents? Please? The last time I ever saw my dad was when I was six."

"Your mom was my supervisor. I worked in cosmetics, and she was over the whole department."

"My mother worked in cosmetics?"

"Yes. Does that surprise you?"

"Well, yes. I never remember my mother wearing makeup."

"She was an artist with makeup. But then your mom had a lot to work with. She was a natural beauty. What man wouldn't be attracted to her?"

Alice noted Mrs. Maxwell's perfect grooming, her high cheekbones, her stately beauty for someone her age although Alice didn't know exactly what age she was. Her makeup, the perfect shade for her complexion, melted into her pores as if it was a part of her and not something separate, something highly definitive of a cosmetic specialist. Maybe if she had removed her gloves, Alice would have been able to tell her age. If nothing else, a woman's hands almost always told her age or maybe even her occupation. Alice's own hands, her bony fingers with no rings and short nails, could easily pass for those of a gardener even though she had not gardened in two years.

"She was going through a nasty divorce when she met your father."

Alice almost dropped the coffee out of her hand. "My mother was married before?"

Mrs. Maxwell reared back in her seat, shock written all over her face, revealing creases not there before.

"You didn't know?"

"Mrs. Maxwell, I mean, June, I know almost nothing about my family."

"Well, maybe I'm not the one to tell you this."

"Please," Alice said, placing her hand on Mrs. Maxwell's arm, realizing it was the same grasp Clara Jenkins had used on her. Alice pulled it back. "I'm sorry. It's just, everything changed when my father left. And the sad part is, I don't even know what changed. All I know is I think we had a normal home. Then one day some policeman came to our house, and suddenly, both my father and Jack Jr. were gone with no explanation. And even though my mother was still there, the mother I knew had vanished. It was if she had been replaced by some kind of clone."

Realizing her voice had grown louder, Alice looked around, but no one was staring. She felt cold tears running down her cheeks. If she had been in BUCKY'S DINER, time would have stopped, patrons frozen in a stare, forks holding country-fried steaks inches from their mouths. Even the gravy smothered over the bites of steak would have clung in amazement at the people airing their dirty laundry in public. Dirty laundry was saved for the web of gossip that held the rural spot on the map intact. But this was STARBUCKS in New York City.

"Your mother told you nothing, not even after you got older?"

"Nothing. She almost went into spasms if I brought up my father, and mentioning Jack Jr. made her angry more often than not. I don't even know what my father looked like. You say I look like him. I saved three faded pictures. They reveal next to nothing."

"Alice, if you have time, I have pictures of both your father and mother. I also have pictures of her with Jack Jr.'s father."

"We have a different father?"

"Oh, dear," she said with a heavy sigh and a shake of her

head. "My husband and I live in Manhattan. Why don't you let me hail a taxi, and I could show you if you like?"

"Oh, Mrs. Maxwell, I would like nothing better."

JUNE MAXWELL LIVED in an apartment building across from Central Park, the kind with a doorman, the kind Alice knew went for five figures a month. Mr. Maxwell had to be wealthy. Working behind a makeup counter in a department store couldn't buy this kind of luxury.

June removed her coat and gloves, revealing only the slight onset of age spots, but the huge ruby ring surrounded by diamonds made them unnoticeable.

"Can I take your coat, Alice? Offer you something? Another coffee? Some wine?"

"Oh, no, I'm fine." Alice removed her coat, embarrassed as she handed it to June. A woman with her taste could see it came from a discount rack in a bulk clothing store.

"Please have a seat." She directed Alice to a large white couch covered with cushions in the mainly white open studio apartment with a view of the park, the kind of apartment everyone in New York aspired to have.

"My first job out of college was at MACY'S, working under your mother in the cosmetics department. Your mother taught me everything I know about cosmetics. Soon after your mother left, I rose to take her position."

"Your apartment is beautiful."

She laughed. "I know what you're thinking. How can someone working in a cosmetic's department afford this? My husband is a stock-market analyst."

Alice smiled.

"If you'll excuse me, I'll get those pictures. They're in a box in my closet."

Alice tried to relax, but all the questions racing through her mind and the revelation of finding out she and Jack Jr. were only half brother and sister was tying her stomach up in knots. The thing that hurt the most was the fact her mother never told her any of this.

Alice walked around the room, looking at the tranquil scenes of the park hanging on the walls—real paintings—before strolling over to the large window to take in the actual view.

June came back into the room, and Alice took her seat once again on the couch with June sitting beside her. "Sorry. I had to find the stepstool to reach them." She shoved a pile of *Architectural Digest* magazines aside and set a wicker box on top of the glass coffee table.

Alice watched nervously as Mrs. Maxwell sifted through the picture albums, all neatly labeled with dates. She pulled out an album entitled 1990 to 1995.

"1990 is when I went to work at Macy's. Priscilla was going through a nasty divorce. But then, aren't most divorces horrid? Luckily, I've been fortunate in that regard. I remember Jack Jr. was seven. He was a handful even then."

"Handful. That's what my mother always said."

Mrs. Maxwell smiled. "I guess I remember her saying it."

She flipped through the pages and removed a picture from the cellophane. "This was my first Christmas party at MACY'S." The back of the picture said *Christmas, December 1990 at Tavern on the Green.* A list of names covered the back. The name Priscilla Black drew instant recognition.

"My mother's first husband's last name was Black?"

"Her husband's name was John Black." She flipped over the picture, showing a group of people at a long table. "There was always the main party, but we had small individual department parties, usually went out to eat together somewhere. This time, we brought our husbands or significant others. Most of the girls who worked in cosmetics were young. Most had boyfriends. A few of the girls were married. I was surprised your mother and John showed up together."

Alice studied the picture Mrs. Maxwell had handed her the way someone nearsighted might do.

"Can you pick out your mother?" June asked.

Alice scanned the picture, going over each face individually before pointing.

"Correct."

"She was beautiful. I almost didn't recognize her. I'm not used to seeing her wear makeup."

"The man sitting next to her is John, her husband. They were still married when that picture was taken, barely."

Alice perused the man with gray hair and a gray beard. "He looks so much older."

"That's because he was—twenty years older. Your mother was twenty-two, I believe, when she met him. And he was in his forties. Now, what I'm about to tell you, don't hold me accountable for all of this being true. While I know it's mostly true, still, this *was* office gossip, and it happened, the way she met him *that is*, long before I came to work at MACY'S. From what I understand, John was going through his own divorce at the time and was dating someone else. He was at the makeup counter with the woman he was having an affair with when he met your mother. From what I hear, it wasn't long until he dropped her and started seeing your mother."

Alice looked at Mrs. Maxwell as if she couldn't believe what she was hearing. She looked back down at the picture, grasping it so strongly she was putting a crease in it.

Mrs. Maxwell pointed to the woman sitting next to her mother. "And this is me."

"You look so young."

June laughed.

"No, I don't mean…"

"No, it's okay. I know what you mean, and I *was* young then, twenty-one, fresh out of college. My degree was in art. I wasn't sure what I would do with my degree. I thought painting women's faces would suffice until I could find something more permanent, like a job at an art gallery, but David came along. My children are grown now."

Alice raised her head, looking at the paintings, and saw the signatures she hadn't noticed before. "Those are yours?"

"Yes."

"They're good. I was admiring them when you went out of the room to get the pictures."

"I'm not so good that I sell many, but fortunately, my husband allows me the freedom to indulge in my art."

"You don't work at MACY'S anymore?"

"No." She laughed. "I miss it sometimes, but I keep busy enough. I quit shortly after becoming pregnant. David and I have two children who live in the city. Both are at Columbia right now."

"Oh, that's nice."

"Yes."

"So how did my mother meet my father?"

June pointed to a man in the picture, the one Alice was still grasping.

"The man sitting next to you?"

"Yes, that's Jack."

"But, he has his arm around you."

"I know. This is all a lot to take in. I was dating Jack when this picture was taken."

"Do you mean my mother…"

"Took him away from me? Yes. There is really no other way to put it."

"He looks young too."

"Yes, Jack is my age, fifteen years younger than your mom. I don't know, maybe after John, him being so much older and all, Priscilla thought a younger man would be better. Wait, I have another picture in here somewhere of your father and mother together."

Mrs. Maxwell flipped through the pages and pulled another photo from underneath the cellophane. It was a closeup shot of them both. They were smiling and looked happy. Right off, Alice noticed the same hair color on her father and her own eyes staring back at her.

Alice took the second picture from Mrs. Maxwell, placing it over the first.

"You see why I recognized you?" June asked.

"Yes."

"This picture was taken, I believe, when she first found out she was pregnant with you. You can keep it if you want."

"Thank you. So my mother and father were married then?"

Mrs. Maxwell's didn't nod or anything but said, "The affair began the night of the Christmas party. Oh, I don't mean they left together, but the way they looked at each other, and well, your mother and John were fighting. It was obvious before they even got to the party John had been drinking. I think he might have been an alcoholic, or if he wasn't then, he was on the road to being one."

"That would explain my mother's strict rule of no alcohol in the house."

"Yes, your mother was a teetotaler. Never once did I ever see her drink any form of alcohol."

"You said you and my mother were friends?"

"We were, later. I even came to your house to see if I could help when I got the word Jack left, but she didn't want my help. I think she was too ashamed."

"I'm sorry. This is all so confusing. I had no idea my mother was married to anyone other than my father or that Jack Jr. is only my half-brother. Or that my mother was some kind of hussy that stole other women's husbands and boyfriends. And wait,"

Alice said, finally letting go of the first picture. "Why is his name Jack Jr.?"

"His name is actually John Jr., but Jack is the nickname for John. Everyone called him John, except for your mother. I think it was your mother who called her husband John and her son, Jack, so as not to get them confused."

"Okay, so my father was Jack White and not Black?"

"Yes," June said.

"Then why isn't my last name White?"

"Alice, that is something you would have to ask your mother."

"Yeah, well, too late for that one, not that she would have told me."

Mrs. Maxwell put are hand on Alice's shoulder.

Alice again remembered Clara Jenkins agitation and how she kept yelling out *White*. It was what she was trying to tell her. Her mother must have confided in Clara. No wonder Clara acted around her the way she did. So many days Alice came home to find Clara sitting with her mother at the kitchen table, Clara babbling on about what she would have done in her mother's situation, only to stop in dead silence when Alice came through the front door, all hush-hush, so morbid. Alice wanted to ask, "Who died?" but thought better to keep her mouth shut. Really, the question she should have been asking was, "What situation?" But then, Clara's bony liver-spotted hand, smelling of lotion, would have held her even tighter, admonishing her, "Be good. Your mother has enough troubles." So she endured the shorter version of the perfunctory arm squeeze and hastened to her room.

Alice felt as if she could burst and wanted to let out some kind of primal scream. June must have sensed this, still caressing Alice's shoulder.

"Alice, why don't you go into the bathroom and run cold

water over your face? I will make us both some chamomile tea. The bathroom is at the end of the hall."

Alice laid the picture of her mother and father aside, letting it drift slowly to the couch. She looked toward the window as she got up and saw flakes of snow coming down.

Alice didn't know exactly how long she was in the bathroom before Mrs. Maxwell knocked on the door to ask if everything was all right. No, it wasn't. Maybe she was better off not knowing the truth. Possibly, she could have dealt with it if it had hit her in incremental spurts over the years, beginning when she was six. Alice always heard kids were resilient. This truth came like a construction beam falling on her head.

Alice opened the bathroom door, and Mrs. Maxwell said, "Alice, you look as pale as a ghost. I'm so sorry I am the one to tell you all of this. Listen, why don't you lie down for a bit?"

"I *am* getting a headache. I'm so sorry. I don't mean to be a burden."

"Oh, no, dear. Like I said, your mother and I were friends at one time. Here, let me show you to the spare bedroom."

A few moments later, Mrs. Maxwell came in carrying a cup of tea. "This should help with both your headache and your nerves," she said handing her the cup. "Can you take a sleeping pill, just one? It might help."

"Yes, that's fine." Alice put the tablet in her mouth and followed with a sip of tea.

"Mrs. Maxwell," Alice said, sitting up in bed against the pillows, "why do you think my father left?"

"Alice, it's so hard to say. But, I believe he may have been having an affair. Jack was like that. You don't change a person's stripes. Your mother, besides being crazy about the man, had a blind eye when it came to him."

"Tell me, did my mother marry him before or after she became pregnant with me?"

Mrs. Maxwell had the same pitying look on her face as Clara

Jenkins. "After, maybe," she said with a twist of her lips and a raised eyebrow.

"And he just walked out of our lives…"

"I cautioned your mother against Jack. But she thought it was jealousy. I never loved Jack. And by the time I could see she had her sights set on him, no matter what, I was already dating David and deeply in love with him."

"All this time, I thought he must be dead. It even crossed my mind, I'm sorry to say, more than once, that my brother, my half-brother, may have killed him. I mean, I woke up when I was six years old to find that both my father and Jack Jr. had vanished. The police had been there the day before. That night, I saw my father and Jack Jr. go out to the shed. And just weeks ago they found the skeleton."

"Skeleton?"

"It was at our old house on Tucker Street in Queens. They're tearing it down for a strip mall. The construction crew dug up a skeleton, and they wanted my DNA. I thought… Well, you can imagine, but then it only turned out to be old bones, Native American ones. And why is my name Black and not White?"

"Alice, about what I said about them marrying after your mother got pregnant, well, I'm not so sure your father ever married your mom. And when your father left, Jack Jr. went to live with his father or his father's sister. I think by that time, Jack's father was a full-blown alcoholic. I heard he died of liver failure."

"They had to be married. I have my mother's wedding rings. The engagement ring is so beautiful. It has sapphires around the diamond."

"I'm sorry, Alice, but those were from her first marriage. I remember those rings well. She told me the sapphire was her birthstone. To this day, I remember your mom's birthday, September 12."

"Oh," Alice cried, placing her hand over her head and closing her eyes.

———

THE SOUND of voices woke Alice. She walked into the living room to see Mrs. Maxwell's husband was home.

"Alice, this is my husband, David."

Alice extended her hand. "Hello, Mr. Maxwell."

"Hello, Alice."

"Alice, I asked David to bring home some food. I thought you needed to eat."

"I hope you like Chinese," Mr. Maxwell said.

"Chinese!" Alice exclaimed. "Oh, shit, what time is it? Oh, I'm so sorry. I don't usually curse."

Mr. Maxwell laughed. "If someone told me what June told you about your family—I hope you don't mind, but June told me over the phone—I would have said a lot more than shit. And to answer your question, it's nine thirty."

"I had a date at eight. I was supposed to meet him at the restaurant."

"That good-looking young man at NATURE'S BLUSH, the one who came running after me."

"Yes."

"I'm sure he will understand. Why don't you call him? You can even invite him here if you want."

"I can't call him. I don't have his number. It was a first date."

"Oh," Mrs. Maxwell said with that same pitying look that had been so prevalent all evening.

"If you don't mind, I think I will head home. I'll just get my coat. Thank you for everything."

"There is no way you are taking the subway or a bus. David, notify the doorman and have him call our service."

"Oh, no, you've already been too kind."

"We insist," Mr. Maxwell said.

Mrs. Maxwell handed Alice her card before she left. Alice took it out of her pocket while in the car—JUNE MAXWELL'S OILS. As she was putting it back into her pocket, she noticed an arrow pointing to the backside. She flipped it over.

Alice, it was so nice to meet you. I miss doing makeup. Please call me. I would love to give you a makeover, nothing too audacious, just something to bring out those beautiful eyes of yours and set off your hair even more than it already shines.
We only covered the bad stuff. There were so many wonderful things about your mom and your father. I'll tell you all I remember the next time we meet.

The writing was tiny, indicating Mrs. Maxwell was practiced in the art of writing personal messages on the backs of her cards.

A part of Alice, the part that wanted to leave her past behind, wanted to call Chen and see if she knew anything about Tom. Charlie was more than likely working, but she felt as if the life had been drained out of her. She only wanted to sleep and wake up to a fresh new world.

At least she knew where Tom worked. She would go by and explain.

26

Tom

Tom left Dragon's Den with takeout he had no appetite for after occupying a table for well over an hour. Simon and Garfunkel would feast. As for him, he wasn't sure if he could ever stomach Chinese again, and he had absolutely been craving it since he stepped out of Nature's Blush.

The waiter with the name tag of Charlie, who spoke perfect English and kept pouring him pots of tea, finally said, "Not that it's any of my business, but I know the feeling. I've been there."

Was the fact he was being stood up that obvious?

Tom had been singing "Here Comes the Sun" to himself ever since she said she would go out with him. She was so perfect. He thought there was a spark between them for sure. Why did she say she would go out with him, even pick the restaurant, and then not show up? Did he totally misread the situation? Was he so screwed up when it came to women he thought they were saying one thing when they meant another?

He had visualized the whole evening in his mind. They would talk over dinner like they had known each other all their lives. Possibly she would tell him about her meeting with the lady. There was definitely something going on about her father, and she would confide in him.

Afterward, they would walk across the Brooklyn Bridge like all the other lovers. Stop in the middle and maybe he would get up the nerve to kiss her there if she gave him any sign. At the very least, they would take a selfie although Tom wasn't much on selfies. He might ask another couple to take their picture. Proof he wasn't dreaming her up. Something to show Burt, maybe even post on FACEBOOK after a few dates. Yes, he had already been thinking long-term, maybe not at their first meeting at the construction site but definitely the second time he saw her. So cheesy.

Maybe he should walk across the bridge and throw himself off. Contrary to popular belief, throwing oneself off a bridge was not an easy, quick way to go. Before death, the impact of the water would cause ribs to break, organs to tear apart, and then the drowning part after which fish would eat a good portion of his body, the remains more than likely never to be found. His parents would be devastated. Or his cell phone would go off mid-fall. He would use all his strength to pull his phone from his pocket to see it was her calling, to tell him something terrible happened that prevented her from coming. Her final words before the big splash would be, "What's that sound? Is it terribly windy?" Then he remembered he didn't give her his cell number. Why hadn't he? So stupid. With the way his luck was going, he would survive, only to be mutilated, blinking once for yes and twice for no for a morbidly long existence. Everyone on both sides of his family had a propensity for prolonged lives. His family even boasted of two centenarians.

If he knew any country-and-western songs, he would be singing one of them about now. They were always about heart-break, weren't they?

Tom boarded the bus, the aroma from his Chinese takeout mingling with the stale odor of the interior and its occupants.

There was a different group of people on it than the last time he rode, but he could almost tell each of their stories by their looks, their mannerisms, and the way they sat or slumped in their seats. For the first time, he no longer felt like the ghost on the bus. He belonged.

———

LAST FRIDAY, he had been so optimistic. Right after Burt said he would get the woman's name, the woman who turned out to be Alice Black, Burt asked about his family, and he had opened up about his life, one of the few times. He gave him all the particulars, that they lived in Georgia and how he came from a long line of teachers. He had been the odd duck in the family. Tom knew both of Burt's parents were dead and that he had a brother in Connecticut he hardly ever saw. His brother also worked in construction.

"How'd you end up in New York?" Burt finally asked after Tom finished singing the praises of his family.

How did he end up in New York? That was a long story, and one he didn't want to get into, but he felt he owed Burt some kind of answer as he had been so kind to him from the start. "My wife went to school up here."

"Wife?" Burt almost fell off his bar stool. "And here I thought you were the shy type. You couldn't be too shy, married and all."

"It didn't last long. She got her degree. The marriage ended, and she returned to Georgia. I stayed."

Burt gave a nod as if a broken marriage could explain most circumstances. Burt possibly detected they were in the same boat, husbands whose wives had found someone better. Burt took another gulp of beer. "Life can be a bitch."

YES, Sarah had slept around, and they fought plenty about it, but he was willing to forgive. That hurdle he could get over, maybe because he had never really been in love with her. Not the way he envisioned love to be anyway. It was like Sarah had managed to convince him he was in love until they were married. Then she convinced him he would never live up to the man she wanted him to be. Even without the affairs, his life with Sarah was like fingernails scratching against a chalkboard. If he had been madder about the affairs, Sarah might have cared for him, and they could have had some semblance of a marriage, but he wasn't, and she didn't.

He was about as opposite from the bad-boy type Sarah went for as anyone could be. Why Sarah even wanted to marry him, he didn't know, but it was her who did the proposing and him who should have said no.

What really tore the marriage apart was Sarah's constant berating of him, about how he was a loser, about how he would never amount to anything. And the sad part was, she was right. At least staying in New York, away from her and his family, his family that were doing so well, he didn't have to be reminded of it, not as much, that was.

"You went to college, and you don't even use your degree," she reminded him constantly. The ones who should have been the angriest about it should have been his parents, but they never pushed or questioned him. As far as he could tell, they only wanted him to be happy.

Working with his hands were the times he was the happiest. Anything wood, he was drawn to; the different textures, grains, colors, hardness, versatility, flexibility. Would it be more suitable for a desk or a chair? What tone would it emit if it was fashioned into a drum, violin, or guitar? It wasn't that he ever hoped to achieve any great success at playing a guitar, but he loved the feel of one. Each had its own unique personality from the curve of the wood to the spacing of the frets. Even the varnish could alter the sound. Every instrument he had ever handled gave off its own unique vibrations. He was sure even the reefer burn on his current guitar contributed in some way to the tone. He picked and strummed, and Sarah complained, "Why do you waste your time with that stuff?"

"SO TELL ME, Tom. You're still young. You have a marriage behind you. Had to have learned from your mistakes if any of us ever do. What are your goals? Do you plan on working in construction all your life?" Burt asked.

"No," he said. Why he said no, he wasn't sure, but the word rolled off his tongue easily enough. He supposed a good paying job was a means to an end.

"So what then?"

"I guess my dream would be to live out in the country some-where, working with my hands, maybe raising a garden, and having a shop full of tools I could do woodworking with."

"Have you ever done woodworking?"

Tom remembered the time he had once ordered a guitar kit in high school. It turned out pretty good, but he had sold it for rent money when he and Sarah first got married.

"Not really. But I think I could."

Tom wasn't sure if it was the second round of beer that made him chatter more than usual or the fact Burt offered to find out who the girl was. His brief encounter with her at the worksite sent butterflies through his stomach, something he never had with Sarah.

MAYBE THERE WAS a logical explanation why she didn't show up. He had to think so because he truly felt something come alive in him when he saw her. He stepped off the bus and noticed a homeless man sitting at the corner. He forced a smile, thinking his life could be worse, and handed him the Chinese takeout.

Tomorrow was Friday, and Burt would ask him to go out for a drink. Sure, he could use a drink, but he also knew Burt would want to know about his date, and he didn't want to tell him what happened. Burt was a straggler when it came to leaving work. Tom would somehow manage to be among the first to clock out, not giving Burt the chance to ask him to go have drinks. He could only hope Burt would think the reason was because the date had gone so well he was rushing out to see her again.

27

Alice and Iris

I ris held the door open for Alice when she came dragging into work nearly thirty minutes late.

"I was worried about you. I called your phone, but you didn't pick up," Iris said.

"Oh, sorry." Alice pulled her phone out of her purse. "I turned it off. I meant to turn it back on but forgot." She looked down to see Iris's call and a message and another call from Chen, no message. Maybe Chen saw Tom last night. Maybe he said something, described her, but no, Chen called every few days and texted several times daily, nothing important, usually passing along some funny meme with a line of emojis, something Alice struggled with. Picking out the proper one to use was like deciphering Egyptian hieroglyphics. For Chen to call rather than send a text meant it was something important. She probably had the paper finished. She had promised to let Alice read it first.

Tina, in her usual bubbly manner, came rushing up to the front of the store. She asked, "How was the date? Give us the details."

"Date?" Iris asked, surprised.

"There was no date, and I don't want to talk about it," Alice said.

"Tina, will you please go to the back and get my massage table ready?" Iris asked, motioning her off. "Not to worry. There's other fish in the sea," Iris said to Alice.

So cliché coming from Iris. Some Buddhist philosophy or Chinese proverb was more what Alice was used to hearing from her. But Alice knew she had been having some lengthy talks with her ex about their son. Talks that probably threw her off her metaphysical game.

"We need to check our stock and get those orders in. I have to hand it to you. These gift baskets have been a godsend. You realize you have single-handedly doubled our business?" Iris added.

Despite her own problems, it was like Iris to interject a positive spin when there was a tense situation. Maybe it was the rippling waterfall sounds already coming from the back, the pretend cascade of water falling, missing the mark when it came to the real thing back in West Virginia, that caused Alice to let out a small squeak along with a tear. Hadn't she completely cleaned out her tear ducts last night when she violently cried herself to sleep? Around any other person, Alice could have contained it, but Iris had this way of pulling emotions from people. She had a deep-seated need to fix people, and Iris knew instinctively who needed fixing. Iris knew it on that first day Alice walked into the shop though Alice didn't know it herself. Chen would label it *unresolved issues*.

"I think you need to talk about whatever happened last night," Iris said. She took Alice by the hand and led her to the back. "Tina, if you don't mind, please go up front and mind the store."

"But, I thought…"

"Up front is where I need you now."

Tina let out a sigh as she turned and walked away.

"Get up on the table," Iris said, patting it.

"Iris, no." Alice shook her head.

"I insist. Whatever it is, I want you to talk about it while I knead it out of your body. Let it all go."

"I'm not sure you can knead this away."

"Well, we'll try," she said, removing Alice's coat and almost pulling her to the massage table.

Iris stuck her head out through the curtain. "Tina, it will be awhile. Please tell me you can handle everything."

Alice had her face comfortably positioned in the breathing slot and heard no comment from Tina but surmised that Tina had responded with her typical thumbs-up.

"She's been doing better. She really has," Iris said to Alice although Alice knew Iris was repeating it to reassure herself, the way her mother always repeated, 'You'll take care of me, won't you, Alice?'

Alice breathed in the smell of lavender essential oil coming from the diffuser. After an hour, with surprisingly no interruptions from Tina, Alice felt relief—relief Iris had quit pressing into her feet with those pressurized thumbs of hers. Sometimes she thought Iris was releasing some of her own stuff with each push of the heel of her hand and thrust of her thumb. But she had to admit, after enduring what sometimes felt like torment, the aftermath of Iris's touch was magic. Alice poured out her heart, telling her in a voice that had become increasingly sluggish all that had transpired since June Maxwell and Tom Walker had entered the shop yesterday.

"Just lie there for a while. I don't have a massage appointment for another hour. Consider this a vacation day. We can do the orders tomorrow morning. They'll still be here by the weekend."

"Vacation day," Alice droned. "I haven't been working here long enough to have this many vacation days."

"Oh, hush," Iris said. "You've done wonders for my business. We even had to hire Tina."

Alice laughed, and Iris followed with, "Okay, I know. Maybe hiring Tina wasn't doing me any favors. But with all this extra business, we had to have someone else over the holiday season," she said, keeping her voice low.

Iris stuck her head out of the curtain again. "Everything going okay out there, Tina?"

"Thumbs-up?" Alice asked quietly.

"Yes, and she was smiling. She didn't hear a thing."

Iris gave Alice's shoulders an affectionate squeeze. "Sleep. I'll wake you right before my massage appointment."

28

Lunch

W hen Alice got up from the table, she definitely felt lighter. So much so, she agreed to Iris's suggestion of going to the worksite to find Tom and explain.

"I could be wrong, but I'm getting the message Tom is your fate, plus seeing the property again, the one you associate so many bad memories with looking entirely different, can be a powerful symbol toward healing, especially now that you know the truth about your mom and dad," Iris said.

Alice would like to hope Tom might be her fate. She definitely experienced something akin to butterflies swirling around in her stomach both times she saw him. Two times—neither conducive to falling head over heels in love. If there was a third meeting, it could be the fate Iris suggested.

She definitely had to find him and see if he was willing to give it another go. She reached out her arm to get her coat from the rack, getting a whiff of her underarm, trying not to gag. She didn't shower last night, nor did she this morning when she saw she had overslept.

ALICE WAS ALMOST to the bus stop when she heard someone call her name. It couldn't be. She turned.

"Doug!"

The voice was definitely Doug's, but as for the rest of him? The guy she knew with the serious blue eyes behind the wire-rims with the rough beard had transformed. The beard and unkempt hair falling to his shoulders, along with the faded blue shirt and jeans she was so used to seeing him in were all absent. He looked like one of those carbon copies of men one would see on Wall Street, perfectly groomed and tailored to the ninth degree. Her eyes scanned over him from his salon-style gelled haircut to his smooth angular face minus glasses (he must be wearing contacts) to the perfect knot in his blue silk tie lying against his light blue (she was glad he hadn't given up the blue) Brooks Brothers shirt encased by an immaculate charcoal suit with a long black woolen unbuttoned overcoat. His appearance revealed a superior fashion sense to which Chen would've said bravo, but to Alice, everything about him looked branded and contrived, the kind of thing the Doug she knew despised. Alice spied a trace of fancy argyle socks, blue and black, melting into shiny leather shoes, the kind that got polished by those men in airports, not that she had ever been in an airport, but she had seen it in old black-and-white movies. When he held out his hand to wave, the watch that probably cost as much as a compact car glowed in the sunlight. This was not Doug but anti-Doug.

A slight shiver went through her upon seeing him again, this new creature he had become, and the shiver turned into comfort. Comfort was her word to describe Doug; naïve was his word for her. Then she laughed. She needed to laugh. It was a release, but Doug would more than likely construe it as happiness in seeing him again, and she couldn't deny it was that too. "How long have you been back?"

He reached for her, bringing her into a tight hug. The metal of his watch pressed against the back of her coat. He stepped back. "You smell like lavender, and also, a little like…"

"Like the outhouse back at The Farm? I was just headed back to my apartment to shower. You smell like some kind of expensive cologne."

He laughed. "Apartment? You no longer live with your mother?" he asked.

"She died."

"Alice, I'm sorry." There was only sorry, not *so sorry*, as Doug knew the relationship she had with her mother.

She shrugged. "You know."

"Yes," he said with a slight nod of his head and a half roll of his eyes. "I've been planning on looking you up. I wanted to get paperwork settled first. So much has happened since I've been back."

"Okay, but why did you come back?"

"Do you want to go somewhere to talk?"

"Doug, I really want to. I have so much to tell you, too, but I had a rough night, actually, a rough couple of weeks. Now I need to get that shower. Can we talk this weekend?"

"I'm totally tied up this weekend. I'll go back to your apartment with you if that's okay. My schedule if free until three. No funny business, I promise." He grinned.

"Okay," Alice said. She couldn't imagine what Doug might want to discuss. "I was on my way to the bus stop when I heard you yell my name."

Before she knew it, Doug ran up the street and whistled down a taxi, a taxi that would have more than likely passed her by if she had tried hailing it.

"SMALL, BUT NICE," he said as they entered the living room. "I see you have entered the world of technology. A flat-screen tele-vision, no less." He nodded his head in approval.

"Yes, and I even have a laptop and cell phone now. I can give you the thirty-second tour."

Doug laughed.

"You have to admit even though it's small, it has more amenities than The Farm," Alice said, grinning.

"Yes, it is nicer."

"I didn't say nicer."

"No, you didn't. Of all of us, Alice, you were the one who belonged there the most. You had an affinity with the land. The view at The Farm is much better," he said, looking out her bedroom window at the brick wall.

"Make yourself comfortable in the living room. I'm going to step into my shower where hot water comes out with the turn of a handle. I have a feeling it's not as fancy as your shower, but it gets the job done. I'll be quick. I still can't make myself take long showers after having to conserve water for so many years."

"Yeah, I know what you mean. Same with me."

Ten minutes later, Alice returned wearing her robe and with a towel wrapped around her head. A strand of wet hair was hanging down the side of her face. She tried to tuck it under, but it wouldn't stay. So she unwrapped her hair and toweled it dry.

"That's how I knew it was you," Doug said, rising from the sofa.

"What? Oh, my hair."

"You are the only one I know with that color hair."

"Doug, you didn't answer my question. How long have you been back?"

"We folded up shop about a month after you left."

"Seriously?"

"Yes."

"And I gather from your attire, you're practicing law. How is your dad? Have you healed old wounds?"

"You gathered right, and he's doing great now that I've come to my senses."

"*Have* you come to your senses?"

Doug did that thing where he twisted his mouth when he was thinking. "I guess the jury is still out on that one, but I'm leaning toward yes. Let's face it. I never was much of a farmer. You, on the other hand…"

"Maybe not a good farmer, but you were good at managing, and I think you could convince anyone of almost anything."

"A lot has happened with me since I've been back."

"If we were playing poker, I might call you on that one," Alice said.

"Oh, really. I want to hear all about it. But first, Alice, I want to tell you…" He hesitated a moment before saying, "I'm engaged."

Alice stood rigidly and let the towel she was using to dry her hair drop to the floor.

"Are you shocked, hurt, or maybe all right with it?" He stood as if he wanted to reach out to her, stepping forward but at the last moment, resisted. She was fresh out of the shower, wearing only a robe. It was only common sense to keep a respectable distance. Doug had always been a common-sense kind of guy.

"Listen, let me go get dressed, and we'll talk."

Alice shut her bedroom door behind her and sat down on her bed, dropping her head into her hands. She reached for her pillow and wanted to scream, but even with the pillow, she thought Doug might hear. It wasn't like The Farm where she could go out in the woods and scream to her heart's content, which was what she did on some days. Nature was good for absorbing anger and heartache. So she satisfied her primal urge to release something with a deep groan into the pillow.

It wasn't as if she wanted Doug. The shiver she experienced upon seeing him only lasted for a moment. He didn't even look like the Doug she knew. This was an entirely different man standing there in his lawyer suit, hailing a cab with the ease of one of the New York elites.

Alice, still in her robe, turned the corner to the bathroom, looked into her bathroom mirror and decided some makeup might not hurt. She applied mascara, powder, and lip gloss, her entire repertoire of products, and thought about Mrs. Maxwell. She moved around the corner to her bedroom and looked through her pile of freshly laundered clothes still in the laundry basket and pulled out the black stretch yoga pants Chen had talked her into buying. She put on a yoga bra and her long periwinkle sweater. Chen said it brought out both her eyes and her hair. This was her most striking outfit, according to Chen. Alice wasn't sure if she was trying to impress Doug, who there was no way on earth she could impress. The *old* Doug, maybe, but not the *new* Doug, the one he was destined to be. The Doug she had met in the coffee shop that day was the one embarking upon his extended Rumspringa.

Tom. She *did want* to impress him, and she had to admit she felt like Guinevere to his Lancelot the way he came to her rescue in chasing down Mrs. Maxwell. She realized it wasn't for Doug but for Tom that she was dressing in the outfit.

"You look pretty," he said when she walked back into the living room. His eyes perused her from the top of her head down to her sneakers and stopped. There was his trademark twist of the mouth.

"What's your fiancée's name?" she asked.

"Constance," he said.

"I thought maybe I saw you one day with her at the METROPOLITAN. Is she blonde?" Such a general description could have been almost anyone in New York.

"She works there. Sometimes we meet for lunch."

"Then it *was* you."

"You should have said something."

"I wasn't sure. I only saw a brief glimpse of you turning a

corner, and well, you had changed so much. If it was you, I found it hard to believe. Plus, I thought you would never leave The Farm."

"*The Farm.*" He laughed. "We never decided on a proper name for it."

"No, I guess it doesn't matter now."

"Oh, I don't know."

"So is being engaged what you wanted to tell me?" Alice asked.

"Do you want to go out to lunch?"

"I guess I am a little hungry. I haven't eaten since lunch yesterday."

"Well then, we have got to get you fed."

"I know a great Chinese place."

"Okay, I'll call a cab." He pulled his cell from his pocket.

"We won't need one. It's across the street."

MR. WANG SEATED them in the back at Alice's request. As he handed them the menus, he eyed Doug over the way a surrogate father might, sizing him up as a future husband, and it was plain to tell Mr. Wang wasn't buying it.

"What's good?" Doug asked while carefully hanging his coat on the coat rack a few steps from their table before sitting. Alice threw hers over the back of the chair.

"My favorite is the Kung Pao Chicken."

"You can eat chicken after The Farm? I remember how squeamish you were when it came to decapitating them."

"As long as I don't have to see their heads being chopped off, I'm fine."

He laughed.

Mr. Wang brought a teapot and poured them both tea in the tiny cups.

"We'll both have the Kung Pao Chicken," Doug said.

He nodded and walked away.

"So this rough night you spoke of?"

"It started weeks ago with a fortune cookie from here."

"Oh?"

"It said I would meet a tall dark stranger who would answer all my questions."

"I take it you had a date with this tall dark stranger last night, and he didn't answer your questions?"

"Oh, no, she did."

"She?" Doug's eyebrows rose.

"It wasn't a date."

Alice told Doug everything that had transpired from the bones being found on the property of her former home to how she was going back to the worksite to find Tom to apologize when he called out her name. She poured out everything over the Kung Pao Chicken, fried rice, and three pots of tea, she with her fork, Doug with his chopsticks. The only thing left was to open the two fortune cookies atop the bill.

"I'm not sure after all you told me if I want to open mine." He slipped it aside and removed his wallet from the inside of his jacket, removed one of several credit cards, and placed it inside the black leather folder without looking at the bill.

"Thanks for lunch, Doug."

"You're welcome." He shoved the check to the edge of the table where Chen's uncle promptly picked it up. "Alice, do you *want* to find your father?"

Alice looked at Doug blankly for a moment. "You know, if you had asked me this before yesterday, I would have said yes, but after last night, I don't know. I'm not sure what the point would be. Clearly, the man wanted no part of my life."

"Well, if you decide you do, my law firm has the resources, all pro bono of course."

"That is so nice of you, but no, I don't think so." She shook her head.

"Well, if you change your mind…" He pulled a card from his inside coat pocket, wrote his private cell number on the back, and handed it to her.

"I'm sorry. I've talked and talked. I know nothing about your fiancée except that her name is Constance, she's blonde, and she works at the METROPOLITAN MUSEUM OF ART."

"I would like for you to meet her. I've told her all about you."

"You have?"

"Certainly. You were a big part of my life for five whole years. She would like to meet you too."

"Here." He handed her the fortune cookie nearest her. "Let's get this over with." He broke open his cookie and looked at the piece of paper. "Mine says, *You will be hungry again in six hours.*" He laughed. "I see what you mean. These are highly accurate. Now yours."

Alice broke open her own cookie and pulled out the paper. She read out loud, "*You will receive a much-needed gift.*"

"We don't want to break the streak of accurate fortune telling. I have time for one more thing before I head back to my office."

"Oh, and what is that?"

"An early Christmas present from Constance and me. Let's get you a decent pair of shoes. If I'm not mistaken, those look like the same ones you wore on The Farm?"

"They are, but not the only ones."

"Yeah, I noticed you left the farm boots behind when you left."

"I didn't figure I'd be needing them in the city."

"Well, I got you a decent pair of farm boots. Now, I'm going to get you something suitable for the city."

29

The Way They Were

"If you're determined to only wear one pair of shoes, you need something you can wear with everything and get you through a New York winter," Doug said.

Who knew Doug was so knowledgeable about fashion? It was like he had two different personas.

"These are stylish and practical. They will go with most anything," the sales clerk said in an exasperated voice, the whole while trying to smile. Alice had said no to several pairs after looking at the prices on the bottom. She was distinctly a different breed of woman when it came to shoes, especially a woman accompanied by a man willing to pay for said shoes, one who was oblivious to price tags. And as far as going with anything she had in *her closet*? If only he knew how scant her closet was…

Doug looked at his watch and whispered in her ear as the sales clerk handed her a pair to try. "Alice, these are nice. I know you're worried about the cost. Don't. These cost the same as we would bill a client for one hour of work. Think of it like that."

"Riding boots! But I don't plan on riding a horse," she said. The clerk had feigned a smile, a smile she knew was entirely for

Doug, not that the clerk was gay but because he knew Doug carried the purse strings and maybe to show he approved of Doug's choice in a girlfriend although he clearly didn't.

She wore the riding boots out of the store, carrying her sneakers in the intended bag for the boots. The sales clerk had looked at her old shoes with disgust and asked if he could deposit them in the garbage can.

"No, those shoes have lots of memories," she said. Doug smiled.

All she could do was thank Doug. She gave him her cell number, and he kissed her on the cheek before leaving her outside the shoe store in Manhattan, a few blocks from his office. One day, she would like to see his office but not today. She was on a mission to find Tom.

He wanted to hail a cab for her, but she told him she wanted to walk, try out her new boots. Chen would be impressed. And while she wanted to impress Tom, she kind of thought he was the type who would be okay with her old sneakers.

ALICE LOOKED DOWN at the black leather riding boots, the boots that cost almost as much as her monthly rent. She had to admit she liked the fact the small chunky heel made her taller. Any narrower of a heel she might have been wobbling down the street. But, she wasn't, and she liked how they encased her legs in warmth, not to mention how they stroked her ego.

She walked past the fancy storefronts, occasionally gazing at her reflection in the glass. For a moment, she felt like Julia Roberts in *Pretty Woman,* one of the movies she had seen on NETFLIX. Doug was Richard Gere, but she knew she wouldn't be ending up with Doug nor did she want to. There were days she would have returned to The Farm in a heartbeat. Doug would never go back. It was apparent he was in his element.

With everything that happened, she hadn't even asked about Chris, Laura, Kyle, Renea, and April. And what about the animals at The Farm? Had Doug sold the land and everything on it to someone? It was all too much to talk about in the few hours they saw each other.

Alice could name the times her life had taken an abrupt turn almost overnight. The first time was when she was six and awoke to find both her father and brother gone. The next time was when she was eighteen and met Doug in the coffee shop. The next was five years later when she returned to take care of her mother. Two years after that, her mother died. A year later, she found an apartment and met Chen and Iris. A few months later, within a period of twenty-four hours, she met Mrs. Maxwell, the tall dark stranger who provided her with revelations she wasn't so sure she wanted, got asked out on a date, and Doug returned to her life.

DOUG AND ALICE would have never come together in a million years if it hadn't been for several factors conspiring, much like the way he described the way the conspiracy theories he believed all came together.

She truly believed fate had them meet in the coffee shop that day. Alice didn't frequent coffee shops, but she was convinced destiny had guided her there on that particular day. Doug offered the escape hatch she was looking for.

In the beginning, she had hopes of something romantic happening between her and Doug, but those aspirations fell by the wayside, and as the first months on The Farm passed, the longing for something with Doug became nonexistent in her mind. But like most coincidences, all the angles were coinciding in their own good time to make something between them happen. The most obvious was the fact there were three females and three males, all roughly the same age except for Alice, who was younger. Laura and Chris went to The Farm as a couple. That left Kyle, Renea, Doug, and her. After Kyle and Renea paired up, that left her and Doug, still an unlikely pair. The Farm —a paradise on some days, a struggle against nature to survive on others—entwined them like Adam and Eve.

Doug was her teacher and mentor. It wasn't until she boarded the bus on that next fateful day to return to Queens to take care of her mother, having the time for hours of reflection over the previous five years, did she realize she might be substituting Doug for her father. Had Doug known all along? Chen with her proclivity toward psychoanalysis had merely confirmed what had already been in the back of her mind.

One of the nightly debates, though Doug preferred to call them discussions, was about nature versus nurture. Was human behavior determined by one's genes or their environment? Alice only knew if she had stayed in Queens, she would have evolved differently, possibly even devolved. Even the way she saw Doug in the coffee shop changed after a few months in West Virginia. The teenage crush Alice had on Doug faded with the realities of their day-to-day existence. She boiled part down to teenage hormones and part to plain and simple logic—dropping her schoolgirl notions of life.

Alice couldn't give a specific date or time to her maturation or when Doug might have recognized her womanhood. A casual touch, their sweat mingling while pulling weeds from the garden. A shared moment of pride upon pulling a gigantic cantaloupe, the biggest any of them had ever seen, from the garden. The first time she voiced her own ideas with confidence on some matter of farm operations. Or maybe it was the way they had all stripped away the pretense of their former lives. Nature had a way of leveling the playing field.

During those first summer nights, Alice lay awake, marveling at the chorus of tree frogs, katydids, crickets, and sometimes the howling of wild animals. She concluded humans were totally outnumbered by a massive population of creatures well-developed in coded pillow talk during the night and in undercover camouflage during the daytime. Alice couldn't pinpoint the exact moment the conductor with one abrupt sweep of his baton halted the orchestra, but she knew it came with the cold, the crisp air that seeped through the cracks and crevices of the uninsulated house. The new sounds were the results of humans: the footsteps of Doug, Chris, and Kyle against floorboards stiffened by the cold, the thuds of logs thrown on the hearth, and the occasional loud crackle of the fire.

Bleak winter nights could provide the most intimate of moments or the rawest of self-reflection or agonizing soul-searching moments. It was January. The complete silence brought on by six inches of snow made every turn in bed and each nightly visit to feed the fire more pronounced. It was close to midnight and her nineteenth birthday. Everyone had stayed up later than usual, talking around the fire, celebrating with her.

"Alice, are you awake?" She could see his face in the full light of the moon as he stood in the doorway. The soft light revealed the kindness in his face.

"Yes."

"I wanted to wish you happy birthday one final time before you fell asleep. "

"Thank you. "

"Are you cold?"

"Yes."

He moved over to her bed, sitting on the edge. He bent over and kissed her tenderly. "Is it okay?"

He had both hands on her face, looking into her eyes. She nodded, and he moved his body under the covers alongside hers.

"Alice, it's up to you," he said, his body pressed against hers for the first time. She could feel his hardness. They had swum naked together, but this—even though they were fully clothed under a pack of covers—was different.

Alice knew little about sex. Oh, there was sex education in school, girls talking about their experiences in hushed tones and giggles in the hallways, and what she saw on movies with every move choreographed, none of which could convey the actual physical experience or raw emotion of it. She supposed most knew little until they experienced it. Doug had taught her about most things. Why shouldn't he also teach her about sex? There was no tremble in her voice when she said, "Yes."

"I'll be right back," he said.

As he moved from underneath the covers and slipped on his boots, hearing the creak of the stairs as he traveled down them at a rapid pace toward his own room, she wondered if maybe *yes* wasn't the answer he was looking for. But within a matter of minutes, she could hear his boots almost leaping up the stairwell. He held up a small package when he walked through the door. "It's a little old but it should work." The thought of getting pregnant hadn't occurred to her.

Doug removed his shoes once again and snuggled up next to her, this time kissing her fully on the mouth, pressing her own mouth open. Article by article, they removed each other's clothes until he was on top of her, still kissing her, both of their bodies sweaty beneath the heavy layer of blankets.

She knew the others could hear, but she didn't care. She had heard the others often enough.

The next morning, he asked her if she was okay. She nodded yes, then it was business as usual. The only difference was they would now share the same bed.

He piled his multiple layers of clothes back on and she hers. Both joined the others for their usual routine.

Doug brought in more wood from the porch and stoked up the fire in the fireplace. Laura and Renea were already in the kitchen, smiling when she entered.

"Are you sore?" Laura asked.

"Yes."

"It's normal. Don't worry. The soreness will go away after a few more times."

Normal. Yes, normal. She was trying to act normal. She went over to the counter. With her back turned to them, Alice couldn't help but smile. She measured out the flour, shortening, and milk for the biscuits, mixing it and flattening it out on the wooden board with the rolling pin, no longer feeling like the little girl of the group. Last night was more than her first time. It was her initiation as a member there.

AFTER BREAKING in her boots sufficiently, she opted for the subway into Queens instead of the bus. She arrived at the work-site at exactly four o'clock, just as everyone seemed to either be packing up or already gone.

"I'm looking for Tom Walker," she said to a young guy coming from the site.

"I think the crew Tom was on already left."

She let out a heavy sigh. "Are you sure?"

"Yeah, why? Are you his girlfriend? Didn't I see you here the other day?"

"Yes, I was here. And, no, I'm not his girlfriend."

"Sorry, ma'am." He walked by her and was about to get into a car parked across the street.

Alice yelled out, "I really need to talk to him. I kind of stood him up the other night, unintentionally."

The young guy threw his hard hat and lunch bucket into the back of his car. He stood with the driver's door open. "How do you stand someone up unintentionally?" he yelled across the street. She had piqued his curiosity.

She ran across the street during a break in the traffic. "It's a long story, but I met a woman, a woman who knew my mother and my father. My mother died last year, and I had a very emotional evening. When I realized the time, it was too late to meet him, and I didn't have his number."

"Well, you don't seem psycho or anything. On Fridays, he and Burt usually go to CCB."

"What's CCB?"

"It's a bar, a popular hangout for construction workers. It's in Manhattan."

"Okay, thanks a lot."

30

The Bar

T he thought of looking for someone in a bar seemed creepy to Alice, but the only alternative was to ask Iris for more time off to go back to the construction site again on Monday. Iris had already been more than kind in the matter, even motherly. It's funny. At the present moment, she had three people in her life: Doug, who was her surrogate father; Iris, her surrogate mother; and Chen, who was like the older sister she never had even though Chen was younger. It seemed rather disturbing in some respects to think of Doug as her surrogate father. Maybe he was the replacement for Jack Jr. instead, but that was still inappropriate concerning the circumstances.

Chen! Why had she not thought to call Chen? She hit her speed dial.

"Hi, how ya doin'?" came the voice on the other end.

"At the moment, not so well. A lot has happened since we last talked."

"I'm on the subway on my way to the restaurant. Are you still at work?"

"No, I'm kind of in limbo at the moment. I just left Queens where my old house was."

"Why?"

"Chen, this has been a crazy week. I need to go to this bar in Manhattan but don't want to go by myself. Could you possibly go with me?"

There was a momentary pause, so unlike Chen. "Well, I guess. What is the name of this bar?"

"It's called CCB."

"How do you spell that?"

"C as in cat, C as in cat, B as in bar."

"Oh, okay. I'm looking it up." There was another pause. "There is a STARBUCKS at the end of the block. Can we meet there first so you can fill me in on what happened and why we are going to this bar?"

"Yes, that would probably be good."

"I'll call my uncle and tell him I'll be late. See you soon."

CHEN WAS WAITING when Alice arrived at STARBUCKS, having her usual green tea Frappuccino with one pump of white mocha and extra whip. Where she deposited it, Alice didn't know. There wasn't an ounce of fat on Chen's five-foot petite physique. The only thing she could figure was Chen had the metabolism of a hummingbird.

Hummingbirds have the highest metabolic rate of any animal, one of those facts Doug taught her. Alice only had a high-school degree but felt like she should have earned a few college credits after having lived with five university students who liked nothing better than delving into long-winded discussions about anything and everything to pass the nights on The Farm. And there were the books, the massive collection that Doug had shipped in increments to the general delivery address they used in town. This collection included all the greats that Doug said everyone should read, which she did, although she couldn't get into Doug's most favorite author, Joseph Conrad. Not to read them resulted in group censure by the others at their monthly book discussion nights.

Alice ordered a hot chai latte with whipped cream, an indulgence she rarely allowed herself, but after everything that had happened over the last few days, she needed what Chen referred to as comfort food, something Chen rewarded herself with after every class with the one professor she loathed.

"Whipped cream? Must be bad," Chen said as she swirled her straw around the round opening. Suddenly, she shrieked, "Couldn't be all that bad!"

Chen gasped as if she were having some sort of seizure, taking Alice off guard.

"What? Are you all right?"

"Girl, I love those boots." She moved forward in her seat, studying Alice's new footwear before reaching down to feel the leather. "These were expensive. Were they on sale?"

"Nothing in that shop was on sale. A gift from Doug," Alice said.

"Doug? *The Doug*?"

"Yes, and Doug is just the tip of the iceberg."

Chen moved her body in closer as Alice recanted all that had transpired over the course of the week.

Chen sat transfixed before saying, "My only news is I have the paper finished. But maybe since Doug has returned to the city, maybe you could ask him if he could give me his own perspective on The Farm? It would make great footnotes."

"Honestly, I think he would like nothing better, but for now…"

"The bar," Chen said.

"Yes."

ALICE PUSHED OPEN the heavy dark wooden door with the hand-carved initials CCB into something out of a different era, except for the modern attire of the customers and the flat-screen televisions which seemed to be a staple of every commercial establishment since her return. Chen stood beside her as Alice eyed the crowd for Tom.

"Well, is he here?" Chen asked.

Alice shook her head. "No but I see the guy who works with him."

"Yeah?"

"You see the older guy at the bar?"

"Which one? Most of them are old."

"The one who is looking straight at us."

"Yeah," Chen said as they moved farther in from the doorway, feeling the rush of cold air as two more customers came through the door.

"I think he must remember me from that first day I went to the worksite. He's the one who got Tom for me."

They walked over and stood as there were no available bar stools. "Burt?" Alice asked.

"You're Alice, the girl Tom likes."

Alice blushed. "He told you my name?"

"Sure he did."

"Do you know where Tom is?"

"I kinda figured he was with you."

"No."

The man hem-hawed around, obviously not knowing what to say next. He took a drink of his beer. "Can I buy you ladies a beer?"

Alice had never been a beer drinker. She didn't understand how anyone liked the taste. But it was the drink of choice at The Farm after a day of working in the hay. She looked at Chen who was clearly game. "Sure," Alice said. "What does Tom usually have?"

"He likes those dark drafts."

"Okay, I'll have one of those," she replied.

Chen spurted off the kind she wanted, much the way she ordered at STARBUCKS.

The bartender placed two mugs on the bar. Burt picked up his own beer and his coat that lay across his lap and motioned for them to follow him. "Let's grab that table over there while it's still vacant. This place gets crowded early on Friday nights."

Both Alice and Chen draped their coats on the backs of the chairs, and Burt followed suit.

"This is Chen," Alice said.

"Glad to meet you, Chen," he said, raising his mug.

"You thought I knew where Tom was? I take it he didn't tell you what happened?" Alice said.

Burt eyed her curiously and took another drink. "No, Tom's not much of a talker."

"I kind of stood him up. I didn't mean to, but something happened that prevented me getting to the Chinese restaurant to meet him. I've been trying to find him to apologize, but I don't have his cell number. I don't suppose you might give it to me?"

"I don't have it to give. Guys at the job don't usually exchange cell phone numbers, only beers."

Alice looked down at the beer she had only taken one sip from, her chin dipping to her chest.

"So what happened that made you stand Tom up? Or is it none of my business?"

Alice summarized in a few ubiquitous sentences, not wanting Burt to relay the dysfunctionality of herself or her family to Tom.

"I'm sorry about your mother," Burt said.

Alice nodded and raised one corner of her mouth in a smile. "Do you think Tom will understand?"

"If there is one thing I know about Tom, he's more than understanding. Yeah, to answer your question, I think he'll understand. But I don't know how you can get in contact with him. The best I can do is give him a message you want to talk to him when I see him on Monday."

"That would be great," Alice said.

"If you trust a questionable old man with your cell number, I'll give it to Tom. As for Tom, I can personally vouch for him. Normally, I would advise a girl like yourself not to go to construction sites looking for a man, but you could do a lot worse than Tom. If my daughter weren't already married, I'd be setting her up with him."

Chen whipped out a notepad from her backpack, handing a piece of paper and pen to Alice. Alice wrote her number down and handed it to Burt with a smile.

"I'll be sure he gets it."

Alice finished her beer and looked at Chen, the signal to leave. "Thanks for the beers. It was nice to see you again," Alice said.

"Same here. I can't buy you girls another round?"

"No," they both said. They turned back to wave at Burt as they pushed through the heavy door of the bar back out into the chilly street air.

31

Chen's Paper

Over steamed dumplings, mushroom fried rice, and a pot of jasmine tea, Alice read Chen's paper while Chen studied her facial expressions between her skillful and rapid lifting of bites of food with her chopsticks.

Alice lay the paper aside. "So I'm Allison, and Doug is Douglas? Chris is Christopher. Laura is Lauren. Renea is Rea. Kyle is Ken. The last one at least is not so bad. Do you really think people won't put two and two together?"

Chen gave a reassuring nod of her head. "Yeah, we can change the names. I had to keep everyone straight."

Alice read out loud, "Plagued by his father's hostility to him both as a child and as an emerging adult, Douglas, feeling saddled with the high expectations set for him and his own inner self-contempt, dropped out of society, escaping to the Appalachian region of Kentucky to live amid hillbillies." She moved the paper to her lap and sighed. "This would never fly with Doug or the others. You also might want to keep in mind he's a lawyer. Lawyers sue, you know. And, if he didn't, his father might."

"I could possibly tone it down. You noticed I changed the

state. Do you think Kentucky might be too close to West Virginia?"

"Laura is from Kentucky."

"I say she's from Wisconsin in the paper."

"Yes, I saw where she grew up on a dairy farm. I'm surprised you didn't throw in that the state of Wisconsin crowned her the Cheese Queen."

"Was she?"

"No, of course not. Kentucky doesn't have cheese queens."

Chen rolled her eyes.

"And this stuff you have in here about my mother…"

"What do you mean?"

"My mother wasn't that bad," Alice said.

"Why are you defending her?"

"Because she's my mother."

"Oh, I see. You can say things about her because she's your family, but someone outside the family can't?"

Alice frowned. "Maybe, I suppose, but it wasn't all bad."

"Well, I can certainly see where there might have been extenuating circumstances that caused her to be the way she was after what you told me about your visit with Mrs. Maxwell. But look, all of her gloominess has rubbed off on you."

"What do you mean? I've gotten this apartment, decorated it beautifully. I've even got a fantastic job and a more than understanding boss."

"Yeah, but it's Christmas, and you don't have one Christmas decoration. You told me your mother didn't even put up a tree after your father left. Is having no tree a family tradition now?"

"I've been thinking about Christmas, or I was until the life I planned turned upside down during the last couple of weeks. I mean, learning about a skeleton in your back yard, finding out your mother wasn't even married to your father, and having a date for the first time in ages only to mess it up? I mean, who could think about Christmas decorations with all of that going on?"

Chen reached over and hugged her friend. "I'm sorry. I suppose not. Listen, why don't I leave the paper with you? It's a copy, anyway. You mark through it and write in some things you want to convey. Change the names and the state to whatever you like. But, keep in mind, it's a psychology paper, not a novel. When I write the novel, it will be with a human element. Everything will be different. And when it's discussed by book clubs, it will be their job to bring out all the different psychological reasons as to what motivated the characters."

"You still want to write a novel?"

"Yes, someday. I would want to meet Doug first, and even Laura, Chris, Kyle, and Renea."

"I don't know what happened to the others. I meant to ask Doug, but like I said, everything has been happening so fast."

"I tell you what. What do you say we go out and look for Christmas decorations tomorrow? You get off work at noon, right?"

"Yes, you know I do."

"It will take your mind off of Tom. I know you're counting down the hours until you can talk to him."

"I guess so."

Chen shoved Alice's shoulder. "Come on. It'll be fun."

"Chen, I said I guess so."

"You're still mad."

"I'm not mad."

"I know. We can call Mrs. Maxwell."

"Why?"

"To get the makeover. You need someone skilled to teach you how to wear makeup."

Alice called Mrs. Maxwell after Chen left. Alice wasn't surprised that Mrs. Maxwell couldn't do her makeup tomorrow.

She explained she had appointments back to back, asking Alice if next Saturday would be okay.

"I could do it early in the morning," she said.

"Next week will be fine," Alice responded.

But after Chen left, Alice went over the pros and cons in her head and decided she would cancel with Chen and work a full day on Saturday. She sensed Iris was feeling overwhelmed, partly from the increased business, but mostly from dealing with her son's addiction, and then there was Alice's current dilemma, which wasn't helping matters. Chen, who liked nothing better than remaking Alice, would be disappointed.

Christmas decorations would have to wait another week. Putting in the extra time would help if she were to be late on Monday morning. She planned on being at the construction site no later than nine. Maybe Tom wasn't meant to be at all, but the thought of going to work on Monday and being distracted by her cell phone not going off while imagining all sorts of scenarios, like maybe he was just too busy to call, Burt forgot to give him her number or hadn't yet had the opportunity to talk to him, or the worst, he wasn't interested enough to give her a second chance.

Too, she was a tad miffed at Chen. She hadn't expected Chen's paper to portray the dark side, or what she conceived as the dark side, of everyone's psyches.

Alice spent a good two hours, armed with a red pen, marking through Chen's paper the way a professor might. She wrote copious notes between the lines and along the margins with arrows pointing to the back where she listed all the good quali-ties of everyone, including herself. She knew little about Doug's father but assumed he was well-educated and smart and a loving husband. Doug had said nothing to the contrary. In fact, Doug had never said he was a bad father. Doug's main intention was to drop out of the system. Alice was glad she had never mentioned Doug's obsession with conspiracy theories to Chen. Doing so might have steered Chen in a whole different direction. Nor would it be good now that Doug was back practicing law.

Alice even went so far as substituting names. For Doug, she wrote Alfred. For Chris, she wrote Malcolm. To Kyle, she gave the name Charles. She marked through Laura with the red pen and wrote, Carol, above it and for Renea, she penned in Charlotte. For herself, she chose Winnifred. All good English sounding names, she thought, and they were not attending Columbia but Oxford, and Doug's father was not a lawyer but a barrister. And they flew to Georgia to a desolate area to begin their farm experiment. No, she crossed Georgia out and put Indiana. Chen had mentioned the harsh winters, and she didn't think the temperatures in Georgia were that harsh. Also, Indiana was farming country, and the inhabitants were referred to as hillbillies. If Chen needed to disparage a state, let it be one Alice felt no connection to or love for.

Alice reread the paper with her edits, no longer feeling it was a betrayal to the place that had given her some of her fondest memories. She wiped a tear away. Iris had said houses had personalities and carried the vibrations of its occupants. They had made improvements over the course of five years, brought it back to life, and now, once again, it sat unoccupied. A sense of dread went through Alice, thinking within a decade there could be little left of the one place she truly felt was home.

32

More Skeletons

A lice didn't recognize the number coming across her cell phone and almost didn't answer. Chen had warned her against telemarketers. She didn't think telemarketers called at nine on Sunday mornings though. "Once they get your number, you might as well hang it up," Chen had told her. *That's a funny analogy.*

The thought it could be Tom sent a shiver down her spine.

"Hello."

"Hi, is this Alice?" It was a woman's voice.

"Yes."

"Hi, this is Nancy from PINE RIDGE NURSING HOME."

"Oh, yes," Alice said.

"You asked me to call when Clara was having a good day. She's been talking up a storm ever since breakfast. Complaining too. Says she always heats her syrup for pancakes. Doesn't like it cold."

"Oh," Alice said rather startled. Yes, that was the old Clara she knew.

"Well, I don't know how long it will last, but if you can get here as soon as possible, you may be able to have an actual conversation with her."

"Oh, Nancy, thank you so much. I just stepped out of the shower. I'll get dressed and get there as soon as possible."

Alice hurriedly dressed, thinking she could put off doing laundry no longer. She pulled her boots on over her tights and grabbed her coat, purse, and key ring with two keys now—her house key and the key to NATURE'S BLUSH that Iris had entrusted her with—and headed out the door.

ALICE ENTERED the nursing home out of breath, having practically run from the bus stop. "I'm here to see Clara Jenkins," she told the receptionist.

"Nancy's on duty today. I'll ask her to bring her out." She hit a button on her phone and spoke into the speaker, "Nancy, Clara has a visitor. Could you bring her to the lobby?"

Alice sat in a seat where she was sure to see Clara being wheeled out. Clara looked straighter in the chair, and she was wearing powder and blush and a dab of lipstick. Her bluish-gray hair was even done up nicely.

Nancy stopped in front of Alice. "Doesn't she look nice today?"

"I'm sitting right here," Clara retorted.

"You do look nice, Mrs. Jenkins," Alice said.

"On Saturdays, a hair stylist comes in and does their hair," Nancy said to Alice. "I picked it out a little and added a touch of makeup. Said she wanted to look nice when I told her you were coming." Nancy turned and bent down facing Clara. "Sometimes, when their minds come back, they can get a little feisty. Isn't that right, Clara?" Nancy said in a loud voice.

"I'm not hard of hearing."

"Well, good luck," Nancy said as she walked away, impervious to talking to Clara in the third person.

"I know you," Clara said.

"I hope you do," Alice said.

"You're Priscilla's daughter. How is Priscilla? Why doesn't she come to visit me?"

"I'm sorry, Mrs. Jenkins. My mother died over a year ago."

"Oh, yes, I remember. How could I forget something like that? Poor Priscilla, so young."

"Mrs. Jenkins, do you remember my father, Jack?"

She huffed. "Of course I remember your father. Do you think I'm senile?"

"No, Mrs. Jenkins, not at all."

"He just up and left her as if she didn't have enough troubles with that no-good nephew of mine."

"Nephew?"

"Jack Jr. Who do you think I'm talking about?"

"I don't understand."

"I convinced Priscilla the best thing to do was to ship him off to my sister. His father certainly couldn't take care of him."

"Mrs. Jenkins, I don't understand."

"You were good to your mother, weren't you? I warned you enough. Your mother didn't need any more trouble after all she went through."

"Yes, Mrs. Jenkins, I came back and took care of her."

"Yes, I remember when you came back. It broke your mother's heart when you left."

"It did?"

"Well, of course, child. Your mother thought the sun rose and set on you."

"She did?"

"Why are you asking all these questions?"

"Because, Mrs. Jenkins, I found out my parents weren't even

married, and that she had been married before, and that Jack Jr. is only my half-brother."

Mrs. Jenkins seemed to stare off into the distance, but then she blinked, rolling her eyes over Alice before focusing in on her face. Clara finally spoke. "I told your mother she should tell you. A child has a right to know."

"A right to know what?"

"A right to know about her parents."

"Tell me, Mrs. Jenkins, when you wrote that letter, you knew Jack Jr. was working up the street. How did you know that?"

"John may have been an alcoholic, but he still kept tabs on his son. After his death, I took on that task. Jack Jr. was probably why he drank the way he did. It's hard to face that your son has been in prison and is on probation. But then, you can't blame the boy too much for the way he turned out. His father didn't set much of an example. Once a cheater, always a cheater is what I say. Oh, your mother put up a good front, but John liked the younger women. I warned her before they married, but did she listen? No. Warned her again when your father came along. Partly revenge, I reckon. Wanted to show John she was still attractive, even to a younger man."

"You knew John, my mother's first husband?"

"Knew him? He was my brother."

"Your brother? John Black was your brother?"

"More than my brother, we were twins."

Alice slid backward in her seat, and Nancy came rushing over. "Miss Black, are you okay?"

"I don't know. Do you think I could have some water?"

"Sure." She called out to an orderly to bring some water while she massaged her neck. "Don't pass out on me now."

Alice tried to laugh, and the orderly handed her a plastic cup. The water was cold.

"Now, take a deep breath," Nancy said. She turned to Clara. "You haven't been upsetting her, have you?"

Clara didn't answer.

"I'm sorry. I think she's gone again. Moments of clarity don't last long," Nancy said.

"I guess it lasted long enough," Alice retorted.

"You sit here while I wheel her back to her room."

Alice watched Clara slump over in the chair as Nancy wheeled her away.

After a little while, Nancy was back, holding an apple. "Here, this might help. Do you want me to take your blood pressure or check your blood sugar?"

Alice took the apple. "No, I'm better, really. Clara knew my mother. When my mother died, I had no way of knowing parts of our family history. Clara knew though."

"Oh, I see. Skeletons in the closet revealed, I'm guessing?" Nancy said.

"You guessed right."

"It happens a lot here. Well, I have to get back to my duties. You sit there until you're able to leave, and if you should need me, you tell Jill over there to buzz me, okay?" She pointed to the receptionist.

"Okay, and thank you so much for calling me, Nancy."

"You're welcome, sweetheart. You have a good day."

"You, too."

33

The Date

8:15 a.m. - Alice was downing the last bite of toast and slurp of coffee when her phone buzzed.

"Hello."

"I'm really sorry about your mother."

"Tom?"

"Yes. Can we try this again? But this time, I will pick you up at your house. It's only fair you give me your address, don't you think?"

"You talked to Burt," she said. Was the smile on her face bouncing from cell tower to cell tower?

"Burt put in all kinds of good words about you."

"Okay, you're right, you *do* deserve my address. I'm in the apartment building directly across from the Chinese restaurant, sixth floor, number 602."

"Maybe I should have waited longer. I might have seen you come home."

"I can't tell you how sorry I am. How long did you wait?"

"Long enough to lose my taste for Chinese food. I need to get back to work. Can I call you during my lunch break? You decide what you want to do on this date and when, okay? Oh, again, I'm sorry about your mother."

"Thanks."

Alice clicked on the little *i* for information next to the number and then *add contact* and typed in Tom Walker and pushed *save*.

Alice had seven contacts on her relatively new phone under favorites in no order of importance. Now, she would have eight.

1. Chen Wang
2. Landlord
3. Dragon's Den
4. Iris/Nature's Blush
5. June Maxwell
6. Pine Ridge Nursing Home
7. Doug
8. Tom Walker

"YOU'RE EARLY," Iris said as she came through the door. "And I could have sworn I heard you singing."

"You did."

"I'm glad to see you're feeling better."

"I talked to Tom this morning."

Iris looked at the table behind the counter, eyeing the row of gift baskets. "How long have you been here?"

"A little over an hour."

While Iris got everything ready to open, Alice filled her in on the weekend's events.

"Things are looking up for both of us then," Iris said, a grin on her face.

Alice displayed a quizzical smile and tilted her head in anticipation for more of an explanation.

"Chad is out of rehab and is coming home for Christmas."

Giving Iris a hug, Alice said, "That's wonderful news."

"What are you doing for Christmas, Alice?"

"I don't know. I haven't thought about it. I know I'm always welcome at Chen's."

"You are welcome at my apartment, too. I would love for you to meet Chad, and if you should be dating Tom, he's welcome too."

The chime on the door sounded, letting them know someone entered the shop. It was Tina. "Good morning. You two look happy. What did I miss?"

THE MORNING RUSHED by as Alice worked on more baskets and talked to customers. The whole time, she racked her brain for somewhere to go on this date. Although all kinds of romantic ideas popped into her mind as she selected soaps and essential oils and tied raffia into pretty bows, the only one she thought appropriate was letting him pick her up at her apartment and walking across the street with him to DRAGON'S DEN and possibly going back to her apartment for coffee if everything went well. She made a short list in her head, shorter than her usual lists, on why this would be best.

1. She didn't want him to have a bad taste in his mouth concerning DRAGON'S DEN.
2. She wanted to be surrounded by her surrogate family.
3. If Chen should be there, she would give Alice her opinion of Tom.
4. If the date went well, and she invited him to her apartment afterward—but only for a short while as they both had work the next day—Freddie would be near enough in case her intuition about Tom was

totally off. She wasn't sure what Freddie might do other than have Isis, his Siamese cat, attack Tom.

Scratch all of that, most of that, no, all of that. She was making something that needed to be casual, informal, and relaxed into a big ordeal, sure to fail. She would suggest walking, talking, stopping in the nearest coffee shop, nothing too fancy. But, it had to be tonight. With each passing moment, the apprehension was building. Waiting until the following weekend would make her a nervous wreck.

"WHAT TIME IS YOUR DATE?" Iris asked.

"Seven," Alice replied.

"You came in early. Tina and I have everything covered. Why don't you head out? Take some extra pains in getting ready."

"Do I look bad?"

"No, I'm not saying that at all. You're just so nervous. Take a relaxing bath beforehand."

"I don't have a bathtub."

"Okay, then lie down and take some deep breaths."

"You're right. It's been so long since I've had a date. Actually, I'm not sure if you could say I've ever had a date. I'm not sure what to call Doug. But thank you. I'll see you tomorrow."

BY 6 P.M. she had used almost half a tube of makeup and coated and recoated her eyelashes so many times she had lost count. Was this how her mother might have done it when she worked at MACY'S? She stepped back from the mirror as far as her small bathroom would allow, appraising the new face she had created. It wasn't perfect, but she didn't want to start over. Restaurants would be dimly lit she told herself.

She still had an hour.

She tried lying on the bed and taking deep breaths the way Iris recommended, but within a minute, she sprang back up for fear of getting her blue periwinkle top wrinkled. She turned on the television and flipped through program after program, unable to concentrate. She had on her best outfit with her new boots. What if he asked her out again? She couldn't wear the same thing. Even Iris, who didn't put much stock in outer appearance, gave her odd looks when she wore the same jeans three days in a row.

Five more minutes had passed. Conversation, something, or someone to take her mind off of the date was what she needed. She took her keys and walked down a floor and knocked on Freddie's door. He came to the door, holding Isis. He stepped back in alarm, withdrawing his hand from Isis's back. She purred in anger.

"Oh honey," he declared.

"What?"

"Went a little overboard on the mascara and eyeshadow, didn't we?"

"I did?"

"Well, it depends. If you were a drag queen, it'd be fine, but it's just not you. What are you all made-up for, if you don't mind me asking?"

Freddie asking permission to ask anything or offer his opinion was an anomaly, and something he didn't mean. Alice knew he demanded an answer.

"Oh, Freddie. I have a date. What should I do? "

Out of all the neighbors, Alice knew Freddie best. Freddie had been the one to fill her in on most of the residents. He knew them all. The artist guy proved to be rather eccentric, keeping to himself. The younger couple kept such odd hours, Alice rarely saw them, only to say hello in passing. The lady Alice suspected to be a gypsy owned a clothing shop in Soho. Freddie told her she designed the clothes herself. Other than Freddie, she had conversed with Mrs. Callas a few times. She brought Alice some stuffed grape leaves when she moved in. "Just something to say welcome to the building," she had said.

Freddie, in his sixties, worked in theater, both as an actor and behind the scenes. He knew makeup, and why she had never thought of asking for his advice, she didn't know.

"I have a date, Freddie. And I'm really nervous."

"First date?" he asked while stroking Isis.

"Yes."

"Well, don't stand out in the hall. When is your gentleman caller due to arrive?"

"In thirty minutes."

"Then we have to hurry. You're giving eyeliner a bad name." He put Isis down and shuffled Alice off to the bathroom as fast as his shuffle could go. Swaying his hips only slowed him down.

Alice had never been inside Freddie's apartment. It was almost twice the size of hers. He had both a bathtub and a shower as well as a whole table dedicated to brushes and palettes of color along with a magnifying mirror, resembling the table she once saw Cher sit at during an interview. Cher was one of Freddie's idols. He pulled out the chair.

"Have a seat. Thirty minutes, you say? We can do it in twenty. You have a natural beauty. A girl like you is not meant to wear a lot of makeup, especially on a first date. Now tell me how you met this guy while I work."

Alice gave Freddie the CliffsNotes version between him telling her to look this way or that way, to close her eyes or lips until he finally held up the mirror and told her she could look.

"Oh, Freddie, you work miracles."

"Well, I don't know about that, but come back another time, and we'll trim your hair, chop off those dead ends."

Alice put her hand to her hair. "Does it look bad?"

"No, no, it looks fine. Don't you worry." He held up his hand and squeezed his forefinger and index fingers together and said, "We might take off just a smidgen, though. Don't give it a second thought. You look marvelous."

Isis had wandered into the bathroom, rubbing against Freddie's legs. Isis was lonely since Freddie's other two cats, Juniper and Comet, had both died of old age last month. He picked up Isis. "Now, give Isis a pet for good luck, and promise to come back and tell me all about it."

"I will. I can't thank you enough."

"Okay, off with you. Have a good time."

Alice had just closed the door to her own apartment when the buzzer went off. "Hi, it's Tom."

His voice sounded shaky. Was he as nervous as her? Burt did say he was shy.

"You look pretty," he said when he arrived at her apartment.

"Thank you."

"Nice place."

"It's small, but yeah, I like it. A lot different from where I used to live. "

"Oh?"

"Yeah, I could tell you about it while we walk," she suggested.

"Sounds good. Which direction?"

"I don't know, maybe toward Manhattan?" Alice asked.

"Okay."

The conversation started out slow and cautious for both of them. Alice's thought of bringing up The Farm was interrupted when Tom turned suddenly.

"Alice, I want to be upfront. I was married. Way too young. Divorced for a while though."

Okay, a little bit of a surprise but no deal breaker. Not once had she even wondered about his past. Everyone had one.

"So tell me about it," she said.

Once he got started, there was never a lag in the conversation. By the time they had crossed the Brooklyn Bridge, Alice knew more about Tom than she knew about her own family, which wasn't perhaps a good comparison. And although she dangled her hand clumsily by her side, still, he hadn't reached for it.

"Are you cold?"

"Not really," she said, thinking he noticed how thin her coat was for this time of year.

He seemed disappointed. She had misunderstood the sign.

"Maybe a little," she said, grinning shyly.

He smiled. "Do you want my coat?"

"No, you'll freeze."

He took it off, wrapping it around her along with his arm. They walked haphazardly through Manhattan and found themselves by some twist of fate in front of THE JAVA BEAN FACTORY, something about its orange exterior calling them toward it like a beacon.

"This brings back memories," she said.

"You've been here before?" he asked while opening the door for her.

"Yes."

Both of their eyes went directly to the corner, lured in by the smooth melodious sound of the woman performing.

"She's good. Reminds me of Eva Cassidy," Alice said.

"A GUILDED SONGBIRD," Tom said.

"What?"

"It's the name of the guitar she's playing. I think it was actually the same one Eva Cassidy used."

"Do you play?"

"Just a hobby." He smiled.

"Do you want to eat here or go somewhere else?" Tom asked.

"This is fine."

They found a table in the back. "What memories?" he asked as they sat then his eyes grew big. "That's it," he exclaimed.

"What?"

"You looked so familiar to me that day you came to the construction site. It drove me crazy trying to figure out where I had seen you. It was you. You were talking to a college guy. He was asking you to go off with him. Am I right?"

"Wow, you were *here* that day? That would have been, let me see, seven years ago."

"Yeah," he acknowledged. "And did you?"

"Go away with him? Yes, I did."

"Did you marry him?"

"Doug? No. But we were together for five years."

"That is longer than my marriage lasted. I remember thinking how pretty you were."

Alice held her head down, blushing.

"So five years, huh?" he asked.

"We lived on a farm."

"I would love to live on a farm."

"Seriously?"

"Yes."

"I can't believe you were here on the very same day. Iris would say something to the effect that this is how the universe works."

"Iris?"

"My boss."

"Tell me what you want. I'll order then it's your turn to tell me all about you."

"Whatever you're having is fine."

"I have to warn you, I've been trying to go vegetarian since Thanksgiving."

"Chen's vegetarian, and whenever she gets us takeout from across the street, it's vegetarian. So, whatever you're ordering is fine with me."

"Chen?"

"My friend."

"Okay. Coffee?"

"Yes, black."

He smiled. "Black coffee, another thing we have in common besides loving farms. You like farms, right?"

"SORRY, we close at ten on Monday's," the girl said, interrupting Tom and Alice's conversation.

Alice looked over to see the singer packing up her guitar and the other two customers donning their coats. The time she had spent with Tom seemed like minutes, not hours.

Tom still had hold of her hand across the table. "I guess that's a hint," he said as the waitress walked away

"I worked as a waitress after I came back from West Virginia," Alice said.

"I think that would have to be one of the hardest jobs there is."

"The key is having good shoes," she replied.

"Shall we head back to Brooklyn?" he asked. "Do you want to take the subway?"

"I'm fine with walking if you are."

He smiled, making her think he wanted to talk more.

IT WAS at the midway point of Brooklyn Bridge when Tom stopped. "Are you tired?"

"We can stop for a while," she said. "Normally by this time, I'm in bed." She blushed. "I didn't mean…"

He smiled. "I know you didn't."

He looked at his watch. "I guess I am too since working the construction job."

"Oh, maybe we shouldn't have walked. Your apartment is in Manhattan. You have to go all the way back."

"I don't want to go back. I feel more exhilarated than I have felt in a long time."

She could feel heat growing in her cheeks and looked down at the water. "Christmas is coming up, and I haven't even thought about a gift for Iris." Why she brought that up, she didn't know. She turned her head up from looking at the water and stepped back, almost bumping into a late-night jogger who hastened past them. Before she knew it, his arm was pulling her to safety, the way he had that day at the construction site. He put his other arm around her.

His lips were moist, and his embrace felt so warm and comfortable. She had been anticipating a kiss all night. And it happened the very moment she wasn't expecting it.

She was still feeling dizzy and lightheaded when he hugged her again and said, "Why don't you knit her a scarf? You said you had learned to knit." He smiled.

"I don't know if I would have time." Were her words slurred?

The way he kissed her was nothing like the way Doug kissed her. It had a ferocity and fierceness about it, sending an electrical charge through her, but at the same time, it was tender. Iris might say they were twin souls, which was much better than soul mates, which is what Iris said she and Doug were.

"I don't know much about that stuff. But you're right, you might not have time, especially if you agree to see me again. You will go out with me again, won't you?" She could feel his grip loosening on her, the shyness Burt spoke of rearing its head. He seemed nervous, like a teenager, not like someone who was capable of that kiss or had been married before. But then, she was nervous too. Nervous that somehow she might blow it, that there might not be a second date.

"Yes," she said, taking the initiative herself to kiss him again. His arms tightened around her.

34

The Holidays

Like a horse out of the gate at the Kentucky Derby might be how Laura would describe the way Alice and Tom's relationship took off. Tom had thought about going to Georgia for Christmas but said he couldn't bear to spend it apart from her. They made love for the first time in her apartment on Christmas morning before going over to DRAGON'S DEN for an early Christmas dinner with Chen's family. Her surrogate family took to Tom, especially Charlie. Tom even taught him a few riffs on his guitar.

Alice ended up getting both Iris and Tina gift certificates to eat at DRAGON'S DEN. Iris never treated herself to meals out. She sent June Maxwell a Christmas card and apologized she had to cancel their appointment to learn makeup, telling her she met a man she really cared about, and they were spending every spare moment together. *Yes, it's Tom, the one who chased you down that day,* she wrote on the card.

Since meeting Tom, the urgency she felt in learning more about her biological units, what she had resorted to calling her parents, had taken a back seat.

It was the day after Christmas that Tom suggested they fly down to meet his family.

"I've never flown before," Alice said.

"There's a first time for everything," Tom replied. "The only problem is Simon and Garfunkel. I could have them boarded, but I'm already spending so much time away from them."

"What about Freddie?"

"The guy downstairs?"

"Yeah, I bet he would watch them for you."

"I guess that would be fine short-term, but I really need to find a more permanent solution."

"Actually, I bet Freddie would take them if you offered. That is, if you want to give them up. He still hasn't gotten over losing Juniper and Comet, and Isis could use the company."

ON DECEMBER 30, Tom squeezed Alice's hand as the plane took off from LaGuardia en route to Atlanta. The nonstop flight only took two-and-a-half hours, but the whole process was like driving to West Virginia, considering the time to get across town to the airport, the wait at the airport, and all the hurdles one had to go through. Tom had a driver's license, but Alice not having one, had to get an airport-issued ID, the least of her concerns. All of Doug's conspiracy theories haunted her after having been made to feel like a potential terrorist going through the TSA checkpoint. She wondered if Tom might share the same views but thought the airport wasn't a good place to bring them up. And then there were the constant announcements about leaving your bags unattended. It was more like some cold dystopian universe than the place movies romanticized it being with passionate lovers separating and reconnecting.

THE WAY TOM'S family absorbed every word she offered about her experience of living five years on The Farm was like Brad and Ellie at IKEA all over again.

"So you lived like the Amish?" Mark asked.

"More or less," she replied.

And although Tom's family welcomed her with open arms and she felt as if Tom was her other half, the one she was destined to spend the rest of her life with even though he hadn't openly said it but only implied it, she did feel like she had to close the chapter in her life concerning her father, whatever that might involve, before she could truly move on.

It was Carol, an adoptee, who said she should take up Doug's offer to find her father. "It will bring you closure," she said.

Alice mulled it over for a week before she made an appointment to see Doug. She made one of her usual lists, the ones the others at The Farm said was one of her little quirks. After living so closely together for five years, the five of them knew each other's eccentricities better than they knew the backs of their own hands.

1. A dream bringing back a long-forgotten memory. Her mother was rocking her in her arms on her bed after a nightmare about her father. Her mother said, "Shh now, we won't speak of him anymore." Alice woke with perspiration dripping down her, realizing she was the reason her mother never mentioned her father. Her mother was trying to protect her.

2. Seeing him, that is if he were still alive, might bring a real release, not the ones she had been having lately, the ones resembling false labor pains, not that she actually knew what those were. At least if she did see him face-to-face, he might ask her forgiveness.

A short list when compared to her others. Then she thought of one more thing, something Tom told her on the trip back. "Alice, whatever you decide, I'll see it through with you."

Alice had given what he said plenty of thought over the last week but decided this was something she needed to do alone—the seeing Doug part of it.

1. She wasn't ready for Doug to meet Tom just yet. They hadn't even dated a full month. Maybe she had a deep-down fear he might leave the way her father did. She hadn't even realized this until now. Another reason she needed to resolve this thing with her father.
2. The promise of Tom's support. Tom said if he should be out there somewhere, he would take off work and take her wherever she needed to go to find him even if it meant another country. It would involve a passport. Alice could only imagine flying overseas after the hassle of such a short flight. Both Doug and her mother were right about the system.

It was Thursday when Alice got up the nerve to make the call. She could have called Doug directly but thought a business approach would be better, a way to sever the intimacy she had once shared with him. She called his office.

"*The* Alice Black?" the receptionist asked.

"I don't know if I'm *the* Alice Black, but I *am* Alice Black," she replied.

"Please let me get your number, and I'll call you back as soon as possible," she said.

"Doug, I mean, Mr. Barton, has my number."

"Okay, I'll call you back."

THE RECEPTIONIST ASKED, "Can you be here by eight tomorrow morning?" *Great*, she thought. She didn't have to ask Iris for any time off. She should be able to make it back across town by ten.

35

The Office Visit

A lice passed these people every day on the sidewalks, rode the subway with them, and occasionally talked to them in NATURE'S BLUSH, but never had she been invited to their lair and seen such a pronounced congregation of suits. Alice got off the elevator on the thirty-third floor, feeling out of place among the gray, black, and navy clad women and men, all clones of each other, the women austere and hard-looking, trying to look like their male counterparts, and the men with their gelled hair, perfectly groomed fingernails, and the right splash of color in the form of a fancy silk tie that spoke power. The smell of leather—not from the saddles, holsters, and boots of gunslingers of the Old West poised to shoot down their opposition but rather from their designer unisex briefcases—permeated the air.

"So you're Alice," the receptionist said. Was it Alice's imagination or was the receptionist sizing her up?

"Yes."

"Mr. Barton has spoken highly of you. Please have a seat. I'll let him know you're here."

The waiting area was a spacious monochromatic gray with

distressed blue leather seats. Alice could tell the furniture was new, the worn look purposefully manufactured by the factory to give that air of oldness and respectability that came with a successful law firm.

Even though it was the first week of January, a Christmas tree—a miniature version of the one at Rockefeller Center with the lights turned off—towered in the high-ceilinged corner.

"Would you like a coffee or pastry while you wait?" the receptionist asked.

"Maybe some coffee," Alice said.

"How do you take it?"

"Black."

"Of course." She smiled. "I'll be back in a moment."

Alice, having second thoughts about what she wanted to ask Doug, moved from the chair and began to pace even though she had walked six blocks from the bus stop to the law office. Alice came to a halt, frozen in awe, and was totally engrossed in the photographs that lined the wall when the receptionist startled her by tapping her on the shoulder.

"They're superb, aren't they?"

"They're more than superb. These photographs represent my life for five years, and if it were possible, I would step into any one of them at this moment."

"I know what you mean. I've often wished that myself."

The receptionist handed her the blue mug that matched the blue chairs with the firm's emblem stamped onto it. Everything about the office had Doug's signature on it.

She studied the photographs with double bevel-edged matting in gray weathered frames, not real wood, but the manu-factured kind that tried to look real, even with the added touch of fake termite holes.

Doug had captured every season. How could she have forgotten him carrying his camera around, a HASSELBLAD, a brand she had never heard of. She only knew it had to be top of the line if Doug owned it. Who knew he was so good? "Old style," she remembered him saying. Nothing digital but scads of rolls of film. "The only way to take pictures," he had also said. He hadn't bothered to get the film developed while she was there. She could almost name the month and the year each picture was taken.

She went down the row. The old truck, did it really look that bad and that good at the same time? The oddly angled image allowed Alice to see the torn leather seat, the one that pinched her rear each time she moved her foot to press on the clutch. She could almost smell the rounded hay bales spread across the rolling hills. Doug had captured the sunlight on them just right. She smiled, thinking of how they tried to manage the mowing and baling the hay themselves until they found out the farmer down the road had the equipment and manpower and would not only bale the hay on their property but pay them a fraction of the cost for the bales. It was one of the few things they made money at.

The foot of snow piled up against the weathered house looked beautiful, but living through that particular winter was a different story. The scene brought back the stillness and quiet that Alice so relished. There were still spots on earth that when nature said *shh* the inhabitants—humans, animals, even old barns and farmhouses—obeyed.

She was just coming to the last picture when she heard Doug's voice behind her. "That one is my favorite."

She turned. "I remember the day you took it. It was the first day of spring."

"That's right. We were just getting ready to take a dip in the lake."

"I'm glad you took the picture before we stripped to swim."

Doug laughed. "The lighting was perfect that morning. All the colors are perfect, the highlights in your hair, the glow of your complexion, and that radiant smile of yours when you're truly happy. Like today. You're glowing."

They came to the next one.

"And that is my least favorite," he said.

"The day I left."

"You let your hair cover your face because you were crying. I was crying, too…on the inside." He paused. "I'll never forget our experience there."

"Nor I," she said in a reflective voice.

A client came through the door. Doug walked over, shook his hand, called him by name, and looked at his watch. "I can see you in about fifteen minutes. Just let me finish up here. I'll have my receptionist get you some coffee."

Doug put his hand on Alice's back and said, "This way," as he led her down a busy hallway past offices with cubicles as workspaces. Doug's own office had an intricately carved mahogany desk. Along the walls were more pictures of Laura, Chris, Renea, Kyle, herself, and Doug in their ragged work clothes on The Farm.

"The people who work here can't believe the guy in the pictures was once me."

"I bet."

"I can make you copies if you like," he said.

"More than anything," she said. "I can't believe I forgot about you taking pictures."

"I have a darkroom in my apartment."

"I'm not surprised."

"So, Alice, why did you want to see me?"

"Do you remember saying you would help me find my father?"

"Yes."

"Are you still willing to help?"

"Absolutely."

36

Facebook

I t had been a month since Alice last stepped foot in Doug's office. The Christmas tree was down, and a blue leather chair was in its place. Valentine's Day was right around the corner, and she wanted Doug to be the first to know, other than Iris, about her engagement. Tom's family knew. They video chatted with them the day following his proposal.

She pulled her hand from her coat pocket and looked at her ring. It was not as ostentatious as the one Constance wore, but she was more than happy with it.

Tom had wanted to give her the ring on Valentine's Day but said he couldn't wait.

Alice hadn't even met Constance yet. She had only seen a picture of Constance showing off her ring, one she had posted on FACEBOOK. Alice was surprised to see the friend request. Chen had said Constance requested to be friends with Alice to keep tabs on her. "She's jealous."

"What? I hardly think so," Alice replied.

It was the *duh* look, so characteristic with Chen, the face implying she agreed with Doug. Alice *was* naïve.

Alice had a grand total of twelve friends on FACEBOOK, most

of whom were Tom's family. Some moments, she felt sad not to have one blood relative of her own as a friend. She had looked for Jack Jr., but there were a zillion Jack Blacks, and none of them appeared to be her half-brother.

Tom's parents didn't do FACEBOOK. Iris thought it was rather ridiculous but had agreed at Alice's urging to let her set up a page for NATURE'S BLUSH, which now, through recommendations mostly by Tina even though she no longer worked there, had over 2,000 likes.

Tom and Doug were rarely on social media. Chen posted something every day as did Charlie and Tina. Freddie mostly posted pictures of his cats, which now included Simon and Garfunkel along with Isis. Mrs. Maxwell promoted her paintings on FACEBOOK. Alice hadn't had the nerve to post but put likes on what everyone else posted.

Constance sent private messages saying how they needed to get together, but the holidays were too hectic, and now with all the stress of planning her and Doug's wedding in June, she didn't know when she could find the time. She also told Alice, being one of Doug's oldest and closest friends, she was on the invitee list. That was certainly one way to put it, Alice thought. "Please, bring a guest," she had added. The urge to call Doug and tell him about Tom had cropped up in her mind frequently, but each time she resisted the temptation, thinking she wanted to experience his reaction in person.

A twinge of guilt crept through her when she checked Tom's page to see he had listed himself as being in a relationship and even named her, but she felt as if she should tell Doug in person rather than let him find out via FACEBOOK.

The receptionist smiled at Alice as she came through the door. Wearing the black woolen coat Tom had gotten her for Christmas along with the black boots Doug had bought her, she didn't feel as out of place as she did before in Doug's office.

"Good morning, Miss Black. I will let Mr. Barton know you are here. Can I get you a coffee? Black if I remember."

"No thanks. I'm fine."

A few moments later, the receptionist said, "Mr. Barton asked that you go on back. Do you remember where his office is?"

"Yes, thank you."

Doug was waiting outside the door as she walked down the hall. He was talking to an elderly man who smiled when he saw her.

"Ah, Alice." Doug smiled. "I would like for you to meet my father."

The elderly Mr. Barton, although he didn't look the way Alice pictured him at all, extended his hand. "I have heard so much about you."

"And I you," she said, taking his hand.

He pierced Alice's eyes with his own as if searching to see if she might have been the reason for his son's five-year vanishing act. He took her right hand with his own and placed his other hand over it tenderly. Time stood still for a moment before he released her. Looking at him was like looking at Doug thirty years into the future.

"I will let you and Doug discuss what you have to discuss."

"It was so nice to finally meet you, Mr. Barton."

"You too, Alice," he said before turning and walking across the hall into his own office.

Before he closed the door behind him, Alice could see the office that would one day be Doug's. It was twice as large as Doug's and had a view of the park.

"Have a seat," he said. Doug sat in the leather swivel chair behind his desk and opened the manila folder that lay conspicuously on the top. Alice felt her stomach twitch.

Doug paused and looked at her as if ascertaining if she could handle it before proceeding. "He's married, has been for twenty years. He has two children, both boys. Both are following in their father's footsteps and working with him in his carpentry business."

Even though Doug's voice took a quieter tone as he gave her this information, everything was so matter-of-fact, like he was informing a client of his or her rights.

Alice's whole body shivered.

"Alice, can I get you some water or something?"

She shook her head and looked down at her lap.

"I think he was having affairs when he was with my mom. That is what Mrs. Maxwell suggested."

"I think you're right. He married the woman after finding out she was pregnant."

"Which would be about the time he left." Alice could hold back the tears no longer.

Doug got up from his seat and moved over to hug her. He released his hug and sat in the chair beside her, taking her right hand into his.

"Did you meet him, Doug?"

"No, I didn't. Our firm's private investigator took pictures. Do you want to see them?"

"No, not really."

"Alice, there's more." He held her chin up and looked into her eyes. "The investigator found out he came back to visit your mother once. It was roughly a year after you graduated high school."

"I would have been in West Virginia with you."

"Yes."

"What did he want?"

"I'm guessing he wanted to see you."

"My mother never told me."

"From what I understand, he joined A.A. shortly before he went to see your mother."

"Doug, don't A.A. members have to apologize to people? Isn't that one of their steps to recovery?"

"I believe it is."

"Do you think that's why he went to see my mom?"

"I think more than likely that's the reason."

"What about me?"

"Alice, remember, your mom didn't know where you were other than somewhere in West Virginia."

"Maybe that's the reason he never came looking for me. Do you think leaving us the way he did could have been the reason he drank?"

"I think it's a good possibility. Also, Alice, your dad was so much younger than your mom. He probably wasn't mature enough to handle things."

"I guess you're right." She wiped the tears from her face. She knew her mascara was running.

Doug handed her his handkerchief. "You're wearing makeup."

She tried to smile. "You didn't notice when I was in your office before?"

"I knew there was something different about you. You glowed. But then, I always thought you did when we were on The Farm. The country agreed with you."

"I miss it."

"I do too sometimes." Doug released her hand and stood up. "I have your father's address and phone number if you want it."

"I don't know if I do."

"You might not today. The news is too fresh, but one day, you might. One day, you might have a child who wants to know who his or her grandfather is."

"You're right." She took the manila envelope Doug handed her.

"Now, as for your mother."

Alice wiped around her eyes with Doug's handkerchief. "I almost forgot about my mother."

"Alice, after what I found out, you shouldn't be so hard on her."

Alice took in a big breath and let it out.

"You know about your mother being married before. And you know she worked at MACY'S before you were born. What you don't know is she never knew who her parents were. She was given up at birth. She went from one foster home to another. Your mother had a hard life. It isn't difficult to see why she married a man who was so much older than her. She was looking for a father figure."

"And then she went in the opposite direction, picking a much younger man," Alice said. "I wonder why."

"There is no way of knowing that now."

"I always thought my grandparents were German."

"Who knows? Maybe they are, or maybe at least on your father's side. I could try to find out, but sometimes, these things are sealed. I could give it a go. All you have to do is say the word."

"No, you've already done enough for me."

"Not really, Alice. I sometimes feel guilty."

"Guilty? Why?"

"I stole a young girl's life away from her. Dragged her off to a farm out in the middle of nowhere, taking her as my common-law wife."

Alice laughed and blew her nose.

"I never thought of myself as your common-law wife. I thought of you as my partner and my teacher."

Doug smiled. "I'm glad you see it that way. Now, as for Jack Jr., I'm afraid there is more bad news."

"Go ahead. Give it to me. I think after the other stuff I can take it."

"He's in prison. Petty theft."

"I guess I'm not surprised. My mother always said nothing

good would come of him." Alice got up from the blue leather chair. "Doug, I can't thank you enough for doing this for me."

"There is no need for your thanks."

"Doug, I want to tell you something before I go. It's good news."

"Oh?"

"Yes." She held up her ring. "I'm engaged."

His mouth dropped. She couldn't tell if there might have been a twinge of jealousy or surprise. He quickly regrouped whatever feelings she thought emanated from him and smiled, but it was a forced smile. Alice knew Doug well enough to see through it.

"Alice, I didn't even know you were dating anyone. This seems rather quick."

"I told you about Tom once. At least I think I did."

"Yeah, I seem to remember. You never said any more about him, so I guess I…"

"We've dated since two weeks before Christmas. He asked me two days ago, and I said yes."

"That is quick."

"Possibly, but we both feel like we've known each other all our lives. We have so much in common, and I've met his family."

"What's his last name?"

"Walker."

"And what does he do?"

"He works in construction, but he's had every kind of job imaginable."

"Oh?"

"Yes, it's really kind of funny. He has a college degree in business."

"So why isn't he doing something along those lines?"

"It's not really his thing. Tom loves working with his hands."

"What about his family? How old is he?"

Doug kept shooting questions at her.

"Wow. I didn't realize you would give me the third degree."

He hesitated. "Alice, I don't want you to think the wrong thing, but this isn't some kind of rebound or competition is it?"

"Rebound? Competition? Rebound from what? And are you saying I'm competing with you? I hardly think I could compete with you." Alice held up her arms and looked around. "I mean, seriously, Doug."

"I'm sorry. I'm sorry," he repeated.

She laughed. "You realize you sound like a father, don't you?"

Doug wasn't smiling. "Maybe. I guess, but I want you to be happy, find the right guy."

"He is the right guy. I'm sure."

"Okay, but I want to meet him."

"You will. I promise."

Doug forced another smile. "Well, when are you getting married?"

"We've been talking about May. We'll probably get married in Georgia. That's where he's from and where his family lives. Both his parents and two brothers and their wives are professors. Well, his parents are retired now. I've met them. They're all great."

"How did you meet them?"

"Tom and I flew down right before New Year's."

"You've never been on a plane before."

"There's a first time for everything."

He smiled. "I guess you're right."

"Doug, I keep meaning to ask you, but the few times we've seen each other, there's been so much other stuff going on. Do you know where Laura, Chris, Renea, and Kyle are? I would love to catch up with them."

"Yes, they're all friends with me on FACEBOOK. I'll make sure they friend you. I couldn't tell you much other than generalities, so I'll just let them tell you."

"Thanks again, Doug, and I'm sorry I ruffled your feathers with my news."

"No, Alice, I'm the one who is sorry. I overreacted. You've overcome so much and turned out to be one of the best, one of the brightest, and most beautiful women I know. Tom is one lucky guy."

He hugged her and kissed her on the cheek and looked at his watch. "I would walk you out, but I have a client who has been waiting for nearly thirty minutes."

37

Long Overdue

Alice and Tom spent Valentine's Day watching old movies on NETFLIX, eating popcorn, and making plans for Tom to move in on Saturday as his lease was running out the following week. Alice, abandoning her pros-and-cons list, told him it was only logical to pool all of their resources together since they were planning on marrying in May anyway. And besides, he was already spending most nights at her apartment.

On Saturday, she got off work at noon expecting to see Tom already moved into her apartment, no, *their* apartment. After going through the logistics of moving Tom's stuff, they decided to sell all but the essentials. Adding one more stick of furniture might cause a cave-in. She thought, poor Freddie, Isis, Simon, and Garfunkel, directly below them. Luckily, everything Tom was bringing would fit in a taxi.

Where was he? Maybe he stopped for bagels. Alice smiled and looked down at the ring on her finger.

TOM HAD DEVELOPED both an addiction and morning ritual when it came to his bagels. Having to leave for work earlier than Alice, he made his own breakfast, black coffee and an everything bagel from the bagel shop three blocks away, which he claimed was New York's finest bagel shop ever since he and Alice had breakfast there after a rather passionate night of making love. Tom was in the habit of buying two at a time because any more and they would lose their freshness, he said. He would slice the bagel then pop it in the toaster. Once the bagel was toasted, he walked around their small apartment, coffee in one hand, bagel in his other, leaving a trail of the tiny black poppy seeds, garlic flakes, pretzel salt, and sesame seeds all over the floor and white surfaces. Even though he cleaned up after himself, he was sure to miss some.

It was Thursday morning, and Tom had come into the bedroom as usual and kissed Alice goodbye before heading out the door for work. She should have gotten up then but rolled back over for another ten minutes.

Alice walked barefoot into the kitchen, feeling the bagel toppings sticking to the bottom of her feet. She had intended on going in early and getting a jump on Valentine Day's baskets, but that wasn't going to happen. Maybe it was because her feet now smelled of garlic and she was already running late or the fact she was getting cramps that put her in a foul mood causing her to resent cleaning up after Tom, something she did on most mornings without complaint. She was down on the floor, using a paper towel to wipe her feet, wondering what it would take for him to stop this ridiculous habit of his. Then she started to cry. Through some serendipitous moment, Tom burst through the door. "I forgot my hardhat." He stopped, and knelt down, "What's wrong?"

"I found myself getting so mad at you for making this same mess every morning."

"Oh, Ali," he said. She loved that he had shortened her name to Ali, usually in their most intimate of moments. It was his name for her, something special. "I'm always in such a hurry in the mornings. I didn't realize…"

"No, you don't understand," she interrupted. "I suddenly thought what if you weren't here to make a mess. That's when I started to cry."

"I'll always be here. For as long as you let me. I'm not your father, Ali. Here." He lifted her up from the floor and had her sit at the kitchen table. "Stay there."

"You need to get going. You'll be late."

"It'll be okay. First time being late, they're not going to fire me for it."

He came back after a moment, holding a small black box and got down on one knee. "Alice, I want to spend the rest of my life with you. And I promise, from here on out, I will clean up after myself. Will you…"

"Yes, Tom, I will marry you," she said amid both tears and laughter.

He opened the box and pulled out the ring.

"A sapphire with diamonds?"

"Tiny diamonds," he countered. "I've been looking at rings for, well, I'm embarrassed to say how long. I knew from the moment we first met you were the one."

"I did too, on some level."

"I kept seeing this one in the window on the way to the subway. Loved that it was shaped like a heart. I looked up the meaning of sapphire. It protects from harm and represents loyalty and trust. I know that's what you want above all else. And I remember how disgusted you were the night we saw the documentary about diamond mines, about the exploited workers and child labor. I was hoping small diamonds wouldn't be so bad. I know how you feel about certain things. One reason I always try to go for the fair-trade stuff.

She smiled. "It's perfect. Did you know the sapphire is your birthstone?

"No, I didn't. But since you told me your mother and I have the same birthday, it would be hers as well." He looked into her eyes. "I love you, Alice."

"I love you, Tom."

He slipped the ring on her finger. "It's hard to leave now," he said, holding both her hands in his.

SHE WAS STILL LOOKING at her ring when she reached for her phone but then decided it was her insecurities nagging at her, the way they always nagged at her. Tom would burst through the door at any moment, the way he burst through on the morning he proposed. He loved her. He hadn't changed his mind. Then, she looked over and saw his guitar in the corner. She breathed a sigh of relief.

It was the voice of doubt that had haunted her all her life, probably the one she inherited from her mother, that made her think Tom might renege on her, and it was that same voice that had her go over to her desk and pull the manila folder from the drawer. It had stayed sealed since Doug had given it to her.

She grimaced and undid the metal clasp and pulled the papers halfway out when her cell rang. She laid the folder on the top of her desk and grabbed her phone from the coffee table.

"Where are you?"

"I'm in my office but heading home." It was Doug's voice.

"Doug? Sorry, I thought you were Tom."

"Nope, sorry to disappoint."

"No, you didn't disappoint. Is there something else about my family?"

"No, Constance sent you a message on FACEBOOK."

"I haven't been on FACEBOOK."

"Well then, I have a surprise. It's rather short notice, but I hope you can come. You have to come."

"Come where?"

"Constance and I are throwing a little get together tonight at our apartment. Laura, Chris, Renea, and Kyle will be here. Constance mentioned this morning you hadn't got back with her. It's taken three days to make the arrangements. Kyle and Renea are driving down from Albany. Laura and Chris live in Kentucky now, and their flight should arrive…" He paused. Alice could tell he was looking at his watch. "They should disembark the plane about now if it's on time, but you know how that is." Actually, only having flown once, she didn't.

Alice could feel her heart pounding.

"Alice, are you there?"

"Yes, sorry." She took a heavy breath. "I'm just so excited."

"You'll be here, right? Bring Tom." He said it nonchalantly as if Tom were an afterthought. Maybe he wasn't serious when he said he wanted to meet him.

Another call was coming through. "Doug, Tom is calling. Yes, I want to come. I don't know your address. Text me the details."

She switched calls. "Tom, where are you?"

"Sorry, I wanted to let you know I'm only getting ready to call a taxi now. The guy who was coming by to buy the furniture was late, and then he tried to haggle me down. It will be another hour before I get there. Sorry."

"No, it's okay. I'm glad you called. I was worried."

"I love you," he said

She smiled. "I love you too. See you a little later."

A ding came in after she ended the call with Tom. It was Doug's address. Park Avenue, no less. The party was at eight. It would give her and Tom a chance to get settled in with their new living arrangement.

What on earth would she wear? Doug didn't say if it was

formal. She couldn't imagine Laura, Chris, Renea, and Kyle in anything but their farm clothes. She looked back over at the manila envelope with the papers pulled halfway out. Maybe tomorrow, Sunday morning, when Tom was with her over coffee. She walked over to her desk and shoved the papers back in, refastened the clasp, and put the envelope back in the drawer.

She thought of Constance. Something new to wear was a must. And makeup. She called Mrs. Maxwell. She heard the flipping of pages, more than likely her appointment book. "Is 6:30 okay?"

"It's great," Alice said.

She would have to meet Tom somewhere before heading over to Doug's. A million things went through her mind. They should take something. Neither she nor Tom, even pooling their resources, could come up with the wines one drank at a Park Avenue address. And what to wear?

She had maybe an hour before Tom got here. She was four blocks from MACY'S. The thought of choosing something to wear on her own added to her anxiety. She texted Chen.

Going to the MACY'S nearest my apt. Have a dinner party tonight. Need new threads. Meet me there if you can.

Nothing.

She sent a new text, this time to Tom.

Doug has invited us to a dinner party tonight. Have to have something new to wear. Going to MACY'S. Will return ASAP.

Her phone dinged back.

See you there. There was a smiley face. No text from Chen would be complete without an emoji.

A second ding. It was Tom.

Okay.

One thing she liked about Tom was he was easygoing, nothing ever appeared to rattle him.

Alice stepped out onto the sidewalk in the boots Doug purchased for her, wearing the coat Tom bought her. Chen had commented on the irony. Snow had fallen, and the sidewalks were a sludgy mess with salt pellets, such a contrast to winter on The Farm, where hers, other than deer hooves, were the only footprints on some days. The snow there could be soft and wet, hard and crunchy, or powdery, but always pristine, nothing like the dirt-etched snow of the city.

She opened the glass door of MACY'S to find Chen standing between the double-door entrance, looking at her phone.

"Chen," Alice exclaimed.

"What took you so long?"

"I walked as fast as I could."

"Kidding, I only just got here. I was across the street when you texted. The sale rack?" she asked.

"Yes."

Chen pushed through clothes, holding this or that up to Alice, shaking her head no, then returning it to the rack. She went through the entire sale's rack in women's petite before pulling out five ensembles she thought suitable. "Take these to the fitting room."

"They're all black," Alice said.

"You said a dinner party in Manhattan, right?"

"Yes."

Alice disappeared into the fitting room while Chen waited outside, her eyes glued to her phone except when Alice came out seeking Chen's opinion.

"So are you going to fill me in on this dinner party?"

"It was all last minute. Actually, he didn't call it a dinner party. He said get-together. The old gang is meeting up at Doug's apartment tonight."

"Gang, as in the people at The Farm?" Chen's eyes grew wide.

"Yes."

"Take videos for me. I want to see these people."

"I don't know. I guess. You know I'm not good at that sort of thing."

"Is Tom going?"

"Yes."

"Have Tom take them. All the better to see *you* in the pictures."

"Okay, if it seems appropriate."

She grimaced as she tilted her head.

"They'll all be doing it, plus I'll never forgive you if you don't."

"Okay, I will."

"Try on the next one. Wait," she said as Alice was heading into the dressing room, "you said Constance will be there."

"Yes."

"Something blue to bring out your eyes and hair more."

"Chen, really?"

"Yes, really. We got to make this chick jealous."

"I'm not out to make her jealous."

"Okay, a little envious. Try the next one on. I'll be back with something striking."

Alice called from the dressing room, "The sale rack, Chen."

"Yeah, okay."

Chen brought back an oversized teal deep V-neck Shaker sweater, a slim fit long sleeve white shirt, and a pair of high-waisted medium washed denim jeggings.

"Jeans?" Alice gasped. "Do you think jeans will be okay?"

"Trust me. This whole ensemble has chic written all over it. Plus, you said it was a get-together. We don't want to risk being too formal or too underdressed. This says I don't care. I dare to be me."

Why Chen was majoring in psychology and not sales, Alice didn't know, but then, sales and psychology kind of went together.

Alice let out a shriek in the dressing room.

"What?" Chen asked. "Too tight?"

"No, the price of these jeans. Chen, I don't know."

Chen went inside the dressing room and stood behind Alice's door. "Yes, but the sweet deal on the shirt and sweater make up for the jeans."

"Can't you find some on sale?"

"No, not possible with these jeans."

Alice came out.

"Oh, girl, you will kill tonight." She stood back. Her eyes traveled up and down Alice. "What kind of shoes are you wearing?"

"Chen, you know I only have two pair, my boots and my sneakers."

"No, no. You can't," she said shaking her head.

"Why?"

"Because Doug got you the boots. And Constance knows that, right?"

"I think maybe she does."

"The point is wearing them could send some kind of mixed signal."

"What kind of mixed signal?"

"I'm not sure. Like I said, it's mixed. Better to stay away from any sort of mixed signals. You *could* use another pair of shoes, you know."

"Okay, as long as they're not too pricey."

Chen's mouth dropped. "Really, we can get a new pair of shoes?"

"Don't look so surprised."

"Okay, follow me to the shoes."

"Would you quit looking at the time," Chen said with a disgusted look on her face. She had only briefly looked at Alice as she had tunnel vision in going through the aisles, pulling this and that shoe off the shelf, handing each to the floor clerk who followed her like an eager puppy with commission written in his eyes. "Size seven," Chen said.

Chen was off to the far corner when he came out with the stack of boxes. "Where's your personal shopper?"

"Personal shopper?" Alice asked. "Oh, no, she's…" Just then Chen appeared with something from the heavily discounted rack.

"Chen, these are perfect," Alice gasped. The sales clerk betrayed a slight frown.

Chen held up the original duck boot. "Could we get the other shoe?" Chen asked.

"These will be okay to wear to Doug's party?"

"At first, I thought not, but the more I looked at them, I thought why not? They're practical and say to hell with it all. We both know how you feel about practicality."

Alice undid the laces and slipped the one boot on while waiting for the sales clerk to come back.

"What's Tom wearing?"

"Slacks and a jacket probably. We haven't discussed it."

"No, not slacks, jeans. And he should wear a sweater under the jacket."

"The sales clerk asked if you were my personal shopper."

Alice could see the wheels spinning in Chen's brain.

"YOU'RE HERE!" Alice exclaimed when she arrived back at her apartment, rushing over to hug him.

"Yes, and I see you've been shopping," Tom said with a smile after a lengthy kiss.

"Is me shopping going to be a problem in our relationship?" she asked jokingly.

"Remember what I told you?"

"No, what?"

"You're in charge of the money, honey," Tom said as he put

his arms around her and kissed her. "So what time is this dinner party?"

"Eight."

"It's four. So we have plenty of time to christen our home."

"Our home, I like the sound of that. We have an hour. Then we have to get ready. Or I do because Mrs. Maxwell said she would help me with my makeup."

"All this extra stuff you're doing—should I be jealous?"

"No, not at all. Do you know what Chen said on our way back?"

"No, what did she say?"

"She said they'd all be impressed because you're so handsome."

"I never thought of myself as handsome."

"Well, you are," Alice said as she kissed him and led him into the bedroom.

"I HOPE THIS IS OKAY. I only own two jackets, my winter one and my summer one, and two ties. Will I pass Doug's test?"

"I hardly think Doug is testing you. No tie. Chen said to wear a sweater under the jacket and wear your good jeans."

Tom raised his eyebrows. "Okay. If Chen says it's what I should wear, then who am I to say otherwise? And as far as Doug testing me, sure he is. He still cares about you."

"Tom, he's engaged."

"I don't care. He would never have gone to all the trouble to find your father for you if he didn't still care about you. The only thing I care about is how much you still care about him."

"I've told you all of this. The relationship I had with Doug was comfortable. What I feel for *you* is totally different."

"I hope you feel comfortable with me too."

"You know I do."

"Well, you look fantastic. Maybe I need Chen to pick out *my* clothes."

"I'm sure she would be more than happy to. She comes alive when she's shopping for me. Well, more alive."

"Okay, so the plan is while you're getting your makeup done, I'm to find something to take as a gift? And when I find something, I'll come by Mrs. Maxwell's, and then we head on over?"

"Yes. Tell me, was it this hectic when you and Sarah were getting ready to go somewhere?"

Tom backed her up against the wall and kissed her. "Sorry, I can't keep my hands off of you. Us together is nothing like Sarah and me together, and truthfully, the word together is stretching it. Didn't you get a feel for Sarah from Carol and Jennifer?"

"Yes, I just hope they really like me and don't say I'm like your first wife behind my back."

Tom laughed. "Can you imagine Jennifer speaking anything other than her mind? Well, either of them, for that matter."

"No, I suppose you're right."

"Trust me, they like you. And even if they didn't, it wouldn't matter."

"It matters to me," Alice said with her head down.

He lifted her chin and looked in her eyes. "I know. I understand. Family is important. Now, I'm *your* family. Remember *that*."

As Tom hugged her again, Alice sniffled. He backed away. "Now don't cry."

"I'm sorry."

"No, it's okay. Just don't cry after Mrs. Maxwell does your makeup."

She laughed. "I won't. We better get going."

38

The Old Gang

A lice and Tom were the last to arrive.

"Wow! Look at you," Doug said, kissing her on the cheek. "And this must be Tom," he said while reaching out to shake Tom's hand.

"So, Douglas, this is the Alice I've heard so much about?" Constance said as she rushed over.

She was dressed in a cashmere sweater and jeans, and she called him Douglas. Chen would surely have something to say about that, but for right now, Alice was thankful for Chen's good fashion sense. After exhibiting a wide smile, one which Alice construed as forced, Constance moved her eyes from Alice's face to her feet, where the smile faded to a stunned expression upon seeing her duck boots. Alice looked down to Constance's feet to see pointy-toed heels, maybe even from the same shoe store Doug had taken her to that day. Constance instantly regained her composure by offering a formal one-armed hug while balancing a glass of wine in her other, something apparently second nature to her. This party was clearly Doug's idea.

"Your apartment is..." Alice didn't have time to finish her statement as Laura and Renea came rushing over, both taking turns at squeezing Alice so hard it almost took her breath away. And then Kyle and Chris did the same.

"I can't believe we are all back together," Chris said.

"And this must be Tom," Renea said. "Doug told us you were engaged."

"Yes, I know it's a cliché, but it was love at first sight—at least on my part. Alice took a bit of convincing," Tom teased.

Alice held out her ring hand and nudged Tom with her other arm. "He's kidding. He didn't need to convince me."

"I'm fairly confident she made a list of pros and cons although I was never privy to the list," Tom said.

"You're still making lists?" Kyle asked.

"Don't knock it," Doug said. "Her lists helped get us through the winters on The Farm."

"So how did he pop the question?" Renea asked.

"It was over bagels," Tom said.

"Oh, in some romantic out-of-the-way breakfast nook in Soho, or someplace like that?" Laura asked.

"No, actually, I was having a meltdown over stepping on poppy seeds and garlic flakes." Alice smiled. "I was so mad because of the mess. Kind of one of those private moments I won't go into, but Tom had forgotten his hardhat, which he had never done before, but he came through the door at just the right time..."

"Which resulted in me proposing a week before Valentine's Day, which is when I had originally intended to pop the question."

"You would have thought you would have just bought blueberry bagels," Chris said with a straight face.

Laura hit him in the arm with her fist.

"What?" he exclaimed.

Laura shook her head. "Whatever you do, Alice, don't let the romance die." She gave Chris a dirty look.

"Is there a significance to a sapphire engagement ring?" Constance asked.

Alice smiled. "Actually, there is. Sapphire is the birthstone for September, and both my mother's and Tom's birthday is September 12. Can you believe it?"

"Serendipity. Works for me," Renea said.

"You believe in serendipity?" Chris asked, arching his eyebrows.

"Time and experience change us all," Renea replied.

"I know the story, but tell the others how you met," Doug said.

"Let's move to the living room where we'll be more comfortable," Constance suggested.

The sectional couch which circled the glass coffee table was the same distressed leather as the chairs in Doug's office, only brown. Except for the abstract paintings on the wall, which Alice knew had to be Constance's touch since she worked at the METROPOLITAN ART MUSEUM, the theme was neutral tones—a white marble floor with an Oriental rug in browns and beiges and a white table against the back wall with an arrangement of an off-white facsimile of tree branches and beside that two small brown leather chairs matching the couch. There was no greenery anywhere. Something alive would have competed with the artificial. The paintings were the only splash of color in the place except for a bowl of apples displayed like a Cézanne painting on the island dividing the living area from the kitchen. Alice doubted if the kitchen ever got used or the apples ever got eaten. They were probably bagged up and thrown in the garbage and replaced by new ones, sometimes oranges, sometimes pears, by a maid who came in to clean every few days. Wasting anything was not the Doug she knew on The Farm. She hoped the maid took the unused fruit home to her family.

"We met over a skeleton," Tom said.

"Ooh, this sounds interesting," Renea said. "Was it at Halloween?"

"No," Tom said, explaining how they met.

"Wow, skeletons and bagels," Laura said after Tom finished the story.

"Yes, leave it to our little Alice to be unique," Renea said with a laugh.

TIME FLEW by as all of them talked about what they were doing now and about The Farm.

Laura and Chris lived on a few acres of land near Lexington, Kentucky. They both taught at the University of Kentucky, grew a garden, had a greenhouse, and were trying to get pregnant.

Kyle and Renea brought out their cells to show how April had grown. Kyle had a psychology practice in Albany, and Renea worked as a social worker. She said she also planned to write a book, maybe about their experience, but she would have to wait until April got older. Alice thought about bringing up Chen's idea of a book but thought better of it.

They shared one memory after the other. Alice was surprised at how each of them recalled the same events differently. Or perhaps it was the wine that was passed around so freely blurring the incidents.

"You know, one thing we never found out…" Renea said.

"What?" Doug asked.

"Why it was called the Old Crosby Place."

Doug let out a heavy sigh.

"You look like you know something, Doug?"

He looked down at the floor and back up, letting out another sigh. "I didn't tell you for a reason. I guess I was afraid if you knew, none of you would have gone. There were times I thought about telling you while we were there, but then I feared you would leave."

"So, what is this mysterious thing?" Chris asked.

"Crosby was my mother's maiden name."

"So the home belonged to your family?" Renea asked. "Why would that matter to us?"

"It's what happened there, why they left."

"It's not haunted is it?" Alice asked.

"No," Doug said. "My mother's twin brother drowned in the lake we swam in."

"Ooh," Renea exclaimed. "I think if we knew that we might have not been swimming in it."

"Yeah, you're probably right," Alice said.

"But you did, and you all had a perfectly fabulous time," Doug said.

"Yes, some of my best memories were up at that lake," Chris said.

"That was when you were still romantic," Laura scoffed.

"Maybe I wanted to break the curse," Doug said.

"Curse? Is the house cursed?" Laura asked.

"Did any of you feel like it was cursed?" Doug asked.

"I, for one, certainly didn't," Alice said.

"My mother thought it was cursed, or at least her mother, my grandmother, did. She refused to live there any longer after my uncle, her child, died there. They packed up and moved up to New York where my mother had relatives. Didn't even want the possessions."

"So that's why it looked like it was stuck in time."

"Yes. After my grandparents died, my mom wanted to go back and see the place. She still remembered it. My father took us. I was about ten at the time. I thought it was heaven and started thinking about it again toward the end of college."

"So you wanted to prove there was no curse or it wasn't haunted?" Alice asked.

"I suppose, something like that."

"Hey, Doug, remember that time you got the tractor stuck in the creek?" Chris asked, breaking the gloom that had befallen them.

"I thought you were driving the tractor that day," Doug countered.

"No, I'm pretty sure it was you," Laura said as they all chirped in agreement.

"I bet that farmer you got to pull us out with that big monstrous tractor of his is still telling the story of the city dudes who knew nothing about driving a tractor or working a farm," Kyle said.

"We did give that town plenty to talk about," Laura said.

"I bet Betty is still pining for your return, Doug," Renea joked.

"Betty?" Constance asked.

"A waitress at BUCKY'S DINER," Alice said. "We think she had the hots for Doug."

Doug turned to look at Constance who was standing behind him with her hand on his shoulder. "She was practically my mother's age."

Tom laughed, displaying the dimples she so loved, and told a few of his own experiences helping his uncle on his farm in Georgia. Tom blended in like a chameleon. Constance looked uncomfortable, lost, and out of place as Douglas, her attorney fiancé, the one Alice called anti-Doug, turned back into rebellious farm boy Doug. He was even wearing jeans.

Amid the laughter, Alice heard Constance's voice, "More hors d'oeuvres or wine anyone? Whose idea was it for the chocolates?"

"Tom's," Alice said.

"And fair-trade," Renea commented.

"I thought that was the theme of The Farm?" Tom said.

The party wound down around midnight.

TOM WAS STRUMMING his guitar the next morning when Alice's cell rang. "Chen wanting to know how the party went?" Tom asked.

"Doug," Alice said, looking down at her phone. "Hi, Doug, thank you so much for getting everyone together."

"You're welcome," he said. "Is Tom there?"

"Yes, he's right here. Do you want to speak to him?"

"I want to speak to you both. Put me on speaker."

"Hi, Doug, thanks for the party. It was so nice meeting everyone Alice has talked about so much," Tom said.

"I wanted to let you know how great you and Alice are together." He paused. "I really mean that. I'm glad Alice has you."

"I'm glad I have her too." Tom looked in her eyes and squeezed her waist with one arm.

"Alice, that first day we met out on the street, do you remember when I told you I planned on looking you up because I had something I wanted to discuss with you but I had to finish some paperwork?"

"Yes, vaguely. We talked about so much on that day."

"We did. But what I wanted to talk to you about, I kept putting off. Honestly, Constance wasn't too keen on the idea. But last night convinced her."

"Convinced her of what?" Alice said.

"To deed over The Farm to you."

"What?" Alice asked. She looked at Tom who laid his guitar aside.

"After everything we've experienced there, the group of us, I can't see selling it to anyone. The house is going to eventually fall down if something isn't done and quick. If I sold it to someone local, they'd bulldoze the house down and use what usable land there is for hay."

"Doug, I'm speechless. What would the others think?"

"I talked to them after you and Tom left. They think it's a brilliant idea. It would take a lot of work. I know it's a big decision to leave your jobs here and go back into the back country of West Virginia." He paused. "Well, I'll let you discuss it. Like I said, it's a big decision. There are stipulations. It's the home you both live in. You can't turn around and sell the property. And we're all welcome anytime we want to come down if you decide you want to take it. We also all said we would wait to visit until you had electricity and maybe a second bathroom."

"But, Doug, you can't just give us The Farm for free." Her voice was shaky.

"Do you also remember when I referred to you as my common-law wife?"

"Yes."

"Do you realize if we had actually been married and had divorced, you would have gotten The Farm anyway? Well, maybe not," he said laughing. "You would be hard-pressed to find a divorce lawyer who could stand up against our firm. Joking, of course. Tom, I hope you aren't taking any offense to this?"

"No, I was married before, not even as long as you and Alice were."

Doug laughed. "Consider it a wedding present."

"I'm looking at Tom right now, and he is looking stunned, but also nodding," Alice said. "I'm in total agreement with him, but let us discuss it first, and we will call you back, okay?"

"Yes, make your lists, and call me back."

She ended the call.

"Oh, my God, Tom, what do you think?" Alice asked. She placed her hands on her head and paced around. She moved her hands down to her side and shook her head. "I just can't believe this."

"I've always told you my dream was to have a place out in

the country. More importantly, Ali, what do you want?" He laughed. "And sit down. You're so excited."

She sat on the floor, cross-legged in front of him.

"There hasn't been a day I haven't thought about being back there. I was even hoping we could rent a car and visit the place together one last time before it falls down. Now we could really make it into something, even raise a family there."

"After what Doug told you about the place, the child dying there, that wouldn't bother you?"

"It's sad, but you know things like that happen. It's not the fault of the house."

Alice paused.

"What is it, Alice? You have a strange look."

"It's just that I had a thought. I remember blaming the house at 123 Tucker Street for all our problems. It wasn't the house's fault. It's the occupants that make it a home. Oh, Tom, I really think we could make it into a home."

"I think we could, too, Ali."

"Tom, you understand from what I've told you and from what the others were saying how rough it is, don't you?"

"I've camped out in the backwoods of Georgia plenty of times. I *do* have an idea."

"How do you feel about my former boyfriend giving it to us?"

He took in a heavy breath and let it out. "I can't say it does a whole lot for my manhood, but I would be a fool to turn it down. I'd have to make up for it by making it into a showplace. The only drawback is we would need money to fix it up. We both have some saved, but it won't be nearly enough. I've been through plenty of hard times though, living from hand to mouth. We could fix a room at a time. I'm game if you are."

She smiled and hugged him. "I spent the happiest time of my life there, and that was with Doug. I can only imagine what it would be like with you."

Alice tapped Doug's name under favorites while at the same time thinking how strange it was that this was Constance's idea. Chen might say Constance was trying to get her as far away from Doug as possible. And Tom might agree. But she didn't care.

"Yes, we want to take you up on your offer," Alice said when Doug answered.

39

Wood

When Doug said he was a carpenter, he vastly understated Jack White's talents. His desks, chairs, tables, and about anything wooden one could think of were all works of skillful craftsmanship. It was an art gallery of transformed forest—walnut, cherry, maple, poplar, and oak with a mingling of exotic woods.

From the back room, Tom and Alice heard the sounds of a band saw and some hammering. Above the woodworking sounds, Alice heard laughter and someone singing. A rather plain woman who looked to be in her fifties appeared through the doorway. She was smiling, all genuine and natural, privy, Alice imagined, to some joke told in the back room. She and Tom had interrupted a perfectly happy family. Alice looked at Tom with an uneasy pleading in her eyes. Tom shook his head no. He knew she was getting cold feet and wanted to head back out to the car and drive away.

"May I help you?" the woman asked, still smiling. She was looking at Tom. Her smile turned quizzical when she turned her glance toward Alice.

Alice hefted Katie up on her hip. She couldn't help but stare back at the woman in the same fashion. When she realized what she was doing, she turned her head to Tom who was monitoring her reaction. This had to be his wife, the woman her father left them high and dry for. Alice looked back. The woman's face went sour. The hair must have given her away. Or maybe it was the eyes. June Maxwell said she took both after her father. Alice could only surmise from her reaction, this woman knew she was Jack White's little girl, all grown-up. The woman took a breath and regained her decorum.

"No, no," Alice said. "We're just looking."

Tom was practically drooling over the furniture while keeping a close eye on Alice's own fragility during the situation. "Do you want me to take Katie?" he asked.

She might have said yes under most circumstances as Katie was getting squirmy, but the warmth and weight of her daughter's little body kept Alice grounded. Alice's nerves were bubbling to a crescendo, and if it weren't for Katie's dependence on her, Alice could have flown off in all directions at once.

"Are you okay?" the woman asked. "Babies can be a handful. She has your hair and eyes. How old is she?"

"Nine months," Alice said.

Tom put his arm around Alice's waist. "Everything is so beautiful. I would love to talk to the designer."

Leave it to Tom to take the initiative she lacked. Was this right—coming here unannounced? Maybe the woman wished they would turn around and go? Alice couldn't tell. She seemed adept at hiding feelings.

"He's in the back. I'll get him," she said. "He'll be glad to talk to you."

"What does that mean, Tom? Glad?" Alice whispered as the woman walked away.

"Alice, don't overthink it."

"She knows who I am. I swear she does. I don't know, Tom. I thought I could handle this. Do you think she's his wife? She has to be." The woman had vanished through the back door. The band saw was still running. Still, she could hear what seemed to be a jovial conversation between two males, possibly three.

Tom gently placed his hand on the back of her shoulder and pulled her and Katie close. "You've put this off far too long. I'm here with you. Take a deep breath. It'll be okay."

"Da Da," Katie said reaching out her arms for him. She sensed Alice's nervousness. At least she wasn't crying. Alice handed Katie to Tom.

A man came out, wiping his hands on a work apron. "Hi. Emily said you had questions. I'm Jack White." He smiled.

Alice knew the woman knew, but she hadn't told him. He was acting too normal, not that she knew what normal for him was.

A shiver went through Alice. Katie was jabbering incoherently. Tom was holding onto her and standing close enough to Alice that she could feel his hip as it jutted out to balance Katie.

The man was skinny, tall, and angular with short gray hair. He reminded Alice of a younger version of the actor Sam Elliott, minus the mustache. His voice was almost as deep.

If Alice had his hair, it was no longer obvious, but her eyes were staring back at her. They were not only staring back but transfixed on her. June was right. He broke his ogle as if he had to force himself to do so. He looked at Tom and reached out his hand to shake it. "Sorry, my hand still has traces of sawdust. I've been sanding." He looked back at Alice and reached for her hand. She took it. He had a firm shake. A memory of his hand on her back pushing her on her bicycle flashed through her mind. "And who is this little cutie?" he asked, directing his attention to Katie.

Had his voice gotten shaky? Was Alice imagining it?

"This is Katie," Tom said. "Say hi, Katie." Tom was all cool and collected, as usual, her rock.

Alice once asked Tom how he always could remain so calm

during a crisis. He explained to her his life was in shambles before meeting her. "You saved me from rock bottom," he said.

Jack White still was making no overtures toward her. How could he not know? Maybe he knew, and it was business as usual. What did she expect? For him to run out crying and hug her and say how sorry he was?

Katie looked at the man who, unbeknownst to her, was her grandfather and shyly held her head down.

"She's named after my mother," Alice said. She hated the harsh sound of the words coming from her mouth. She shouldn't have to give the man clues. Would he finally make the connection? Her mother's middle name was Kathryn. It pained Alice to think he didn't remember.

"Your work is art. We live in West Virginia, and this reminds me of the pieces we've seen at TAMARACK. Have you heard of it?" Tom asked.

Tom was trying to get her to regroup, get hold of her emotions before she lost it and said something she would regret. On the drive up, Tom had cautioned and drilled her on calmness and civility, and how if the worst happened, it didn't matter because she had him and Katie and his family, not to mention all the friends they both had.

"No," the man said.

"It's a collection of West Virginia's finest made up of the work of artisans throughout the state. There are some marvelous pieces of furniture there."

Tom was throwing West Virginia in the mix of hints or possibly he was talking to the man to let Alice get a better picture of him. Or knowing Tom, he could have been making conversation to keep Alice calm, not realizing he was giving Jack White clues.

"Sounds like a place I'd like to visit. The problem is my sons and I stay so behind, we don't get to travel much."

"Sounds like a good problem to have," Tom said.

Jack White emitted a half-hearted laugh.

The woman hadn't returned from the back. Alice was glad. She was giving them time. Maybe she wasn't a bad person at all. Maybe she had her own regrets about stealing her father away from them.

"Many of your pieces have a Scandinavian influence," Tom said. While Alice knew Tom was truly interested in the furniture, she also knew Tom was keeping her father talking, waiting on her to get up her nerve.

"Yes, and Shaker. Have you heard of Shaker?" he asked.

Alice jumped in. "Tom and I visited SHAKER VILLAGE in Kentucky once when he had a grant workshop in Lexington."

"Yes, we wanted inspiration. We've been fixing up an old farmhouse in West Virginia," Tom said.

Again Jack White stared at Alice as if he was trying to fit puzzle pieces together. Alice wondered why it was taking him so long to connect the dots. He knew Alice was somewhere in West Virginia when he went to see her mom. If he didn't already know, he suspected. Maybe he didn't know what to say or how to say it. His hand was shaking when he pulled out the chair. "My wife weaves the chair seats." He said it with his head down.

Nothing about the scenario was right. A furniture maker would talk more about his craft. He was stalling, fumbling over words. Tom had talked to plenty of woodworkers. They liked nothing better than talking about their craft and the various woods.

There was no point in delaying it. Alice was on the verge of blurting out *you're my father*, or worse, *you left us when I was six* when Jack looked up from the chair. His eyes were wet.

"Alice?"

"Yes," she said.

They both stared at each other, neither of them knowing what to do. Then he said, "Do you still have the birdhouse I made for you?"

Alice shook her head no. She willed away the tears that wanted to come back into her tear ducts. "I suppose it went along with the tree and the house. There's a strip mall there now."

"Everything changes," he said.

"Yes, it does," Alice replied.

The door dinged, and an older couple walked into the shop. Jack White looked up and waved at them. Alice could tell he was trying to smile, but it wasn't coming. "Just a moment," he said. He disappeared to the back.

Alice looked at Tom. "Is he disappearing on me again?"

Tom hugged her with his free arm and said forcibly, "Alice, no. He's not."

Katie was squirming all over the place.

"She wants down," Alice said.

"I would take her outside, but I don't want to leave you," Tom said.

Katie started to cry.

"No, we'll both go," Alice said.

Tom gave her a look that had *no* written all over it just as Jack White came back out. "Could I take her?" he asked.

Alice didn't know what to do. Tom looked at Alice with a nod and handed Katie to him. Her tears dried up almost immediately. She played with the safety glasses around his neck. He held Katie and shouted over to the couple who seemed to be waiting for him to finish up with them, "My granddaughter. I'm sorry. Some family business came up. My oldest boy will be out to help you."

The couple looked both disappointed and surprised but said nothing.

"She looks hungry." He looked down at Katie and smiled. "Are you hungry, little one?" He looked back at Tom and Alice. "There's a diner not too far from here. I'll buy you three lunch, and we can talk."

40

Maggie's Diner

They followed his blue Ford pickup truck into the parking lot of a Cape Cod style restaurant. The sign read MAGGIE'S DINER. Tom motioned for Mr. White to wait while Alice changed Katie's diaper in the car.

They walked into the crowded diner with noisy customers filling its maze of tables. There were tempting pies and cakes under glass at the long counter. On any other occasion, both Tom's and Alice's mouths would have been watering, but even though they only had coffee and toast for breakfast, Alice didn't have much of an appetite. Several people waved and said, "Hi, Jack." Her father appeared to be a popular local.

A row of booths sat against the windows and turned the corner. One lone booth sat empty in the back.

"I see Maggie saved my booth for me. I usually come in here for lunch with my notebook and draw plans for my next piece. I made Maggie's dining room suite."

A young waitress whose name tag read Josie said, "You have company today, I see." She handed them the menus.

"Yes, Josie, there'll be three adults and one toddler. We'll need a highchair," he told her.

Tom fixed Katie in her highchair, and Alice put on her bib then handed her a juice box from her diaper bag, which Katie latched onto instantly.

Jack White smiled. "She's hungry."

Josie sat a steaming cup of coffee on the table. "Strong and black, just how you like it, Jack. What can I get the rest of you to drink?"

"An unsweetened ice tea," Alice said.

"The same," Tom echoed.

"So what would you like to eat? They have great steaks here." Mr. White said.

"Anything vegetarian," Tom said.

"Both of you are vegetarian?"

"Yes," Alice responded.

"I remember when we pulled the wishbone at Thanksgiving," Jack said.

Alice looked down at the menu to avoid the emotions swelling inside of her. Her heart felt like it was on a roller coaster. She didn't know whether to feel elated he remembered or angry he actually did remember and treated the memory she grasped onto so desperately so nonchalantly. "A salad for me. Tom?" she said, not looking toward her father.

"The Portobello sandwich looks good. Katie can have some of mine with the fries," he said.

"Did your mother tell you I came looking for you?" Jack asked out of the blue.

"No, she didn't."

"She said she didn't know where you were except that you were somewhere in West Virginia, but she didn't know where. How *is* your mother?"

"She died five years ago."

"Oh," he held his head down. "I'm sorry to hear that." A tear rolled from his eye, and he wiped it away.

The waitress returned with their drinks. "Do you know what you want?"

Tom told her.

"Your usual, Jack?"

"Sure, that's fine."

The waitress picked up the menus and left.

"I guess none of us are really that hungry, are we?" her father asked.

Alice grimaced and shook her head.

"I'm an alcoholic. Have been for years. I guess the heavy drinking started when I left. But Emily stood by me. Even encouraged me to start my carpentry business when I sobered up. Everyone in town knows."

Alice let out a heavy breath. "I really don't know what I expected coming up here. I guess some kind of closure."

"I wish I could give it to you, but I don't know how."

The waitress brought their food along with a small paper plate for Katie. Tom took three French fries from his own plate and put them on Katie's plate.

"I remember how most of your food ended up on the floor when you were that age," her father said.

Tom smiled. "It's the same with Katie. I should have given her one at a time."

"So how did you two meet?"

"Oddly enough, it was all because of a skeleton," Alice said.

Jack White laughed, the tears illuminating his blurry eyes. "A skeleton?"

"Yes, Tom was working on a construction crew, the one tearing down our old house."

Her father fiddled with his fork, digging it into his steak, never taking a bite. "That house never was *my* house," he said.

"What do you mean?" Alice asked.

"The house was owned by John Black, your mom's first husband."

Alice looked at Tom and back at her father. "I never thought about it, I guess. The deed was in my mother's name when I sold it."

"I'm sure he deeded it over to your mom when I left. It was paid for. Probably thought I might sell it and leave your mom high and dry." Jack White shook his head and sighed, still stabbing his fork into the steak. "And, the sad thing is, I might have," he said, looking up at Alice. "I hate to make light of it, but that was the truth of it. I had a lot of growing up to do back then. You'd think having a child would force me to mature, and maybe I might have, but there was Jack Jr. to contend with."

"You know he disappeared after you left, don't you?"

"I didn't know until later. I always wanted Priscilla to ship him off to his father. She argued and rightly so. He wouldn't be any better off. Your mom seemed to be attracted to alcoholics, maybe something in her genetics. When you found out how to find me, did you find anything out about your mom's family?"

"No, Doug offered, but I didn't really see a reason to pursue it. He said it might be hard."

"Who's Doug?"

"He's the man I lived with—in West Virginia."

Jack White's eyebrows raised.

"Doug is the reason Alice ended up in West Virginia," Tom said.

"I think we have a lot of catching up to do if you'll let me. Alice, I would like nothing better than to be a part of your life, and I've discussed it plenty of times with Emily and my boys. Emily said the day would come when you would show up. She said we should be prepared. I should have come looking for you myself, and so many times I said I would, but kept putting it off. Afraid, I guess."

"I want to hate Emily, but I can't."

"You shouldn't. She's a good woman. She didn't know about you and your mom. Or she probably wouldn't have messed with

270

me. By the time she found out, she was pregnant. If she hadn't been supporting me, I don't think I would ever have sobered up."

"Tell me, why did you marry her and not my mom?" Alice demanded.

Other than Tom, who had taken two bites out of his sandwich, Katie was the only one eating. Tom kept giving her French fries, dabbing them in ketchup for her. She squealed in delight, impervious to what was going on. Alice wondered if Jack White and her mom might have had these same kinds of life-altering conversations around her when she was Katie's age.

"I guess because she demanded it, and your mom didn't. Emily's like that. After a while, she said I either sober up or leave. It was a long hard road. I'd stay sober for a while, but then I'd always fall off the wagon. This last time is the longest I've ever been sober. The wood keeps me grounded. Your mom always hated me spending time in the work shed."

The waitress came by to refill their drinks and saw no one needed a refill. "Is there something wrong with the food?" she asked.

"No, Josie, it's fine. We're not very hungry today, I guess," Jack said.

She walked away carrying her pitcher of tea.

"Please tell me about your lives." His eyes were both sad and pleading.

Tom told him how hitting his shovel against the skeleton in their old back yard led him to the love of his life. He also told him he had been married before. He said they now lived on The Farm, the same place Alice was when Jack White went looking for her. Alice explained who Doug was and how they ended up with The Farm. By the time they got to that point, Katie was drifting off in the high chair.

"May I?" her father asked, reaching over for Katie.

Alice nodded.

He got Katie out of her high chair and held her on his lap.

She seemed perfectly at home on her grandfather's lap, sleeping through the noise of the diner. The waitress came back to the table. "Can I box any of this up for you?" she asked.

"I might take this steak to Abby," her father said. He looked at the both of them. "Abby's my black lab. Do you have a dog on the farm?"

"No, but we've been thinking about getting one," Tom said.

"Dogs are a great thing to have. So tell me more about this farm you live on," her father said.

"Do you want me to go out and get her stroller? Holding her like that might get tiresome," Tom said.

"No, I love holding her," he said.

They sat there for a good hour while both Tom and Alice talked. Tom told him about how they roughed it for a year, fixing up one room at a time, and how they still had a lot of areas in the house to go.

"We didn't have much money at first," Alice said. "We didn't even go on a honeymoon so we could spend the money on the house."

"Not my idea, but Alice's. She kept us on track. She made lists and prioritized what needed to be done first."

"Lists?" her father interjected.

"Alice is notorious for writing lists," Tom said with a laugh.

Jack White smiled and looked at his daughter. "I taught you to do that. You don't remember, do you?"

Alice shook her head.

"You were only four. You couldn't write yet, so we said the lists out loud."

"What kind of lists?" Alice asked.

"Let me see if I can remember one," he said, scratching his chin with the one hand he had free. The other was still holding Katie who was fast asleep, her head on his shoulder. "Oh, I remember. This is a good one. We listed the pros and cons of taking the training wheels off of your bike."

"Did I take the training wheels off?"

"No, I believe we came up with one more con than we did pros."

"Did it have something to do with possibly wrecking and scraping my knee and having to put that stinging red stuff on?"

"Yes." Her father laughed so hard it almost woke up Katie. "I believe you're right. Your mother always put iodine on your cuts, and you always screamed when she did it."

Alice, try as she might, was losing her resolve to hate her father. She laughed too.

"It used to kind of annoy me that Alice made lists for everything, especially when I imagined she might make a pros-and-cons list on whether to marry me or not," Tom said.

"There were obviously more pros," Jack White said.

"Honestly, I didn't even have to think about it, but if I had, there would have only been one con," Alice said. She wasn't smiling.

"Alice has always had this deep-seated fear of people disappearing on her," Tom said.

Her father let out a heavy sigh and frowned. "That would be my fault."

"Maybe even my mother. She kind of disappeared on me after you left."

There was dead silence at the table. Even Katie was still.

"After a while, I came to greatly appreciate her lists. They came with every important decision in our lives," Tom said.

"Not with Katie though," Alice said.

"Yes, Katie was the exception," Tom echoed. "We both knew we wanted a baby. Also, when we moved to West Virginia. We didn't care about the cons, the biggest ones being both of us would have to quit our jobs and the fact we would need money to fix up the house and we had relatively little money."

"But Tom is great with all sorts of handiwork."

"I watch a lot of YouTube videos on how to do things."

"But the problem at first was we had no internet access," Alice said.

"Worse than that, we had only a barely working bathroom and no electricity, except for using a generator," Tom said.

"We went with electricity first. It was only logical," Alice said.

"Alice even suggested we run electricity to the barn so I could use it as a workshop. The next thing was a better bathroom. Our goal was to get both of those before cold weather set in."

"Did you make it?" her father asked.

"Yes," they both said in unison. Tom reached for her hand and held it on the table.

"I don't know if you still aren't hungry, but they make the best desserts in town here—all from scratch."

"The chocolate cake I saw when we walked in looked good," Tom said.

Her father yelled out to Josie in the almost vacant restaurant now that it was a good hour past the lunch crowd. She rushed over. "Yes, Jack?"

"How about you bring us all a piece of that chocolate cake?"

"Yes, sir, and some more coffee?"

"Yes," he said.

"Do you need cream or sugar?" she asked Tom and Alice.

"No, black," they both said.

"I can't believe she hasn't woken up," Alice said. "She will probably need a diaper change soon."

"I'll hand her back then." He smiled. "I do remember changing a few of your diapers. Never did much with the boys though. So, keep telling me about the farm.

"Well, we had planned on a garden, but we were both working on the house nonstop, so we didn't get to that until the following year," Tom said.

"And we were running out of money."

"But a stroke of luck came our way," Tom added.

"It was one of those blessings and curses," Alice said.

"A contractor wanted to buy a plot of our land to build houses on." Tom looked at Alice and squeezed her hand tighter. "We were almost destitute, but still, we didn't want to give up any land."

"Plus, we had made an agreement with Doug not to sell. So we called him. Seeing it was only ten acres and nowhere near the house, he gave his approval. We took everything into account and made a list. We *did* sell ten acres off," Alice said.

"The land they wanted was where the road that was barely a road came onto our property. We liked our privacy and didn't want to look out and see other houses. Fortunately, the hills would block the view of the houses they would build."

"We negotiated things with the sell," Alice said.

"Yes, we needed a better driveway onto our property, along with a bridge over the creek. When the other houses moved in, the county agreed to provide those. Also, a cell tower went up. We were also against that at first," Tom said. "But we knew we didn't really have too much say in the matter. The cell tower is over another hill from us, just on the edge of our property. So, now we collect rent from it."

"And we could use the tower for internet," Alice said.

"Which led to my job," Tom said.

"I never asked what line of work you were in," her father said.

"Here we go," Maggie said. "Thought I would relieve Josie for a bit, come back and say hi. Three chocolate cakes and three black coffees." She set them on the table. "Guess I don't have to ask who gets what," she said, laughing. "And who is this little beauty? Looks to be worn out."

"This is my granddaughter, Katie," Jack White said proudly.

Maggie raised her eyebrows slightly.

"And this is my daughter, Alice, and her husband, Tom," he added. "This is Maggie, the owner of this fine establishment."

"Well, you got yourself a right smart-looking family," Maggie said. "Can I get you all anything else?"

"No, I think we're good," Jack said.

"Well, I'll let you get back to your family."

"People around here knew I had a daughter. It's a small town. Probably came back here to personally check you out," Jack said as she walked away. "So, Tom, what's your line of work?"

Tom already had the cake in his mouth. He swallowed. "This is superb."

"Yes, you gotta try their apple pie sometime."

"I basically coordinate grant workshops," Tom said.

"Oh?"

"Yes, I finally found something I could use my business degree for. It started with the small town near us. They wanted a recycling program. I knew they had one where my brothers worked and knew it was funded by a grant, so I initially contacted them to find out about it."

"All of Tom's family are professors. They suggested Tom could apply for a grant for the town."

"Yeah, I loved doing it. I was helping the town. It wasn't hard setting up the budget and all the stuff that went with it. One thing led to another. I searched online for other grant opportunities."

"He got a website going and travels to give workshops now, helping other small towns as well as individuals in some cases."

"Alice takes care of all the billing. She's good with accounting. It's a great job. The good thing is I can set my own schedule. I do most of the work from home. When I do have to travel, Alice and Katie usually go with me."

"Yes, it's been a godsend," Alice said. "Until I had Katie, I was doing an assortment of herb packets, a mail-order business. At first, I only shipped them off to NATURE'S BLUSH."

"What's NATURE'S BLUSH?" her father asked.

"It's where I used to work in New York. It's a health food store."

"Sounds like you two have a good thing going, living on a farm, getting to work from home," Jack said.

"It got that way after I met your daughter," Tom said.

Alice blushed, and Katie stirred.

"Can she have some cake?" her father asked.

"Just a bite," Alice replied.

"Tell me, how are you set for furniture?"

"Our house is practically bare, but we couldn't afford any of your pieces," Tom said.

"Afford? What is there to afford? I give my pieces to family."

Maggie came by to gather up the plates. "I would ask if it was good, but each of you appear to have licked your plates clean."

"Delicious as usual, Maggie."

Jack White laid his credit card down.

"Thank you for dinner," Alice said.

"I don't think one dinner is going to make up for all the ones I missed, Alice, but I hope you'll give me the chance to do better for this little girl." He bopped Katie up and down, who squealed.

Maggie came back with his card and the slip to sign.

"Wait, Maggie." Alice's father got out his cell. "I'm not too good at using these contraptions, but if you don't mind, can we get a few pictures?"

Alice smiled. "Yes, I think that might be nice," she said.

BEFORE THEY SAID THEIR GOODBYES, they exchanged cell phone numbers, and Alice gave him their address.

He shook Tom's hand and gave Katie a kiss on the forehead.

He reached to hug Alice. She felt awkward but wanted to feel the embrace of the man who was her father. The last thing Jack White said to her as he released her was, "I hope it's okay if I come down and see you in West Virginia."

Alice said okay even though she felt it was the last time she would ever see her father. Maybe it was enough. She had Tom and Katie. Both she and Tom had friends in the community. There was Tom's family. Both Iris and Chen would always be her friends as would Laura, Chris, Renea, and Kyle. And she knew she could always count on Doug if she needed something, but after all Doug had done for both her and Tom, she hoped she wouldn't have to ask anything of him again.

41

Back Home

I t had been a month since they returned from seeing her father. Alice was out working in the garden, and Tom was inside working on his fall schedule of workshops with Katie playing on the floor beside him when two trucks drove up. One looked like a moving truck and had WHITE CUSTOM FURNI-TURE on the side. The other was the blue pickup truck she remembered her father driving.

Alice walked to the end of the driveway and stood with her hand over her eyes, blocking the glare of the sun.

"Not an easy place to find," her father said as he got out of the blue pickup truck. A younger guy with ginger hair got out of the bigger truck.

"This is my oldest boy, Russell," he said.

He held out his hand to Alice. "Glad to meet you."

"Can I?" Her father reached out to her, and she awkwardly embraced him. "I guess this will take a little while to get used to," he said, pulling away. "Well, where's my grandchild and Tom?"

"Inside," she said. "I'm afraid the house is a mess.

Tom's working on his computer, grant stuff, and I've been out in the garden all morning."

"I should have called, but I was afraid you would tell me not to come."

"I guess if you would have called to tell me you were coming, I would have worried you wouldn't show up."

"That's another reason I didn't call."

"We have company," she called out to Tom as she went through the door.

"Not company, family," her father, following behind her, said.

He bent down to Katie who was on a blanket on the floor and took her hand into his. "Hi, Katie, do you remember me? I'm your old grandpa," he said.

Tom closed his laptop and got up from his chair, offering his hand to Alice's father.

"This is Russell, my oldest," he said.

Tom reached for Russell's hand. "Nice to meet you."

Her father perused the room. "IKEA?" Her father said it as if it were a dirty word.

"It's all we have for the moment," Alice said.

"Not enough to fill up this big house," Tom said. "This was Alice's starter furniture in New York."

"We had a tiny apartment in New York," Alice said.

"There we found ourselves tripping over the furniture some-times," Tom added.

"Can I offer you something to drink? I have ice tea, or I could make coffee if you like."

"Tea's fine," they both said.

Alice came back from the kitchen with two glasses and handed them each one. "Do you want to sit down?"

"I've been sitting too long. I need to stretch my legs. How about you, Russell?"

"Either way," he said.

"He's not old like me. Why don't you give us the tour?"

"Sure," Tom said.

He picked up Katie. "She's walking now, but it'll take forever if we let her."

After the living room, their next stop was the kitchen. Alice's heart leapt when she saw her father's eyes firmly glued to the metal lunch box on top of the hutch. He looked at her in surprise. "Is that…"

"Yes, it was one of the few things I kept from my mom's house."

Jack White started to say something but choked on his words.

They took the two men through every part of the house. He inspected the structure the way a sea captain might inspect a ship to determine its seaworthiness.

"It's built good, nice and solid," her father said. "They built houses strong back in the day. Not much on insulation though, and I see you still have a way to go on finishing the upstairs." He scratched his chin with his one free hand. "Here, if you don't mind." He handed the empty glass back to Alice and pulled a metal tape measure from his pocket. He went over to one wall and measured across the baseboard. "Is there a lumber mill nearby?"

"About thirty miles away," Tom said, looking at Alice with a puzzled look.

"I think a month might do it. Do you think you could put up with me for a month? I could get to know you, Tom, and my granddaughter better." He winked at Katie who was rubbing her eyes.

"A month?" Alice asked.

"Yes, I brought a few tools from my shop."

"A few?" Russell said, laughing.

"I brought what I thought I would need. Besides, you still

have plenty at the shop. You said you had more work to do on the house, so I thought I might lend a hand."

"Mr. White, we can't let you…" Tom began.

"Yes, you can let me, or at least I hope you *will* let me. And please, don't call me Mr. White."

"What should we call you?" Alice asked.

He sighed. "I guess that's a hard one. I haven't earned the right to be called Dad. When you were small, you called me Daddy. I'll let the two of you mull it over and decide. I hope you'll let Katie call me Grandpa. I plan on sticking around for her."

"I hope you let Dad stay and help you fix up the place," Russell said. "It'll give Brent and me a chance to show him we can run the shop without him."

Alice flinched. It sounded strange, this young man she had only met today calling her father Dad. Maybe after a month, she could bring herself to call him Father or something. She didn't know.

Katie let out a whimper. "I need to put her down for her nap."

"We have just the thing for that," her father said. "Are you up for some lifting, Tom?"

They followed them both out to the truck. Russell opened the double doors to the back of the truck and lowered the ramp. Tom and Alice looked at each other in shock. It was full of what Alice surmised was furniture, all wrapped in thick gray padding. It was the kind of furniture that would make Doug and Constance envious.

"Now let's see, there is a bedroom suite for a little girl in here somewhere."

"Are you delivering the rest of this to someone?" Tom asked.

"I'm delivering it here," he said.

"We can't accept this. Back at the restaurant, I thought you maybe meant one piece," Alice said.

"I'm not taking it back," he said.

"This is too kind," Tom said.

"Nothing kind about it. I counted up the pieces I would have made for Alice if I had stuck around and been the father I should have, but this was all I could fit in the truck."

"Yeah, and we got to get a move on unloading. I want to get back on the road," Russell said.

"You can't stay too?"

"He's in love. Has to get back to his girlfriend. She rode part of the way down with him. Dropped her off in Morgantown. She has an aunt there."

"Yeah, and I'm eager to get back."

"Well, Russell, climb up there. Let's find that bed and get Katie down for her nap," Jack said. "Russell's taking the furniture truck back. Tom, you and I can unload my tools from the back of my cab tomorrow. Are you too busy to learn some woodworking?"

"Never too busy for that," Tom said.

42

A New Beginning

J ack White returned home after two months. He said
always double the time anyone tells you they promise to
get a job completed. By one way of reckoning, a
month's time was correct as that was how long it took
for Alice to call him Dad. Katie called him Grandpa almost
immediately. She had a lilt to her voice when she said it, and
since it was two syllables, she moved her body upwards when
she said the *-pa* part.

In actuality, the house was completed, if you can ever call an
old farmhouse complete, within a month and a half, but Tom and
Alice asked him to stay for as long as he could. "You've worked
so hard. You need to take a little vacation time. And you can't
leave before Katie's birthday, Dad," Alice exclaimed. She didn't
have to twist his arm.

Two days after Katie's birthday, Alice came downstairs early
to find her father was drinking a cup of coffee and eating a piece
of toast. She saw his suitcase next to the door.

"It's time I go back. Emily has been more than understanding
about me being away for so long."

"We'll miss you so much," Alice said as she hugged her father. "We've gotten so used to having you here."

"I'll be back. Maybe we can make this a summer thing if you're okay with that?"

"I'm more than okay with it," Alice said.

"I'll get Tom and Katie up. Tom can help you load your tools onto the truck."

"They're already loaded."

"But some of them were heavy."

"Already taken care of, Alice."

It was a tearful goodbye for Alice and Tom as her father stepped up into his blue pickup—not so much for Katie as she was holding her new black lab puppy her grandpa had gotten her for her birthday.

Alice had no doubt he would be back. His notebook with all of his plans for The Farm, which included a greenhouse and a chicken coop, lay on the cherry coffee table he had brought down for them.

After Alice, Tom, and Katie had their own breakfast, they took a walk out to the barn. They found he had left most of his tools behind, including his band saw. There was a note attached.

Tom, you'll need these to do any work you might want to do on your own and to build that guitar you were talking about. Plus, no need for me hauling them back down the next time I come.
Love,
Dad

Alice had neglected emailing everyone during her dad's stay. But that afternoon, she sent out emails to Chen, Iris, Laura, Renea, and Doug telling them about her dad's visit along with before and after pictures of the farmhouse.

"They won't believe it," she told Tom.

Over the months that followed, Alice took up journaling again. She wrote a lot about her renewed relationship with her father. She made no lists of pros or cons. She accepted it for what it was.

Alice was reluctant to call it closure, so she wrote on the front of her journal, A New Beginning.

Acknowledgments

I want to thank my husband, Chris, for all of his stories about pizza delivery, along with his other jobs. Getting hit in the head with a baseball bat during a pizza delivery—true story.

Thank you to Barbara Chambers who has been my most faithful beta reader from day one.

Thank you to Melissa Woods who beta read for me.

Patricia Hopper Patteson beta read for me and went above and beyond. So, thank you Patricia.

And thanks to Keith Daniel Roe, my newest beta reader.

Thanks to Elizabeth Childs for her comments on my first three chapters.

Thank you, Harvey Holbrook, for you help when I asked questions about police procedures.

Thanks to my editors Emerald Barnes and Lisa Binion.

I'm thankful to my dad for leaving me the farm. Yes, living here, especially in the beginning, was much like the way I wrote about Alice's farm—only woodburning stoves for heat and cistern water. But living out in nature is well worth it.

About the Author

J. Schlenker, a-late blooming author, lives with her husband, Chris, out in the splendid center of nowhere in the foothills of Appalachia in Kentucky where the only thing to disturb her writing is croaking frogs and the occasional sounds of hay being cut in the fields.

For more information:
https://www.jschlenker.com/
jschlenkerauthor@gmail.com

f facebook.com/J.SchlenkerAuthor
🐦 twitter.com/athursdayschild
📷 instagram.com/jschlenkerauthor

Also by J. Schlenker

Jessica Lost Her Wobble

A Novel Tea Book Club Selection, 2017 Wishing Shelf Book Awards Finalist, 2014 William Faulkner-William Wisdom Writing Contest Finalist, and recipient of a 5 Star Readers' Favorite Award.

At mid-life, Jessica, after many upsets, moves to an island for contemplation of her life and to make a new start. While there, she reflects back on her beginnings in the early twentieth century in England, her move to New York City, and marriage at a young age, while making friends with a girl half her age. This friendship opens up a new world for her and helps her explore her own soul. Jessie becomes a part of the island otherwise known as a local as she reinvents her life there and finds love. But all is not as it seems.

"Jessica Lost Her Wobble" is J. Schlenker's first novel.

Review Excerpts: "Let me get this out of the way.. Buy this book and read it!!" "Exceptional book. I would give it 10 stars if they were available." "This is a book that must be read to the end, meaning all the way through the last big surprise epilogue. I didn't see it coming and it changed the whole texture of looking back on this well-written novel."

The Color of Cold and Ice

A recipient of the IndiBrag Medallion and 2018 Wishing Shelf Book Awards Finalist

Sybil has dreams; the prophetic kind, although interpreting them correctly is another matter. Her latest dream involves her sister Emerald, who wants to pursue her art once more and move on with her life after losing her husband. John, once felt he was making a difference as an ER doctor, but finds himself slipping away in his Manhattan practice as well as in his marriage. Allison, John's wife wants to change her ho hum existence with John into something spectacular. Mark, Allison's brother, a struggling musician, wants to quit rambling in life and find his purpose.

The cold changes everything.

'A powerfully written novel driven by strong characters, plot twists—and color! Highly recommended.'

This has been written by a very talented writer; I will be keeping my eyes peeled for her next book too.

A 'Wishing Shelf' Book Review

Michelle, a white woman stumbles upon her grandmother's journals that have lain dormant in the attic for fifty years. There is a picture of her grandmother alongside an African-American woman. It is inscribed: Sally, born into slavery—my ancestor. The journals relating Sally's story end abruptly. Michelle makes it her mission to find out more about Sally. The quest brings up more questions than answers. Just when she thinks she has come to a dead end, she uncovers the most startling fact of all.

Sally

Based on the life of Sally Ann Barnes 1858 to 1969

'The powerful story of a black woman in the American South and the astonishing life she lived.'

Powerfully written and populated with well-developed characters, I would recommend this book to anybody interested in American history. Or to anybody who simply enjoys a gripping story.

A 'Wishing Shelf' Book Review

Review Excerpts: "Sally by J. Schlenker has touched me with a strength, a grace, and a beauty that belies the sadness that the pages hold." "Mesmerizing Story. Superbly Written." "A Compelling Read." "Should be taught at schools."

The Missing Butler and Other Life Mysteries

A Collection of Short Stories. A 5 Star Readers' Favorite.

Sometimes life is absurd. Sometimes life is serious. Sometimes life is sad. Mostly, life is a mystery. This collection of short stories, along with the author's whimsical art work, humorously explores the absurdness, the seriousness, the sadness and the mysteries of life, or at the very least causes us to pause and think, and maybe even laugh at ourselves.

Review Excerpts: "Great collection of short stories!" "A brilliant collection of outrageous, people in a variety of situation." "Whimsical and Well Written"

A Peculiar School

What if all animals got along?

Miss Ethel Peacock, who lives at a nature preserve, has the brilliant idea of starting a school for all animals. She musters up her courage to take her idea to Mr. Densworth Lion, principal at Cub Academy, who thinks the idea is preposterous. He roars, "Animals have a pecking order. Getting along isn't in an animal's nature."

Ethel is disheartened until her friend, Luce Pigeon, tells her about a tiger, hyena, orangutan and polar bear who live together in the tunnels under the city after escaping from the zoo, and about the badger who helps them.

The two set out to meet the animals. What Ethel finds when they arrive is beyond her imagination. Animals with distinct personalities are working together but barely surviving. She and Luce must help them escape their underground prison.

The night of the escape is chaotic. The animals scatter amid the blare of police sirens. What happens next motivates Ethel even more to open the school. Her plan gets a big boost when the owls, keepers of the sacred knowledge of the forest, give Ethel their blessing.

But, the owls are hiding something about the nature preserve that could change everything.

https://www.jschlenker.com/